LIGHT
OF THE
DIDDICOY

A NOVEL BY
EAMON LOINGSIGH

THREE ROOMS PRESS
NEW YORK

Light of the Diddicoy
a novel by Eamon Loingsigh

First Edition

ISBN: 978-0-9884008-9-4
Library of Congress Control Number: 2013947721

Copyright © 2014 by Eamon Loingsigh

Cover and interior design:
KG Design International
katgeorges.com

Three Rooms Press
New York, NY
threeroomspress.com

The tribe of auguries,
These vehement unkempt visionaries . . .
The men stride upon dirt paths, their glinting weapons sided,
Guard well the motley chariots wherein their kin do dwell
And stare long upon the harrowed horizon far off in Hell
At brood on the gloomy regret childish hope once confided.

—CHARLES BAUDELAIRE

I am come of the seed of the people, the people that sorrow;
Who have no treasure but hope,
No riches laid up but a memory of an ancient glory
My mother bore me in bondage, in bondage my mother was born,
I am of the blood of the serfs.

—PADRAIG PEARSE

It seems to me that we can never have a complete settlement of world
conditions until the Anglo-Saxon begins to realize that he is not of a
superior race but that all races are equal.

—EDWARD J. FLYNN, Letter to Eleanor Roosevelt

I cannot forget
That old home I left
In that town of great renown,
I long to go back
To that old-fashioned shack
In dear old Irish Town.

—ALDERMAN PATRICK LARNEY, Brooklyn Eagle, 12/22/1940

For Mary Regina Lynch, née Sullivan/Gramma
1917–2012

CHAPTER I

Glasnevin Rebelpoets

DOWN UNDER THE MANHATTAN BRIDGE OVERPASS there once roamed a gang I fell in with. A long time ago it was, when I was young and running. It's all I had, this life. Just as yours is yours. Don't let yourself think mine is anything different, anything better. I won't have it that way. It was just a life, and there you have it. But like so many born on the isle of Ireland, I am to die far from home. Though such a grief has since let me alone, as bitterness only cuts into the bone, I'm at ease with it in my age. But to go 'way with all these memories, well, I rush them out here for you to breathe them in. To read with your senses as I lay here in the brood of the night, broad awake to recite my beads, not so dutifully. Because when dying it's no longer duty, it's prayer. So here I am to send a story you true and fair. About blood. And honor. About the code of men, and about empathy too.

This story will both begin and end on a ship as any good run or reel should, but we'll start you here for good measuring.

Cobh wasn't called Cobh when I left it. Queenstown, and a great Atlantic crosser allowed myself and far too many others aboard in the swirling mist. Among the high masts two giant round silos breathed into the air above, black exhaust due from the belly of the iron woman's coal-fired furnaces within. Her long reach a mile wide in black and red faded paint as she sat three-quarters full already from her port in Liverpool on stop to pick up itinerant thirds in the country that made her back in '89. Six-inch black iron gun heads reached from what was once a leisurely deck for more distinguished passengers of another era, ghosts now. The Great War changing and altering all of life as we know it. And just above the rusted anchorhold in sea-weathered letters, a degraded font from that bygone time, *RMS Teutonic*.

Not a day for celebrants, it is the offing of the peasant ceremonial here. Lacking pomp and cheer, instead the heavy request of need and necessity fills their eyes. The hunger of orphans and their low caste beheld in their beams, bony travelers huddling for lands of hope and honey. Desperate for their utopia somewhere far off, they are. A utopia dreamed up by the imaginations of the falling and those without promise. As was true to the time it was the motley beaten Celts, pushed to the western edge of Europe and beyond. Into the sea. Their hopes are as humble as their tattered belongings, with only a meal as their immediate mark. I remember how clear they were to me, standing like statues in my mind, the thin faces with paper passes in palm stand blank and disenchanted with patchy beards and shrunken features and tubular breasts and tumorous growths and black fingernails and crippled feet deformedly ornamented by undermined sandals like a parade of pilgrims crossing the desert if only to summon God himself in the absence of His resources and with a will to survive at least long enough to enter the shrine, America.

The farthest I'd ever traveled previous was to sell peat over in Ennis or through the earth's skullpate known as The Burren for the horse fair up in Ballinasloe. A long ways as far as I knew. My father had just arrived back from the greatest of graveside orations and the displays of rebelpoets at Glasnevin. And when the dawn is come for change and you know it, you must prepare or be swept in by it. Great change is on the wing. Rebellions among wars.

Da nods his head at my departure up the plank, a simple handshake and I am gone to life by him as he turns back into the land. His eyes narrow under the cap and brow like a man hiding feelings. And I suddenly find that no longer will I follow his long shadow round the farm, the turf-creel on his shoulder, the scent of gorse in the air. Older by a year, brother Timothy tips at me nervously. Mother and two sisters stayed back in Clare having said good-byes there to leave the men for the day's ride through the countryside, out in the long hills and stretches of rock-strewn fences where old and forgotten territories are marked like dead dog's piss in aged farm hay.

"Not to werry. Hardest t'ing he ever had to do, send ye away such. We'll give to what comes of it," Mam is tear-smirched in the doorway, sorrowed by the life of things that are far from her control. "May trouble be always a stranger to ye. . . . Whence I gave birth wid' ye some fourteen year ago, I t'ought den and still do now dat ye'd be one day a man to open the door fer many. Take dis, den. Put it in yer pocket and touch it when ye please. Ye'll be grand wid it. Safe keepin', not to werry."

The Saint Christopher is not much more than a tin imprint and once upon it had a hole where to thread a string to tie round the neck, but since then it'd broken entirely. I place it in my pocket. Feel the imprint of his face on my thumb and fore-finger. And that was that, Mam gives my wake with hopes to follow, her teary face blushed with a constant cry from the deaths of her two infant sons, Sean and Colm, born and died before Timothy even. And why does Timothy get the farm and I the Saint Christopher? And I think now that surely it's because his birth and survival was the answer to Mam's praying so hard. Mine was much less, but who has the understanding in their early years to ponder on such things except artists or rich people who are so often one in the same. And maybe the old, such as myself typing away here before I go. But little does she even know that emigrating during the Great War is likely another dead son in the wait. Only luck can make it across the sea lanes with the sea wolves dug in for war, where the *Lusitania* was sent to the dregs just north of Queenstown in Kinsale, just south of five months early upon. Saint Christopher or not, the German has his way on the seas and the war never means to kill a single Irish but then again a dead Irish, incidental or not, won't change the course of things. The Irish and the sea songs though, they are fraught with the romance of death. Not a song I plan to sing, but what word have I in it? Old songs sung by the stink of peat back famine way. Back when times was worse, true. But why I am to suddenly go, no one is to rightly know. Not I. Not Mam either, but Timothy says for soldiering I'm too young yet and I hate him when all I see are the backs of he and Da walking over the hills for drilling with the Volunteers. My Mam says for traveling it's Abby and Brigid that are too young yet. So it's me who goes then.

"When ye can rub yer own two coins togedder, then ye can elect yer destinations," says my Da, who with one arm pulls down the blackthorn from its chimney home; then he and I and Timothy too go off through the fields for the country train to the port city solemnly. Out from the farm. Out to the world with me.

CHAPTER 2

Four Italians

IT'S A LATE AFTERNOON AT THE Brooklyn side of New York, 1915, some week or so before I am to arrive. The motile current of a cast-iron gray October sky slowly shifts in its expanse above the Bridge District where there are barge horns moaning like giant creatures groaning in the waterway distance. Across the East River the canopy of bridges opens outward to reveal the step-stone skyline of Manhattan pushing close on the shoreline's edge. A glass gust turns ears to ice, tilting heads to shoulder and spinning loose papers and dust into pirouettes of refuse along the freight tracks cut into the Belgian bricks. Reaching out into the gray-green suffused shipping lanes below the immense stride of the Brooklyn Bridge stanchions, a floating pier wobbles with the weight of a tied ship at its berth. And under the cold shadow of a Dutch African freightliner at the Fulton Ferry Landing, see a gaggle of some one hundred men come to rest upon a day's hard working. The vessel rising in the East River from the shedding of its cargo, lines of impatient and hungry men now wait their turn for an envelope.

A group of young herding roughs who steer the docks in the neighborhood, "Dinnies" as they are known, taunt the itinerants out of their lazy babbling. Lashing them with tongues, gnashing at them they scatter in a scuttling rush, for the fierce pace demanded by the wartime economy has no time for the

laggard and no patience for the immigrant laborer. Now come
to bear defrayment, these laborermen wait in a single-file line
and upon receiving an envelope from the stevedoring company
that employs them, are met by the gypsy-toothed smile and
brawny, leaning figure of the one known as Cinders Connolly,
the Fulton Street Terminal's dockboss.

Tall in his beam he is, and with a grand smile across his pan,
he barks his demands along the labor line trailing from hull to
plank to train. Here spit in the wide hand and rubbing it into his
knuckles as he come to the end of the stevedore's table to collect
his tribute from the men, Connolly is flanked by the flat face of
the foolmute Philip Large, his right-hand man. Short on stature
with round, raindrop eyes and stubby arms, Large shifts his head
on the neck like a beast of burden and is known to break a man's
back if his hooks are screwed in. Along with three or four other
Dinnies what support them, Connolly and Large are the Fulton's
enforcers for the Bridge District gang called the White Hand.

Among the crowd funneling in a motley shuffle toward the
stevedore's line are four Italians shown early for work and
picked out of need for numbers. With three ships docking at
once in the morn's whistle, the four untried immigrants were
brought upon. Loafing as they could, they offered passive stares
back at the Dinnies who barked at their ears. Whispering in
tongues with words understood only in the ancient villages of
Calabria, did they. The Dinnies only hearing whispers, and a
whisper's not right as it's known there's more to hear in a
whisper than a scream. Chuckling too, in foreign jokes. Sensing
dispute, Connolly nods for The Swede and a runner is off.

Darkness besetting them here, the cold shafts of the new city
gives these guests a shiver scarcely felt in their own past.
Hungered and proud for their work, they are readying a return
to their train station hotel and the unsettled families that await
them as they shuffle to the stevedore's table in queue. Three of
them are brothers with the sunken, bony cheeks of the peasant
traveler. The last is a cousin who is short but healthy in his
paunch and rich in certainty. Together, they speak with agility

and mirth, but are misunderstood by the violent riverside natives as the brassy mettle of salty immigrants, ignorance and remiss.

It is the squat one who the brothers turn to for advice. The lone cousin with the round shoulders and wide face, bow lips and half-dozing, half-daring eyes. He pushes to the front when Connolly points at the envelopes. Not understanding a word, Giovanni Buttacavoli directs the cousins to walk with him around Connolly and Large. Politely as he come, Connolly steps in front of the four and motions again at the envelopes.

"Time to pay up, fellers," Connolly says as he pats down the foreigners for weapons while Large and others stand at the ready. "Nothin' personal, we all pay tribute. Ten percent, then on your own ways ya go. Whadda ya say? Easy, ain't it?"

Not a word knowing, Buttacavoli tilted his head and lowered his brow as Connolly strangely patted down his thighs.

"I already tol' yas, pay up," Connolly showing snarl, this time touching the lapel of Buttacavoli with his pointer and waving his arm behind. "I gotta lotta guys I gotta tend to, now hurry it up. Ya holdin' up the line here."

Backing Connolly at his right, Philip Large stares in his dullness at the feet of Buttacavoli. A tug is heard bleating out on the East River and too, a train passing on the Brooklyn Bridge above echoes its clickety-clacking off the black ice water. Large moves his mouth around from irritation. The passing of long moments make him seize. The tension annexing inside him bursts up and forces him to pass a *maa*ing oxen bawl from his throat to release it. This gawking sound is frowned down by the Italians. They hear it only as weakness, unskillful constraint.

The line of men with pocketed hands that've already received their envelopes and are waiting behind the four Italians is bottled up, and so they air their grievances of it. At the ripe of impasse after his hoarse baying, Large tries timidly to bring his arms together to cross but his jacket being too tight behind, drops them to their natural position wide from his stocky, bovid build.

Whether by confusion or obstruction, Buttacavoli and the three brothers gently refuse to comply. Declined, Cinders Connolly peers over his shoulder coldly. Across the way, listening with great intent, is the man everyone calls The Swede. With a long face upon him and a tow head, The Swede stares with a gaunt scowl at the proceedings as he is perched on the bow's edge of a bobbing tug knotted to the wharf just north the brick face of the Empire Stores and the old Fulton Ferry.

Allowing the dockboss Connolly and Large the fair prospect of collecting their own tribute, The Swede sits. Though he sits, there was reason for his being summoned from 25 Bridge Street by a runner when it got apparent these four immigrants were to be troublesome.

From the tug he pierces the cast in front of him. Beside him stand Tommy Tuohey, a pavee fighter from the boreens of the Old Country, and the dark-skinned mauler, Dance Gillen. These Whitehanders, headed by The Swede, wait while some seventy men bottle behind the line waiting to pay tribute. With nary a blink, The Swede first motions for Dago Tom Montague, a half-Italian who grew up in the neighborhoods.

A cold chill runs through the thick uncombed hair of Buttacavoli as those behind him grumble, casting slurs. He finds there is coordination among the locals. Not one to give in to low-class thieves dressed as grown orphans with atrocious manners, he stands chin up. In his land, a brute is met with refined grace. Not even an enemy knows your thoughts and when revenge is struck with blood, a shrug is all that comes upon the face of the victor when blame come his way. When a half-breed with a terrible accent sputters in his language of needing to pay a portion of their earnings, Buttacavoli lowers his daring eye and opens his legs, straightening his stance. Asking elegantly why he would have to do such a thing, he flicks his fingers and turns his head away. His brothers agree. No one takes family money, and again make around Connolly and Large.

The Swede unfurls his limbs and stands in his long span from the tug loosening his tie with a knuckley fist and a groaning sigh.

"They from Navy Street o' Red Hook? What? Bay Ridge?"

"Not sure, maybe jus' immigrants," Dago Tom shrugs.

"No such thing, coincidence!" The Swede snarls back. "They wanna invade us? See wha' happens."

Stamping to the front of the line he elbows through the insolent Italians, past Connolly and Large. Berating with abuse the laborers waiting to give tribute, "Every damn one o' yas who got'n envelope an' ain't paid they shares yet, give it back this very second!"

"But what fault it's mine dese stupid wops. . ." one navvy pleaded.

"Give 'em back now!" The Swede explodes in the man's face that silences all and screaming down into the backing faces of the obedient, "Now! Now! Now!"

Gillen grabs two laborers coatwise and shoves them back to the table while Tommy Tuohey claps his mitts, "Back-up, bhoys!" and tosses backward five and six at a time as the hungry trip among themselves to let go their pay.

Standing above all else at six feet and five inches, The Swede stomps on the pier planks waving his gangly, muscled arms and clubbed fists in front of the stevedore's table as they all rise from their seats in awe at his roaring and his convulsing, "I'll beat ya alive! Back up! Now! Back up! Back!"

"Back-up, bhoys," Tuohey repeats. "Back-up, ye feckin' sausage!"

Pushing faces back so the circle widens, kicking with boots at men with blatting disgust, The Swede makes his territory. Makes it a circle around the untried four Italians. The fighter's circle. Spitting at its edges, daring a cross of it; until finally in his comfort, puffs his long trunk and the angular slant of his splayed chest and shoulders for a grunt in the air that of a bull ape's summoning.

"AAAAaaawwwwwwwhhhhhhh!"

All quiet on the Fulton Terminal it was after that. Even the tugs and barges on the water hastened their bleating. The drays stopped struggling over the cobbles. The trains on their tracks and on the Els and bridges disappeared and Dago Tom stopped pleading in the foreign burr.

"Pay up, or pay up! This is what's said! Final!" The Swede moaned like a giant spider-ghost into Buttacavoli's face as the words echoed thinly into the windy air. "Ya wanna take this neighborhood, ya gotta kill us all. See us? All o' us? Takes more'n four o' yas. 'Til then, pay up! Rules is rules. Tribute, now!"

A Calabrian's patience and honor having been beckoned and then split by the rush of waterfront wind through face and coat from under the bridges into the gaggle of labormen assembled. Buttacavoli shivered, blinking his eyes yet still decided. Summoning the firmness in the roots of his honored society, he softly protests the lack of respect afforded him for space. Calmly, and in the middle of the ancient circle, he places his envelope in coat and folds his arms.

In an athletic attack, The Swede leans into a long right cross that explodes under the jaw of Buttacavoli, whose arms and legs straighten and stick in place as he is felled. Yet as he goes down, a left-handed fist lands and quickly blats with a thud to jolt Buttacavoli's defenseless, white-eyed face. To the dock he slaps, stiff as a tree slams to forest floor.

The crowd quickly surges into a rollicking fervor and bellows as advancing soldiers into blood. Still in one motion, The Swede kicks one of the brothers in the gut and pounds him with strides of clubbed fists. As the brother comes to the ground himself, he receives the boot and the lace of labormen taking their turns. One of which snaps his head back so violently that the crowd bucks in excitement. Amidst the affray, Philip Large hooks another scurrying brother by the waist from behind and dead-lifts him high, slamming him backwards on his head, and in the middle of a ravenous circling crowd of wild dogs feasting on live bloodied prey. Fancied by the chaos, the dockworkers are brawling and elbowing and snapping at one another from the murk and bedlam for their own meat-seeking kicks. The stevedore's table upended, Tuohey grapples the last terror-stricken Calabrian and holds him tight while Cinders Connolly takes potshots off the skull, laughing all the way. As The Swede finishes up with his second, he asks with respect for Connolly to step aside among the flailing turmoil, cracks his right hand into a tight fist and spears the last in the throat with a force that sends Tuohey backward a step, who then gave the fool to the ground to have. Struggling for air this last brother too receives the dockloaders' work boots to face and lips.

And the men of the piers had a wild time of it, hooraying The Swede. His gaunt face standing firm among the facile cheers and with his clubs still clenched at his hips to show all the stance of justice meted out down here on the Brooklyn docks he proclaims, "A message to Frankie Yale!"

"Go back to Sackett Street, ya fookin' guinea wops!" Another agrees.

But little do they know, and less do they care, that these four were fresh off the boat and not at all known among the Brooklyn *coscas*: the Camorra of Navy Street, the Cosa Nostra of Sackett and Frankie Yale's down in Bay Ridge and Coney Island.

Behind The Swede, Dance Gillen jumps in the air feet high, stomping Italian face and gullet simultaneously. Holding his hat in hand, while a flounce of half-curly African hair spills over his forehead and temple, he comically loses his balance, hence the moniker Dan the Dock Dancer, aka Dance Gillen.

The dock men tear at the immigrants' clothes. A broken-faced watch is pulled and so too a meaningless letter tossed aside like feathers off a fowl's carcass. Some foreign coinage jingles uselessly on the pier and falls through the wharf slats to the water below. Strange hairy charms used for summoning luck and good travel are plucked and cast too.

Emerging from the crowd is Eddie Gilchrist, the gang's accountant hard at work. Forcing himself upon the devouts bent down over the prostrate victims, Gilchrist rifles through each Italian's coat pockets alongside them. He rummages for the envelopes or else demands them from a scavenger who beat him to it. Gilchrist is supported by Connolly and Tuohey. As a matter of superstition, Gilchrist refuses to reach into the coat of Buttacavoli, whose chattering teeth bite deep into the meat of his flabby bottom lip, convulsing in a fit from the blows to head. And so instead Connolly dips his fingers in cautiously, as the others stare at the flailing foreigner. Then hands over this last envelope slowly and with only his fingernails touching it.

As Gilchrist finishes his gathering, The Swede and Cinders Connolly immediately begin reorganizing the men for tribute, ordering the stevedore's table be righted and breaking the circle into a line.

Supported by Dago Tom and Dance Gillen, Gilchrist abandons the injured and steals under the Manhattan Bridge for the headquarters of the White Hand where they and many others report to Dinny Meehan on the second floor of 25 Bridge Street just above a whiskey dive called the Dock Loaders' Club.

CHAPTER 3

Ship to New York

THEY MAKE ALL MALES BETWEEN THE ages of eighteen and forty-one step out of the line to be saved for the conscription. I lean up the plank and onto the *Teutonic*. Men with the choppy language resembling the landlord's pay taker corral us like cattle. They are stewards, and they are English, and they shove us down the dark stairwells of the ship with swinging oil lamps by their ears.

"Get along niy, 'urry up niy!" They say with tall ruddy smiles over the rat-haired heads.

"Slime," one of them counts the passengers by grabbing them by an arm and pushing them toward the stairwell. "Glad to see y'off. Slime. Glad to see y'off. Slime. Glad to see y'off. Slime . . ."

Another young official up ahead of him laughs at his wit and throws an echo down the long hall, "At's a way Currington. Oi Whatley! See 'ow Currington's countin' the 'eads 'ere, would yu! Funny innit?"

"Slime. Glad to see y'off. Slime . . ."

I too am swung by the elbow toward the stairwell and counted, "Slime!" Behind me I hear a man threaten the officials not to touch him and an affray breaks out with a piercing whistle that summons the meanest in the Anglo stewards. They rap the rebel on the head as he stands his ground with a few wild swings he'd been saving for them. A group of women go to yelping as he is dragged back where from he come and out of sight.

There is only one entrance and we are funneled like heads of beef from the planks and thin hallways and through tumbling metal stairwells in the dark to the stern dorm. To the back of the big girl. And as we are last to board, we are not split by gender nor age. It's the size of a ballroom, lacking the ornaments and chairs and tables and musicians and dancers. Steel walls, iron floors and not a single facility in sight save piss pots. Not even a sheet for a woman's privacy. By the time we fill the hall with some ninety souls there's nary enough cots for the amount of us and so I go without and sit instead against the great unpronounced tin wall. By placing my ear on it, I can hear the gentle laps of salt water touching off on the opposite side and wonder how loud the sounds will become when far out and into the deep.

After some great wait, a backfire explodes somewhere below us and toward the bow. I hold the Saint Christopher in my fingers and feel as though my life is in God's hands as I am such a stranger to this great floating vessel. Little do I know that for the rest of my long life I'd be a stranger in strange places, filled with my green, West Ireland memories of childhood.

Hidden men yell at one another like apes as they stoke a fire in the belly of her. From somewhere, propellers turn over, kicking off the rust and spinning begrudgingly in the salt. A great horn blows above our blindfolded ears outside with a trembling in my chest. Voices above seem to be sarcastically saluting the people of the land as we lurch backward to our staggering. Mothers filled with the ignorance of the Old World and the superstitions against anything mechanical yelp again at the sudden movement and hold on to each other in their fear. Old men too who've never seen yet even an automobile in their long lives, now in the hold of a great and mysterious metal monster about whose whim they haven't a clue. After some thirty minutes of passengers bogging their strange good-byes outside, we must finally give leave of the shore and head south. The waves at the iron wall behind me now spanking and echoing through the chamber dorm.

The sea is hidden. And to us, doesn't exist. The great expanse of it is nothing more than rivets and squares of iron sheets and slats along the whole of the room like the blank canvas of the art of the forgotten. An old highwayman is gumming a potato he's hidden in his humble packs. Chewing as lines and muscles in his temple and pate flex like iron cords to crush the tuber in his gnawing gate, leaning off his cot with legs wide out and swaying with the expanse of the ship as if he'd made countless journeys like it in his days.

Eight hours go by, my stomach turns with hunger until a child hardly out of infancy hands me a share of bannock bread, "Me mam says 'tis fer ye," and runs off among the other steerage crew before even I can thank her. But I say it anyhow for it is only right to give thanks, particularly to those who give when take is in the need.

By now, the fireman's castle is ablaze at sea and the iron sheets become too hot to lean on. Devils of men bellow out from somewhere we cannot see. "Feed that bitch!" I hear a man proclaim in the tin distance. "Feed 'er! Feed 'er! She's a hungry one! Shovel ye're mightiest boys! Feed that bitch and give'r what she wants for the love of ye!"

I peel off my coat and wool sweater and yank down my tie in order to free the sweat that accumulates on my back and chest. Not wholly understanding why there is such a great blaze on board, I tremble with the thought of a ship fire at sea and just when I feel we are all to die by the flame, she moans a great sigh through the pulse of the deep in an abyssal ecstasy. So deep and so long you'd think it's a mother dragon receiving the bulbous, tyrannical cock of a sex-crazed wandering wyvern bullmale from some arcane and wretched lore. I stare ahead with a crazed look upon me, ears dedicated to defining all the cryptic sounds around us.

Now growing angry, the *Teutonic* pushes forth through the froth. I can hear the men again feeding and stoking in some mysterious contest, "Yeah! Yeah! Yeah!" We pierce the water at a pace of twenty knots. The width of the sea gulps at us in hopes of devouring our negligible souls for its evil quota. The Atlantic foam sucking at us in its great vaginal drink far worse than could ever be imagined in the old seafaring songs of my peat-fire childhood. Never at rest am I, as the hull of the cruiser staves on, flexing and bobbing and oscillating afloat, incising the folds and rocking through the brine as the ancient deep barely acknowledges our shafting it.

"T'ink dis here's bad, do ye?" the man with the potato calls. "Ye'd a try it back den when a clipper's all ye had. The creakin' o' swolled wood and the swayin' fore an' aft. T'ink dis here's bad, do ye? Nar! Hell I'd take dis over a coffinship any day."

Listening intently to the water, I try to distinguish the sounds of a U-boat. I hadn't a single idea what a U-boat would sound like underwater of course, but any sound that comes to mind brings a flash of anxiety to me anyhow. My palms are so wet I wipe them on my thighs and knees so that my pants have the look of being soiled. My jaw sore from grinding, nails raw from biting. An hour later and I see the potato man with his nose to the air, shaking his head.

"Smell a storm," says he in my direction.

Sure as anything, we next hear the crack of the cloaked sky above as the Atlantic crosser makes her way into the teeth of it, or so we are led to believe. All of us sit in wait, warbling our eyes up like owl heads to feed our ears. Billowing rippled waves of some imagined proportion lap and lick like holy fires on the stretch of mankind, forcing the vessel's long genuflecting and seesawing.

Children and drab-dressed women are sent flaying off their backsides with legs and feet asplayed in the air and are sucked into a corner where loose remains gather like storm water sent fleeing for the sewer collect. The floor quickly changes to the color of the inside of our stomachs. Now the pinkish viscid innards spread along the steel bottom and soon enough we all are sliding in it, skittering off the slippery sheet and slamming against the wall, potato man among us. The cots too, as they are not secured to the floor, go flying toward the collects with the open-legged peasant women and clumsy children holding tight on their kin.

Screams of panic echo off the steel faceless walls. When the ship pitches high into the air, the inevitable down-splash of its great tonnage sends the population across the room but with nothing to grab on to. As the diving and swaying becomes longer, the force of ninety humans and their scattered belongings and fifty cots all slam against the uncaring steel with accumulating power. I see a woman completely unconscious with blood lines trailing from her ear and three of her brood holding on tight to her as if they don't realize she is dreaming a dream from her concussion.

Along with everyone else, I lose track of my bag that holds my life's worth inside it. As I look around for it and between being sent to opposing sides, I see boys around my same age stick their hands into others' belongings and pull out coins, stuffing them into their own pockets. Two men begin berating each other and stand in the center of the moving floor gummed with mucus and previous meals. One punches the other and they pull on each other's clothes for balance and dominance. Fighting and fighting in their beleaguered state like two cats that have been tied by their tales upside down and next to each other, brawling and hissing as if the other is to blame for their condition.

When the lightning finally passes, the swells calm too and soon all are slogging through the half-inch puddle to collect our soiled rags. A week goes by like this and only three times do the doors open with the mean stewards yelping for us to queue up as we grab for our cups. The soup is no more than water and stock, leftovers no doubt. I wait in line looking ahead impatiently and with only three in front of me the ship tilts deep into the sea as I drop my cup. I scramble for it before another can snatch it, but when I return to queue I see that the barrel holding the soup has tipped over and without cleaning the spillage, the stewards double back and lock the doors behind them. Some children around me scoop up the stock mixed with the dried vomit as their mothers cry out at the state of their lot. I look for the sweet child with the thoughtful mother and the bannock shares, but cannot find her. When I come to my place along the wall it is then I see my belongings have disappeared entirely, hungry eyes staring at my dismay like hidden hyenas protecting their earned pilferings.

Without normal sleep nor food and feeling the ship slowing, in a sudden four doors are opened above that I had yet to realize were even there. Appearing from them are the Englishman officials and their yelling.

"Out! Out! Out! Out yu goes!"

"Where are we?" One man calls up to them.

"Out! Get out!"

And so we again funnel obediently toward the single-door exit leaving behind us unclaimed trash, upturned cots never used for sleep, sopping blankets and overturned piss jars and rancid fecal buckets where somehow flies had made their way into the steerage hold or had created life itself from the stink of the third class.

A few hours later, I wait in line but for what I do not know. The ship backs away from us. There is land on either side in the distance of the island house packed with fellow ragged travelers pale with the sea's nausea and a childhood of peasantry. I give my name. "Liam."

"Whole name," he demands.

"William James Garrihy, born 1901, Clare, Ireland."

"Calling or occupation?"

"Laborer."

"Name o' relative or friend ya joinin'?"

"My uncle, Joseph Garrihy."

He hands me back some papers and that's when I find out someone misheard me and therefore changed my name. I am Garrity now. They then take my clothes so they can see the whole of me; sunken belly poked, tongue pulled and genitals picked up with a flat stick and my face flushed in embarrassment.

"Where ya off ta den," Another man says as a matter of occupation.

"Water Street."

"Brooklyn o' Manhatt'n?"

I thought of the two words. Brooklyn sounds more familiar.

"On 'at ferry ova dere, g'ahead."

CHAPTER 4

Mary's Eldest Son

I SHIFT IN MY SEAT AND take from my old man's pipe here, the discomfort weighing on me. It is not an easy task to write of my own life when the humility of my people pulls at me. The tradition of telling stories is a social one, where I come from. But I have become an American over these many years. And though I think as a traveling shanachie, I feel to write as an American does.

Richie Lonergan hops in his stride. He hikes his left leg forward, all the while keeping a strong and equal pace down the tenement low-risers of Johnson Street toward the waterfront in the middle of the night. As he is known, his face is chiseled and without expression like a young stone-faced white Indian among the coarse escarpments of his landscape. His bony cheeks reddened from the cutting winter wind and blond hairs flaying out the side of his cloth cap, Richie pushes on emotionlessly into the night. With fifteen years behind him, the boy is an experienced Brooklynite. Impassive is his wont, he keeps at pace under the elevated tracks. Above him, they are adjoined southward from the Sands Street Station House. He passes under the view of a couple trolley watchtowers like a city varmint mingling in its business among the trash and rails under the eyes of uncaring subway standers.

Through the littered train yard he limps. On a wooden leg with an empty shoe nailed to it, he goes without a fear in him. Jumps on a hitch between an old rusted-out train that lay forgotten for over a year, he then emerges into the waterfront neighborhood: a place most New Yorkers only notice from a train window, as yet another slum down by where the ships let off. When he gets to Hicks Street, he swings to the right and waves one arm in the air for balance but soon slows to cut through a tract of browned winter grass near Middagh Street scattered with the rustling rubbish from the restless night.

When upon he come to the old brick building that houses the picture frame factory, he flattens his back along its side to hide himself in the shadows, to rest a moment and calm his breath. The boy can hear the hearthy laugh and hearty lilt of old William Brosnan, head patrolman at the Poplar Street Station. The station stands opposite the factory by way of back doors, separated only by a thin garbage-strewn lot. As young Richie stands erect upon the brick wall, a long glim of yellowed light appears where Brosnan flicks the ash off his black cigar. Through the crack in the door Lonergan hears Brosnan's brogue as he chews the fat with patrolmen Culkin and Ferris of the local Bridgetown beat, the old Fifth Ward.

What brings Richie Lonergan out this night is a homeless laborer at the picture frame factory who spends his nights there for a portion of his earnings. Dumbly leaving his bicycle out back, Richie eyeballs it from around the dark corner. Richie inches closer to the back door of the factory, closer also to the lawmen of the Poplar Street Station across the way. His breath cools in the smoky cold, and he pulls the cap down tighter over his flat-stone cement eyes and sandy hair. He feels the wind biting at his ears and imagines that the yellow glim of light gives off a warmth. And if it is only his imagination, at least that somewhat warms him even. The boy hadn't the thought to beat his way out of a bad situation, but if pressed, he can summon the cudgel from his pant leg and put a man to God's path if he steps between him and his take. Copper badge or not, though he prefers not for it's a long bit on Blackwell's Island for a teenager to do a thing as that. True too that Brosnan knows him since he was only a child and had more than once put the manacles on him. Even monikered Richie the name the papers love to flap him with, Pegleg. For it was Brosnan himself who'd first responded after the trolley sliced the bottom of Richie's leg off when he was only of eight years fetching bread for his poor old Ma. Brosnan and Bill Lovett too, who helped calm the squirming child that stared at his own blood and limp leg lying motionless between the tracks. An accident so deeply set in the back end of his youth that he rarely thinks on it himself, though others always seem to wonder and whisper about it.

Richie peers around the brick building and hones in on the bicycle, then listens implicitly to the sounds animating the night; the clopping in the distance of old nags pulling their loads along the rocky cobblestones to deliver fish and vegetables and the like for the morning's market; the plucking of standup pianos in local saloons where suds wet the insides of late-night merchant marines and happy barkeeps; the bellowing of old Brosnan again laughing brusquely, mixing in a few jokes before again to blast open an uprooting bellow on the other side of the glimmer at the back door. Richie hears too the rumbling tracks above like rolling thunder in age-old lores where gods show their disapproval of mortal sins by the distant cannonades and clapping above. When the time seems right, Richie limps to the back of the factory, dragging his wooden leg behind, clicks the kickstand back on the bicycle, and walks to the front as though the bike were his from the get-go and nary a nerve jingled in the boy's body nor mind. Unable to ride the thing himself, he pushes it all the way back up Hicks Street against the wind. Through the rail yard he goes limping all the way toward the Lonergan first-floor room on Johnson Street, a wooden frame, pre–Civil War tumbledown that creaks when the wind rings up.

Richie reaches out to open the door, then maneuvers the bike and his leg through the sleeping troupe of ten or eleven sheetless children lying askew on the parlor-room floor. Their light-haired heads dark and wet from the body's oils and fallen asleep they have, exactly where their heads lay now.

Mary Lonergan's back is bent over the bucket of dishes beyond the sprawled children, her hands already wrinkled and

sore from the late-night scrubbing job at a Crown Heights man-
sion. It isn't until Richie drops the bike with a rattle among the
others that Mary turns round.

"And what are ya supposin' we do with all dese bikecycles
you keep findin' in the middle o' the night, Richie? Are ya
makin' a collection?" she shoots off in her Brooklyn brogue.

"Nah, rentin' 'em."

Across the left side of Mary's face is an old scar from hot
grease that had been thrown across her. Under her left temple the
hair has been scalded away and was never to grow again and her
left shoulder too was spotted with burns that had eaten the pig-
ment from her skin to leave the side of her a pale color. In 1904,
when Richie was three years old, his father took a pan of grease
off the fire and threw it on her in a fit of anger. It even made the
papers but that was only for a day. The scars are there still.

"I know da plan, Richie." She lays a fist on her hip. "But do
you think ya can get up a little earlier now an' again to rent'm
out to the kids that need them durin' the day? Ya've got a collection now; next step is the rentin' part you keep spakin' of."

"Where's Paps?" he answers.

"Don't know, saloon I s'pose."

"Anna?"

"Sleepin' in the back room, God let 'er rest. The sweetest
darlin' of a girl, she is. Spent the whole of a day at St. Ann's
prayin' for me," Mary whined her voice a bit at the end to
accentuate that Anna was praying for her poor old mother. "No
one hears a t'ing in this werld, not even a poor mother with
starvin' chicks. But Anna does. Ignore and ignore, that's what
they do. The evil is in the ignorin', write it down fer it's the
truth. Doesn't matther it's yer dyin' breath, they'll just give ya
the blindeye. Yer last dyin' wish'll go unheard and then off ya
take to the groundsweat with ya, and fer the goin' price too.
That's the cure fer ya."

"Why she prayin' for ya, Ma? Wha' happened?" Richie
could tell she had been thinking and plotting all day.

"Yer fadder's a loogin," Mary threw a washrag on the draining board. "He's made enemies of every boxer from here to Hell's Kitchen, he has. No future in promotin' or nothin' o' the sort. We're doomed!" she cries out and turns her back, half acting. "We're doomed to a life o' peasantry, Richie. Ye're da son of a scrubberwoman and a punchy ex-gangster and ex-boxer from the Lower East Side. We won't go nowhere an' with all these childers, Richie?" she spread her arm out motioning along the floor.

"Ma, stop cryin'," Richie hated when she used old words like that, "peasantry."

"I went by the Dock Loaders' Club t'day . . ."

"Again," Richie finished her sentence.

"Yeah, they won' let me in, but Bill Lovett was there and he said he'd send a message to Dinny about helpin' out widda openin' costs fer ya own bikecycle shop, God bless that young man Lovett. Ya know he's a big dockboss for Dinny Meehan now? Did ya know that?"

Richie turned around.

"Even though McGowan's the rightful dockboss in the Red Hook, Bill's proved himself by fillin' in with honor," she continued. "Only twentyone year old and he's showin' his colors as a dockboss, God bless'm. Ran out all them I-talians that tried takin' over the Red Hook after McGowen got sent up for a jolt . . . Saved Dinny Meehan a war against 'em, ya know he did. And Lovett's got just the temperament fer such a place as the Red Hook. But I known it from the day that bhoy was born into those rookeries on Cat'erine Street. That bhoy had swagger and he had a lot of it too. He's a good one, that Lovett. Always cared 'bout ya too since the accident . . ."

"Yeah, yeah, yeah . . ."

"Since before even too, he has, Richie. He always looked out for ya. He's got the ol' can-do, Lovett. And he was the first one there when the trolley got ya and he wrapped his tie 'round ya leg so's it wouldn't bleed out."

Mary stopped speaking as she blushed and the warmth hit her throat, tears blurred her eyes. She had the highest of expectations of Richie since he was her first and since he had

everything it would take to lead her family out of the Bridge
District slums. He had the fight in him and he had the nerve for
it. He had followers and most important, he had the name:
Lonergan, known on the Lower East Side and Brooklyn as a
name to put the fear in people. And Brady too, Mary's maiden
name and the surname of her famous brother, Yakey Yake who
ran things in the old days on the docks by Catherine Street: a
man who could turn on a dime, but fought mostly not for pleasure, but to give bread to his people, his family. Who kept the
Eastman Gang and the Five Points Gang at bay. Yakey Yake
was also the man who employed John Lonergan as one of his
main soldiers that she married at his courting. But when Yakey
Yake died of the consumption in 1904, things quickly went
awry for the Lonergan family.

Most of the time Mary was quietly proud of her Richie as he
fought through his childhood injury, but there were other times
when she hid from him and couldn't stop thinking how far
along he'd be if that accident had never come to them. She
couldn't let him see the terrible disappointment that overcame
her when she thought of it. Gathering herself in front of him,
she continued.

"Richie, ya've five bikecycles in a pile among the children
here and four out on loan. That's a lot o' bikecycles. With ya
own shop on Bridge Street, ya can quit the cutpursin' gimmick
at the Sands Street station and become a legitimate retailer. A
real businessm'n. Out of all me children, you got what it takes
to be somethin' more'n anyone, Richie. Somebody! Ya fifteen
now, Richie. A man o' da werld. Even Anna likes the idea and
swears she'd help. Ya know how she looks up at ya, Richie."

Through his sternness, Richie looks at his mother with a
shade of concern.

"Ya know Richie, people talk. They do, and they're sayin'
one day the gang could be all Lovett's. Can you imagine the
take fer us if ya was his right hand? Like the Romans we'd live!
O' course he's too young yet and that Dinny Meehan's a smart
one too, him bein' as long-lastin' as he has. And Bill's only got

the Red Hook now and who knows what'll happen when they let McGowan out. But that Bill Lovett's a wild one and he'll give Dinny more to chew on, true 'tis."

Richie stared, fidgeted.

"What do I know, anyhow? Just an ol' sow with no hopes. All I want is children that don' go starving their youthful days away. Ya know more'n I do, Richie. Ye'll do as ye t'inks fit, ye'll do . . . Fine then, what do I know? Nothin'. I'll be washing other people's floors while yer own fadder dips his finger into me sugar jar for a drink and a long-shot at the policy wheel."

Without a response Mary continued, but with less anger, "I know ya got yare own gang, Richie. They're good lads too. Who says ya gotta dump 'em? Nobody says. But if I know one t'ing that's good for all o' us it's that if ya gotta go on the lam or upstate fer a stint—God forgive me fer sayin' it—Dinny'll make sure we got food on the table. He will too," she pointed a finger at her son. "Ye'll be good to be in debt with Dinny Meehan. He takes care o' his. I may be a woman, but I'm the sister of Yake Brady and the wife o' his meanest man, John Lonergan. I know what a debt is to the like o' Dinny Meehan. Ya'll owe him, I know it. And ya're a loyal man, Richie Lonergan. Honorable man! But t'ink o' yer mother. T'ink o' Anna and the childers. Best chance we got, the gangs. Always has been fer our like."

CHAPTER 5

The Shapeup and The Starker

I SLEEP ON AN OLD SOFA with springs that have pierced the cushions through and right off I am taken with a fever from the long trip and the new weather and all. For close on two weeks I remain inside and become a burden to my uncle Joseph who tells the truth about things with the drink in him. A scarecrow of a man with his spindly legs, bony hips, and hunching shoulders, he seems to have a right opinion about it all whether someone asks him for it or not. I don't remember much of him from home though, as he'd made his way to New York back in 1908 for the labor work in the building of the Manhattan Bridge. Wasn't around much when he was in Clare anyhow.

I realize that he is a figure among other men, but I am unsure of his crew's place along the docks in Brooklyn. Most of his men are Irish, true, yet I see in all of them a bit of the outsider. With broken beaks and loose teeth, suits that are torn at the seams, sunken eyes, and a hungry look on their mugs, I know that to the bottom of them they are ill at ease. And the more I look on my uncle Joseph for the assurance I need, the more my stomach sags and slides with uncertainty.

Every morning except Sundays he gets up and walks from the brick tenement on Water Street next to the Sweeney factory with his crew of ragged cullies. They then go left on Hicks Street and line up with the rest of the laborers waiting for a ship to rest on the slips to request work. Sometimes they jump a trolley as far down as the barge port at the basin or load a truck off the Baltic Terminal or a train along the Jay Street freight tracks.

Uncle Joseph and his men haven't endeared themselves with the Dinnies who are in charge on the docks and run things from 25 Bridge Street, so they find getting work difficult. It is all quite confusing to me, gangs and docks and such, since I only hear about things secondhand from my uncle and his followers, but the Dinnies are often the topic.

"The Swede an' them put a few good men down at the Fulton Street Landing the other day," Uncle Joseph says puffing from the cutty among his crew. "Four of 'em. I-talians. Just lookin' fer work s'all they was after. Put a good beatin' on 'em too I heared."

His stroppy crew of listeners nod dolefully, and I decide I'll steer clear of the like of the man they call The Swede.

Looking at me then, Uncle Joseph speaks, "Feckin' banditry 'tis. Well then . . . We'll get ours too, but right by the werkin' man t'will be."

In time, I wake with them. Out seeing the city for the first time and walking from Water Street through pier neighborhoods in the morning under the drooping laundry lines and the blur of faces about. Behind the loping of my uncle and the others, we come under the two bridges and down the dock-train arteries of the Columbia Street piers. Bumping into strangers as I look up, nary a pardon to be heard. Families of fifteen are jammed into third-floor windows to peer out the fetid flat for a respite of air. Some tenements holding ten or twenty rooms shoulder-to-shoulder along the streets with tenants shoulder-to-shoulder inside them. An endless stacking of shacks and rowhouses and redbrick buildings at every curve and corner. The Bridge District, heavily industrialized with the crack of tool smiths and cigar rollers, linen makers, dye makers, tie makers, and seamstresses, all singing foreigners' songs by the open shudders. And then there are metal box makers and corrugated-cardboard-box makers and ship-container makers and warehousing units aplenty and gas companies competing for heads and police stationmen leaning back on their heels in the morning cut, suited up in their blue tunics and sidecocked caps.

The sound of the city goes ringing in my ears all at once: the dinging of distant tugs under the bridges, the sounding off of the booming barges, the clopping of horse buggies and drays. The city's orchestra of working-class harmonies mixing with the buzz of automobiles, the winching chains pulling up buckets on the coal wharfs, the *cuckoo-cuckoo-cuckoo* of elevated trains above and the scraping of their brakes on high. Too there is the tenor of arguments upstairs and next door, the soliloquies of the poor pierced by the soprano of the women victims sonorous in her sorrowful dispirit, ancient in their dialects and tongues. There are wild dogs tearing away at metal garbage cans on the sidewalks, footsteps on the creaking stairwells. I hear the drunken beratements of street men who it would seem yell at the paperboys, who themselves bellow from the street corners clamoring of the previous day's headlines in the brume of the late dawn's shuffling. Babies just able to walk and young children are playing with a long stick and a tiny ball in the street and they run shoeless most of the time, jumping over mud puddles with hardly a mother or father to be found standing over them. They play improvised games like stoopball or Kill the Carrier, a form of hurling where a child holding a stick is chased down and tackled by all the others, on the pavement no less. And spilling in their mischievous masses onto the stairwells and in front of draft horses pulling a man and a dilapidated cart, slowly scuffling through the neighborhood to get to the next at first blush of morn.

At every street crossing it seems another elevated track appears above with long stairwells filled with travelers stomping up and down like human conveyer belts. Grocers and tobacconists stand in their doorways smoking under the shadows

speckled with the lattice-light of the trellis-framed Els and
somehow live among the creaking and the screeching and
clicking and hammering of trolleys swooshing and grumbling
by all day and night. They converse with the men who sell
apples from their horse-pulled drays at the end of the sidewalks
and admonish the rag-picking children who walk by shoeless
and the low-placed homeless who splay their junk wares on the
pavement for possible buyers. And when a train comes to a halt
above, a small army of ten-year-old bootblack boys run up the
station stairwells for customers exiting like a gang of brothers,
though they are supposed to be competing against one another
for nickels and for dimes.

A day or so earlier a fire below the street had flames jumping
from each of the sewers, blowing manholes in the air after a gas
leak flooded the pressurized underground. A pre–Civil War
wood-framed building had collapsed over the sidewalk and into
Pierrepont Street some three months before I arrived, and lay
there still untouched. Only the oncome of winter has halted the
advance of weeds, now receding in the rubble. Children gamble
openly against a brick wall below the brownstone stairwells,
laying down the money they've garnered from some under-
handed racket for a chance to double it playing craps and faro.
And bigger kids come by with rapacious intentions and punching
the wee ones to extract their own sort of protection money, preparing themselves for the big show on the docks later in life as
it's the Dinnies who are the heroes on the lips of these shorn-
headed, floppy-hatted lads.

The first liner I ever see fall into dock, scraping its keel against
the wooden pier with a swoosh and a gulp, is a Scandinavian
girl named The Halkinnean full with a load of crated birch
shingles weighing close on seventy pounds each. The flag has
gone up in the waterfront steam, the old signal for labormen to
gather. And the whistle from the pier house blows as men amble
out of their tenements and from the saloons for the need to
work. No more than a skinny stripling standing in line with
larger men of much might, I am lost among the crowd and

quickly can't find my uncle. As I look around in a fright, I hear the callings of the cattle pushers.

"To Pier Six wit' ya's!" They yell. And quickly the hopefuls begin running up the cobblestoned street, a rough road lined with freight tracks along the pier houses that break the waterfront view, "Run! Go! Who's the best among ya!"

As we pile into the landing at Pier Six, a new voice yells at us to run north again. "Up to da bridge'n back, first ten mens guaranteed woik!"

Scrambling, men in dirty suits with broken shoes and hats in their back pockets fight amongst one another for the lead. Their suit ties are in tatters and dirt-rimmed collars flap mistakenly over their bedraggled coat as they take to the wind in hope of winning work for a day. Unknown faces spilling strange languages from their gobs and with eyes empty and bellies falling out of them with hunger to summon strength from their deflated reserves, they clamber with patchwork humility in the early-morning gales. Some men cheat and turn around for the final stretch before making it to the bridge. They are met then with shoulder bumps that put their faces in the ground and kicks that leave them moaning heavily in the cobble mud. Eventually we are led by the Dinnies all the way back where we started and lined up again. Breathing heavy. Breathing deeply with our hands on our knees, we look for the Dinnies and quickly straighten up to show how we are not in the least affected by the sprinting and fighting.

"On the line! Fix ya'self on the line, ya bunch o' spalpeen layabouts," I hear one of the Dinnies yell out.

"Get there! Get there. Quick, quick . . ."

"Ya nothin' but a bunch a rotten navvies!"

"Shape-up boyos, who's the man of the men here?"

"Who's the bee's knees, then?"

As I look up, four of the men barking at the mass of hopefuls push themselves through the group and make a separation to reveal their leader. And in he come. From the grimace of his toughs they clear the way for the chieftain of the dock clans.

Look at the man. Mid-twenties he strides across the face of us with a prominent stare and a fixed grin as his cronies shrink behind him, arms crossed. He does not have a happy grin though. This grin is that of a man staring into the sun. This man who emerges from the parting crowd, he who knows that each pale staring face that peers upon him is desperate for work, does not give the glaring eyes a notice as it's he who looks upon our shoddy like to see how much work can be wrung from us. How hard we'll give. He looks in each face. In each eye and if he finds fire, he moves on. If he finds passivity, moves on. If he finds reason, he chooses. But reason without muscle of course, he moves on.

Lost in the crowd as was I, one of his sluggers approaches and grabs me by both shoulders, pushes me between two men that know each other in line. After a moment, one of them elbows me behind him so he can be on the side of his buddy and I having to force myself back into line again from behind.

The man with men parting around him is, of course, Dinny Meehan, leader of the White Hand. And though it was many years ago, I remember it as if it were happening now and right out in front of me.

It was then, as Dinny Meehan strode through the dock aisles, that I finally figured out that the group called Dinnies were really his own: Dinny's men, that is. And along the line he stalked like some rogue general inspecting his indigent battalion of scamps and scallies queued up as well as they could but stung with the hunger and the cold.

He stands there in my mind as if it were today. Bold and humble, a man of his time and mine. He is standing there ahead of me, scanning the bodies and the faces of the hopefuls in line. Erect like a gypsy traveler appraises a piebald vanner mare with a keen, scrutinizing eye before arguing price. He even asks to see some of the men's teeth and if they possess all the digits on their hands. Behind him, a pier reaching out into the East River becomes filled with a backing ship and four guiding, noisy tugs. This man Meehan did not walk with the gruff demeanor of his roughneck toughs who make order on the labor lines. Instead, he answers his men's questions with a nod or a softly spoken "Nah," or a gentle "Yeah."

His clothing, though a bit patchy, clings to his muscled shoulders, chest, and upper arms and down toward his flat stomach and punchy legs. His boots are soiled, as are all the other men's, and he has the face of a hardened laborman with a wide jaw and the small ears of a fighting dog. His brown hair falls back over the top of his head without the spit or oil some use, though shocks of it are left over his temple and down close to his ear on one side. His eyes though, that's what made Dinny Meehan. His eyes are a very intelligent green and made of a nice shape both mean and understanding.

At the time, no one had to tell me who the tribe-head here was. He carried the weight of the responsibility of things on the Brooklyn docks in his eyes, he did. As had all chieftains among their clan in the olden days back home when they ran wild through the glens, heathers, bogs, and boreens.

Up and down the line bark his boyos. Attacking a loosened piece or a scowling laborman here and there. Hissing at them in the morning wind. Pushing them off balance if they sneer too much. The dockboss of the Baltic Terminal was John Gibney, "the Lark." His right-hand man standing behind him is the slick-haired Big Dick Morissey with the chest of a black ape and the forearms of an anchor chain. Also there, tightening up the line, is the gangly white-haired dooker with the long arms and club fists, the one everyone calls The Swede. And finally Vincent Maher, a handsome masher who was a bit younger than the rest and who smirks with the sport of a skirt chaser yet walks with the same authority as a man in the inner circle of Meehan's larrikins.

From behind with a scare and pushing passed me without mention of a pardon is another taller sort that doesn't have the shoulders of Big Dick or the vulgar bearing of The Swede. This man who leapt through the line from behind me came straight to the ear of Meehan and overhearing him as I did, was taken by the fellow's accent, which can't be mistaken for anything

other than that of a true Irish traveler. A native of the country
roads of Ireland where they claim no territory as their own and
wobble about in covered wagons pulled by gypsycobs from riverside to horse fair. This traveler, Tommy Tuohey is he, a type I
knew all too well as coming from the clans of fist fighting and
knavery who sleep their drink off under the big aimless pale
starry and mooned sky. With logistics at hand, Tuohey speaks to
Meehan as he'd just come from a meeting with the captain of
the ship for a rundown on the goods to be unloaded and an esti-
mate on manpower.

"Fer de sake of an eerly day Dinny, sexty-two strongmen
could give de ship to rest, giverteek, moraless," said the man so
quickly that I barely understand him myself.

Meehan nods to Tuohey. Then appearing from another place
was Eddie Gilchrist who was good with numbers, though a bit
on the soft side. His spectacles at the end of his nose clumsily,
Gilchrist looks up and mumbles under his breath as he gathers
quickly the difference between the money offered by the ship-
owners, money needed by the stevedoring company, and how
much take the gang would get from the sixty men.

For the dockmaster's final line-walk, the others snap to attention and look forward into the distance, pushing their chest out
and standing tall on their feets. When he comes upon me and my
youthful, bony physique, he snorts quietly and grabs my arm,
wrapping his hand around it entirely. Looking in my eyes, Meehan
quickly looks away again without changing the posture on his face
a bit. Then moves on and picks the fellow next to me and a few
others for the job. Gibney the dockboss walks behind Meehan and
every here and there whispers into his ear about a man having put
a dollar in his pocket to get picked, then the man emerges from
the line and stands among those who would work that day.

My uncle Joseph is against the idea of paying to work, and so
is his crew. Consequently he and his are rarely chosen. Across
the gaggle he looks at me with a scowl as the line falls apart.
Some throw their gripes in the air while the firm-eyed Meehan
with all his cronies about him gives his back to us.

The Swede stands and stares into us as the others around him walk toward the ship. He dares any of us to step forward, waits for someone to back up their crying out against the old rules that still have life here on the docks of Brooklyn.

And as soon as The Swede begins to turn back toward the dock, a man runs from among us with a pistol in hand and lets off a wild shot into the gangsters. Everyone ducks except me since I don't recognize the sound of a gunshot. The Swede acts quickly, turns round and pushes the running man off balance and lands on him knee first, then rips the gun from him. Tuohey, Gibney, Morissey, Maher and others land on the man too while Dinny Meehan rolls up his sleeve to look upon his bloody forearm, wounded by the shot.

"It's nothin'," he promises, then waves his men back toward the ship. "Bring 'em over here."

I stare as the groups of men walk in opposite directions, those heading to the docks for work, and those heading back to the saloons. The man with the gun is taken from our lot and dragged screaming. He is apparently insane, soft on the brain, or both. His fate is not for us to know or ask, however.

"Starker," Uncle Joseph explains. "Hired by the shippin' companies or maybe the New York Dock Company, who knows. Anodder who wants Dinny Meehan dead."

"That's a good thing, is it not?"

He looks at me. "They kill union guys too, anyone for the dime. Labor sluggin' has loyalty to no one but the dime."

I wonder if the police are to be summoned, but told that no such law exists along the waterfront. The Poplar Street station is only called upon when a body is found by those who believe in police law.

"Up the street inland, the law is there for most people," a crony of my uncle mumbles while the starker is pulled away by his collar. "Here, no one wants to know what passes in the dark."

We turn round, and without work my uncle and his men curse the gang again. Days go on like this and the only time I ever get work is when multiple ships arrive simultaneously and no other men are to be had. Weeks can go by without working a single day while the same groups of men are picked. Some complain that they haven't the money to pay the gang to be among the chosen and if they did, they'd still have to pay tribute at the end of the day. This would leave them with a small take.

Too many men, not enough ships and jobs. Even in a place like the Bridge District that is highly industrialized. Still, it isn't near enough, as more ships unload the human cargo of pilgrims and defectors and escapees of foreign and obscure hostilities every day. Spilling into the overflowing neighborhoods and exasperating an already desperate circumstance. My uncle and his men explain to me that a few years earlier, many gangs used to war with one another for the right to work. For labor work. But Dinny Meehan brought all the gangs together and since then, it is the White Hand that controls the labor racket.

When we do get picked for loading or unloading, the work is backbreaking and strains my young thin muscles to a burning never witnessed in my body. I am often overcome with the need to drop my carry under the great strain in my shoulders and neck. Winded too, as we are made to run, and the sweat underneath my shirt freezes when it's cold enough. One time Gibney the Lark kicked me to the ground for my lagging in the line. Already tired from the work, I fall like a pile of bones and use the time as a resting point while the others laugh it up at my expense. At the end of the day, when the stevedoring company passes out envelopes that contain my earnings, Gibney and his right-hander Big Dick, show up again with some other fellows and demand a portion. I willingly hand it over. Having heard the story of the four Italians who were dragged off by ambulance cars, I'm not concerned about the morality of it. After taking my portion, Gibney and Big Dick simply turn round and force upon the next victim.

"Have a little dignity, bhoy," my uncle Joseph angrily whispers. "Don't look so feckin' scared when ye hand it over. Show'm yer honor. Give'm the eye. Are ye wid us or not?"

"I am."

CHAPTER 6

McGowan's Wake

ONE NIGHT ON A SATURDAY I sleep on the sofa while white snow
shimmers out the sooty kitchen window. It falls slowly, peace-
fully into the foreground of the bridges and masts and elevated
tracks in the air among the stacked factories and tenements
and brownstoned buildings leaning over the East River. The
dark Water Street shack shakes when the stringed freight cars
drop their loads of raw materials to the Pittsburgh Plate Glass
Company. Rail brakes moan through the halls when ship con-
tainers full of paint cans are delivered at the Masury & Co.
factory and clicking echoes travel through the air shafts when
torpedoes are transported to the E.W. Bliss building up and
down Plymouth Street a block away.

In good spirits after a bout with the drink, Uncle Joseph
brings over a few men to the tenement for a shindy. That
Saturday, the bottom-floor room was to cackle with voices and
was lit with elongated, blooming flames in the dark from sucking
pipe matches. With the drink in them they are blurts, much
louder now than on the piers where I last saw them.

When I am woken by the drinking roars, they hand me the
hooch for a swig; and, set to waking the fireplace too, they
throw broken pieces of wood from the stairwell banister. Cursing
Dinny Meehan and all the toughs who follow him, they resort
instead to lines about worker-friendly environs and the right of
men to organize.

"Fair bein' fair!" they demand. "Civility of the worker's rights!"
I watch them from my springy sofa pounding their fists on
the kitchen counter with their boorish denunciations and their
lavish proclamations. Crooning the melodies of the abject and
summoning the war cries of that time and place.

"Emma Goldman says . . ." and "Gene Debs is a man we'll
vote fer . . ."

It was the pookas lived here too. I'd heard them as they were
still fresh in my old country thoughts. The shanachies who storytell
from village to village had always told me that the Irish are cursed
by them, which explains why we are always on the bottom of every
rung and wrangle, no matter the city we reside. Once we show a
bit of success the pookas come and haunt us and whisper good-for-
nothings in the ears of all. Next thing you know the whole shabang
is overcome with unrest and back we go to the starving bottom of
the rung, having to work day and night to wrangle every gimmick
we can just to hold our lips above the water. That's what the
shanachies say at least. And though I had no idea what they speak
of, pookas and wrangles and such, I am beginning to get a sniff of
it as I listen to my uncle Joseph and comrades.

I can see that hungry look in his eye, Uncle Joseph. He has
the stare of a scrag by the way his thin hairs flap over his baldspot,
skinny neck and sunken cheeks with the opaque pallor of a
half-dead man. He comes upon me close and breathes his
boozy pan in my face, "Yer makin' progress now among us,
bhoy. The men'r noticin' ye as well. They are too! Ye've a fine
werk et'ic 'bout ye."

Impressionable as I am, the compliments open me up. I want
to cry, I really do because the struggle I am going through
internally is a difficult one.

"Not ye to werry, Liam," he says. "We've got ye in our sights
as well. We all see ye, don' t'we fellas?"

"Sure do," they agree.

"Right that."

"T'ing is," he continues, one arm around me on the sofa and
pointing at me with the hand that is wrapped around a bottle.

"We need guys like ye. Sure we do! We need ye here in Brooklyn. Young strong bucks like yerself. Able bodied and minded. The werld was made fer de like o' ye. An' the International Long-shoremen's Association needs good lads like ye. Ye're comin' in at the right time, ye are. I'm goin' to introduce ye to a man's gonna help us all, name's Thos Carmody. He was sittin' right here just a few week ago. Oh yeah, that's a man can get things done, he'll have ye up an' runnin' with a union card an' all. He told us of the German plot, didn't he men?"

"He did!" They agreed.

"The English, they call him the Hun, but what's an Irishman got against the Germans? Nothin', that's what. One million dullers fer a strike in Brooklyn, that's what they're ready to pay us, bhoy. Thos Carmody an' the ILA, they're ready to pay us fer refusin' to work and make weapons for the English to buy. And guess who's to lose power from us strikin', guess?"

"I don't know."

"Dinny Meehan and his band of pikeys 'n tinkers, that's who. We'll take'm down. With no work and full bellies, the ILA's ready to finally take'm down. Are ye wid us, bhoy?"

"Sure."

He points to my cup, "Put a hole in that, kiddo, and have another drop."

I drink and drink, not realizing the brew is so powerful. It's poteen, of course. Handmade in the tub; what we call back home "pu-cheen," the rare ol' mountain dew. Though the taste of it is awful, the feeling is wondrous and with the mingling of compli-ments and the potion in the drink, I become overwhelmed with the happiness. One of the men asks if I am cold in the bones. Standing over the fireplace, he pulls a hot poker and stuffs it into a full glass of ale, takes a sip for himself, and hands it over to me. I nibble on the hot brew a couple times until I am encouraged to take bigger slugs. Within moments I am not only warmed to the core, but happily dizzy from the drink too.

I speak openly about the docks and my new life for the first time. Words flow from me as they hadn't in all my life flowed before. Realizing it all as a big adventure, I see it as one day to be a great story for recounting to my childhood friends in Clare, if I ever am to see them again. Uncle Joseph encourages more and more, and next thing I know I'm at a pitch of excitement what with all the new sights and smells of Brooklyn fresh in my mind. Standing from the sofa and waving my arms about uninhibitedly. It all comes rushing into my mind's sight as articulate as the greatest of writers, or so I feel: the view of the canopy of bridges from our neighborhood connecting us to the mystical place called Manhattan. Manhattan! With its huge buildings erect and virile and austere across the East River from the docks along Columbia Street or right out the kitchen window of our Water Street room. It all makes perfect sense to me now and I am out of my mind with fervor and optimism.

Another of my uncle's friends who'd been sitting in the kitchen with his legs propped akimbo onto the boiler played an old song on his "tenement house piano," as they used to call it. Though it is no more than a simple penny whistle, it is good sounding. The music, the bitter weather, the smell of firewood, and the drink give me to thinking. And then I think again of the vantage point at the docks and its southern skyline of Lady Liberty standing tall over the water and so very proud too, my eyes foam up with dewy-eyed nostalgia. Now drunk, the fairytale comes alive. I realize then that my struggle is that of any other boy becoming a man and if a boy my age doesn't struggle, then he may never become a man. Unable to scoff at my own sentimental epiphanies, I continue forth in my dream-drunk conclusions.

By the time all my thoughts are emptied, the room begins to spin in my head and a fierce sweat comes upon me. My stomach is light and airy and not understanding the predicament, I stand up and burst forward with all the liquor that covered the remnants of my thin dinner splashing onto the wood floor in front of me out of a sudden.

"Ye feckin' ungrateful lil' muck!" Uncle Joseph bellows and abuses.

I'd fallen to the ground among my own retching. Above, Uncle Joseph punches upon my head and face, my reactions to block them are slowed and incompetent, limp. I can't remember all the things he says as he punches and kicks, but I do remember him gnashing and spitting in his fit.

"Yere fadder ain't but Fenian swine from old and stupid ways!"

His boys stand up from their chairs and pull pipes from their faces at the spectacle.

"And yere mother's a country óinseach," Uncle Joseph kicked, pulling me up by my hair. "An' ye're the child of a great ignorance! Can't even see the opportunity of yere life in front o' ye, ye beggar's spawn!"

Dragging me to the door like they did the insane starker on the docks, he opens it and throws me by the collar down the wooden stoops onto the icy pavement out front. When I try and rise, he leans down and punches with a closed fist onto my cheek by my eye. I fall back again and again he drags me across the sidewalk to the gutter by a lightpost, spits in my direction, and turns round.

"Ye don' wanna listen to me? Go an' beg ye're way t'rough life, ye shanty Irish!" As the door slams shut, I can hear him slurring at his followers inside. "That goes for the each of ye, too . . . ."

I can tell that he is angry about other things, but that matters not now. All of this means but one thing; I'd not return to Water Street again. Sent to the snow and the cold and the freezing December night air, disheveled and drunken I wander confusedly, and vomit more in the muddy snowbanks at the edge of the pavement. The ice sheets along it slide the world from under my feet. Dumb from shock, I hadn't even considered the idea of grabbing for my coat on the way out. After a very long hour in the whipping winds that come jettisoning off the East River, my ears begin to sting and my face is frozen in place with tears stuck to my swollen cheek. Gathering balance from the corners of buildings, I begin simply trying to open one door after another regardless of consequence. Finally, at a six-story tenement house on Montague Street, a door is open just a crack to allow a frozen stranger's entrance. Not much cooler inside the halled inner walls, I can feel a bit of heat coming from the bottom of a door on the first-floor. I huddle my frozen hands close to the warm breeze from the floor and finally resolve to lay my entire body along it to fall asleep like a wrecked ship among its own shambles.

A week goes by and I have disappeared from the docks altogether. Uncle Joseph being the connection, I forgave the thought of searching for work there. I lay my head at night in a disowned building along with a huddle of other abandoned children off the Flatbush approach to the Manhattan Bridge. Windows boarded and front door bolted, we steal up a hole in the flooring to gain access from beneath where the smell of old death and winter dirt mix. In the night wind, the wooden two-story building shifts in the air and creaks at the whim of the night gales. Not fearing the danger in it, we light some extra coals and floorboards in a barrel upstairs until one night when the barrel itself burns through the floor and falls to the lower level with an awful crash. We peek down the hole surprised by it all as embers fly below, leaving us cold for a night, scrambling for warmth.

I get by with eating dirty snow for water and stealing bread from horse carts and peanuts from the pockets of sailors that stammer from saloons and into view of a pilfering child. I still owned a dollar bill, so when I do buy a can of beans or so I slip longbread in the back of my pants slyly. I learn to conserve energy and plan out my thin meals, thoughts consumed only on how best to steal. It was many a night I slept on the wooden floor of that shack with a great emptiness in me and from it I come to see the immortal cunning of the thief and his relation to American ingenuity. An art form of necessity and urgency and competition. Breeding it in the child, they do. Bred in these children that sleep next to me with their faces pressed against the cold wooden floor and no sheet to cover them, no pillow for their eggshell heads. Some no more than five and six years of age huddled together motherless in the wintry night.

In a different language it's said where I come from, "The well-fed cannot understand the hungry." And so, not a soul wonders about me or stops to ask a question or offer help, only pitiless smirks and "I'll fan ya ears, kid, 'less ya beat it quick."

I am regularly shooed by shopkeeps even when stealing is not on my mind, like they sense the hunger in my eyes and body language. Where empathy is with them I couldn't know. Back home, my da would sometimes let a hungry wanderer stay with us a day or two and collect free meals so long as he helped about the house and farm. A common thing among the country Irish. But here a wanderer is leered at and cruelty lives in the locals' eyes and in their stance like a mad child's grudge. I swore to my mother's soul never to lose what I learned from my family of mercy, empathy. No matter where I am to live.

I nick a wool coat with a big collar at a restaurant in Borough Hall and inside the pockets are a pair of heaven-sent gloves. Yule tidings for a lost winter gamin. Toward nightfall I wander back to the Flatbush orphanage, wind whipping in the ears. It is a brumal and barren hungry night wherein the streets are hollowed out by the promise of a piercing frost. My face feels dry and cracked. My groin is frozen and there is loneliness in the whistling cold and the dry-freeze of my thoughts. One of the kids at the makeshift orphanage is named Petey Behan. He has short legs with a long torso and some power in his shoulders, thin hips, and a box face with a mouth that never stops its blathering.

"Me and Pegleg an' some others are extablished," he boasts. "We gotta a couple gimmicks that're gonna pay out soon, ya know? You guys should come meet'm, Pegleg. We gotta gang and we're lookin' to expand, but ya gotta be tough. If ya ain't tough, don't think about it. Pegleg's a killer, he'll kill ya. I seen 'em kill one feller. I did too."

"Really?" Two other kids gaped as the light from the fire lit their faces orange in the dark.

"Yeah," Behan says. "Beat 'em wit' his own fists and then shot 'em with a gun right in the face. An I-talian kid that thought he could steamroll Pegleg into sellin' junk for him. Just kilt 'em dead. The cops caught up to Pegleg too, but they let'm go."

"They let'm go?"

"Yeah, they couldn't make it stick. My brother's a
Whitehander too."

"He's one of Dinny's?"

"Yeah, kinda. He's done work wit' both the Whitehanders
and the Jay Street Gang back before the Jay Streeters agreed to
work wit' the Whitehanders. He had to do a job once too, my
brother. Him and Wild Bill Lovett together, they stole a bunch
o' stuff from a warehouse and then sold it to someone in
Manhattan. Like a real job, ya know. They made real good
money doin' that. My brother said he got twenny dollars pullin'
that off. And he did it with five other guys who all got twenny
dollars too. Dat's what we're gonna do, me and Pegleg an' us.
So if yas wanna real job, just ask me. But ya gotta be tough, see.
If ya ain't got tough, ya better go'n get it."

Lying across the hardwood floor with the rest, I shared bits
of bread with a thin four-year-old that refused to speak. Unable
to close her own mouth, or unaware it was open, she just looked
at my hand every time it disappeared inside my pocket, then
poked me on the leg for more bits.

Appearing from the dark and standing over me, Behan says
to me, "Hand over the coat, it's my place to be askin' for it."

I look up at him. "This is my coat."

Next thing I know he's dragging me across the entire room
by the collar and trying to shake me free from the thing with a
couple kicks to my side and some more shaking. Instead of
fighting back, I let it slide through my arms and look up.

"I was the first one here," he says, making a big scene of it in
front of the little ones. "I got rights to charge rent and seein' as
though I know y'ain't gotta a penny to ya name, I claim dibbies
on this here coat."

I watch him disappear to a corner farther away from the
glim of the dying flame in the barrel. The wee one I was just
feeding then realizes I have no more bread and gets herself up
to find a corner to sleep in too. Eventually I do the same.

The week before Christmas and wandering through the
maze of buildings by daylight, I walked around a snowy corner

and was surprised by a man running for his life, striding desperately past me. On his coattails are two others whom I recognize immediately from the docks: Tuohey the pavee fighter and The Swede whom you never can forget once you put eyes on him.

"Ya fookin' better run, Leighton," I hear The Swede yell as the three men continue running toward the middle of the street, moving to the opposite sidewalk. "I catch ya and ya pay for ya brother's ills!"

A main thoroughfare is Fulton Street. It has a terminal and used to be the road that lead to the Fulton Ferry for the Manhattan crossing. In 1915, though, it was next to the Empire Stores, the port warehousing structure scurrying with workers winching pallets of tobacco through the iron-shudder windows above. It ran parallel with the Brooklyn Bridge where the three-story Sands Street train station fed the elevated trains that snaked through the neighborhoods and across the bridge to Park Row, in Manhattan. A city on its own, Sands Street station also housed Richie "Pegleg" Longergan's gang of cutpurses and pickpockets. With such dense commuter transience, it was the perfect headquarters for a gang of teenage thieves. Of course, among this gang was Petey Behan. Himself the thief of my much-needed coat.

A week or so after that, I am wandering over by Jay and York streets on the east side abutment to the Manhattan Bridge with the belly falling out of me in hunger. After long bouts of fasting in the desolate wind and dry crisp air, it begins to seize up in me. I can feel my eyes in my face glowing with visions. New splendors come across my mind and just as soon as they swirl beautifully around my imagination they disappear, and I became enraged under faulty logic. No money and no plan, I am alarmingly unafraid of my fate and when reason does come over me, my stomach turns in concern while my eyes light up in fear.

I go back to Water Street ready to grovel back into my uncle Joseph's good standing and a woman answers the door.

"Don't know any Joseph Garrity, child, must o' moved out," and the door closes.

At Front Street just a few blocks away, I see playing among the garbage and muddy puddles in the cobblestones a motley band of eight or nine shanty children, parentless in the long misshapen shadows of late afternoon. A few of them have their feet dangling in the sewers where the excrement of neighbors mingles in the mud and whatever else accumulates in the rectum of the streets. Remarkable though was, next to the ragged kiddies, a lounging horse that had finished her last breath and lay there on her side retired from her slavery. With a gaping mouth, staring eyes, and a mountainous rib cage in the air with a thin layer of skin over her, the old girl was a daunting figure there in the road sprawled aside the impervious imps and refugee nurslings. The eldest boy stands over the others with a cap over his eyes and his hands in his pockets keeping at a stern stare on me, shoulders hunched under two floppy suspenders. A bit younger than myself, he is the most like a parent among them and orders the others around, ballyragging them for saying dumb things. I feel sad for the beast and believe he does too, so I ask him whose draft horse it was.

"Well it ain't yours is it?"

The youngest, barely able to speak, spoke up to me, "The butche's on he's way ter pick up da ol' nag and make a . . ."

"Shaddup!" the eldest says to the nursling, then motions for me to keep moving.

The child looks up behind him to the eldest and scowls. The type of scowl a four-year-old shouldn't know how to cast just yet.

"G'on, don' get ya'self thinkin'," the eldest reiterates.

A day or so later and still without even bits of food in me I go back to Borough Hall and wander around some more. Hoping maybe someone will see me this time. I think of a plan. Rather, of needing a plan. Needing to come up with some sort of resolution where my daily routine will be more fruitful. A plan is a fine idea. If only I can get something to eat so I can think more clearly so I can make this plan. Snowflakes begin to populate the air like floating crystals. It's all dreamy inside me and I stare ahead while my thoughts turn soft again, lucid. I allow

myself this purposely. Irresponsibly. Without the wool coat, I
stuff my hands deep into the pockets of my trousers and shiver
obviously, significantly. It is Christmas Eve, so I say a prayer
and think about the warm choruses sung on such a night at the
church of Clooney back home to celebrate the birth of Christ
together. I think about my mother too, and sisters so far away.

Moments later I am overcome with distress. Distraught by
pookas whispering in my ear and cursing the fact of it being so
cold. I walk with a wild pace looking around everywhere for
loose morsels or opportunity like a gull circling behind the ferry's foam. I walk myself right out of Borough Hall and toward
Columbia Heights. When I see a lazy dray with a cover over the
back, I sneak up behind it regardless of consequence and rip
open the sheet.

"Hey! The fuck's wrong wit' ya?" the driver belches.

I look at him with cat's eyes and scurry off.

"Kid!" I hear a yell from across the street, then see a young
man crossing the cobbles in my direction. "C'mere, yeah. C'mere.
What ya doin'?"

He looks healthy, fit. Maybe twenty-two years old. Handsome
and with his cap over one eye and a toothpick out the other side
of his mouth, he walks with a rhythm. I recognize him, but
can't remember from where. I stand still, hoping he can lead me
to some food.

"Yeah, ya stealin' in my neighborhood widout me knowin'
first? Is that it?"

I look at him.

"Ya ain't gonna answer me?"

"I'm not."

"Oh yeah? Wha's ya name?"

"Liam Garrity."

"Garrity?"

"Garrity."

"Joe a relation o' yours?"

"Uncle, but I swore him off as he did me."

"You got nowhere to go?"

"Not yet."

"How old are ya?"

"Still fourteen."

"'Still fourteen,' he says," laughing at me, then looks around. "What are ya, right off the boat?"

I don't answer.

"Listen, come wit' me. Ya hungry? Come wit' me. I gotta be somewhere an' ya can come wit'. C'mon," then grabs my arm and walks me quickly through the cobbles toward the sidewalk.

After a few minutes of walking I ask his name.

"'What's my name,' he says," again making fun and repeating. "Guy, just call me Guy."

"Guy?"

"Yeah, or Patrick Kelly, like everyone else around here."

I would get to know him quite well over time, his real name was Vincent Maher and he walked me into a flower shop and dropped some coins on the table, left with a bouquet. "Ya ever been to a wake?"

"Uh . . . I have."

"Good, le's go."

"What if I don't want to?" I stop.

"C'mon, only one better place to catch a girl, dat's a weddin'. Wakes? They get all lathered up about 'em, girls do. And dis guy dat died's got t'ree sisters. T'ree of 'em, let's go. They got scoff there."

"Scoff?"

"*Foooooood*, shit kid, ya don' know nothin' do ya? I can tell ya hungry, though, as there ain't a lick a manhood on ya, fookin' scrawny as ya is. Jus' follow me kid, I'll take care o' everythin', don't ya worry. C'mon."

"Who died?"

"A guy."

"How'd he die?"

"Screw got'em."

"What's that?"

"Shaddup."

As we walk away, he takes off his trench coat and drops it over my shoulders. A few minutes later and we come upon a throng of half-frozen men and women and their children standing in the street in front of a wood-framed, four-story tenement. Maher grabs me by the lapel and pulls me through it as most step aside when they see him and his side-cocked cap. We thump up a thin stairwell together, dark as a forgotten cave. The dusty steps creak in their blackened wood and Maher whispers down, reminds me to keep my mouth buttoned. On the second floor the banister is gone other than some shardlike stalagmites sticking up from the planks. I hold onto the wall instead where I feel the rotted and exposed studs and downstairs I can hear the hum of the crowd reflect from the entrance and up through the stairwell. We hear keening coming from behind a closed door above us and the hushing coos of loved ones like pigeons on a wire. When we make it to the third floor we take a left and pass the doorless lavatory. Maher knocks lightly with a knuckle, then checks up the stairwell toward the top floor in the black.

I huff from the stairs, not so much from being winded but because my body is beginning to give way for not having slept in some two days. And for the hunger, which leaves me only with emaciated energy. With no bed or rest in the coming, my stamina is discouraged though the food is just behind the door, so I am told. Beginning again to dream with eyes open, my thoughts are tumbling from one topic to another and nothing much seems so real or connected, though I try with all I have not to reveal my mind's unsound movements.

"Who is it?" whispers a man from behind the door.

"Maher."

The door opens and a giant leaning figure stands in our path. I know right off who it is from the white hair and the scary look on him. "Who's the kid?"

"C'mon, would I bring any touts around here? I needa talk to Dinny 'bout this one. Let us in."

The Swede bends down from the door frame to whisper in the dustwood hallway, his neck arteries seizing in blue and red,

"Ya fookin' stoopit, ya not gonna bring no fookin' stranger in here . . . who says ya could. . . ."

"Listen, lemme talk wit' ya a second, c'mere," Maher says as calm as anyone could be under such a threat. "Stay there," he whispers back to me, then disappears behind the door with The Swede.

Two minutes and the door opens up violently.

"Put ya hands up," The Swede says walking from the door and confronting me.

"Sheesh," Maher mumbles.

The Swede pushes me against the wall and cups his large hand into my loins and squeezes, then searches underneath me in the back, pats my chest and thighs, his hands easily wrapping around my reedy waistline.

When we come in the door to the kitchen I can't find the scent of food, instead only of fresh-cut wood and flowers that can't quell the rattles in my shrunken belly. I am told to take the coat and hat off and we then walk softly into the opening to the diminutive parlor. Supported by four tattered wooden chairs, there is a long yellow pine coffin stretched under the drapeless window reaching into the middle of the room. Topper shut.

Dinny Meehan glances at me directly in the eye then gave attention back to the woman whose faint hands he holds between the span of his brawny shoulders. She snuffles and her nose and cheeks are blushed with the cry. His gentle confidence attempting to assure her of a sanity in this world, he whispers to her in the sunlight dust. Stacked behind them in the close-shouldered room are thickets of bursting bouquets contrasting the dull grays and dark colors of the parlor. Maher adds his to the confection, gives a distant hug to the mother of the dead. The only light in the entire flat comes from the cloudy window and the dull glim of the gray Christmas Eve day outside.

Three sisters sit on the faded and torn navy blue sofa by the coffin, the youngest on the arm and a widow sat looking out the window in a long stare under an awning bower of lilacs and assorted flowers, her two fatherless dawdlings running from the back room to the kitchen unattended. Six broad men stand at varying heights at the women's opposite like high-rises wedged together in a dumbstruck skyline, hat in hands, thin black ties between tight jacket lapels. The Swede at the pinnacle, his long needle face topped with white feathers like a towheaded city savage. I recognize others from the docks, the pavee fighter Tommy Tuohey among them.

Maher and I take our place in the room's saturnine reserve cast by a dead man's presence. At my side, a pair of eyes look at me in the hush. It is Harry "The Shiv" Reynolds, who I know as the dockboss at the Atlantic Terminal known chiefly as the bloodculler of Columbia Street's bulkhead. My stomach makes a curling sound and I am overcome with a terrible cramp in my bowel. Reynolds looks at me again, then steadies himself.

The Swede leans over us and looks out the window, his attention caught by a gaggle of brown trenchcoated men accumulating around a two-horse dray that stops out front, mingling among the crowd below.

"Everybody get away from the window." The Swede breaks the reserve.

The widow refuses to acknowledge, the mother shrieks knowingly, Maher takes a pan from the kitchen and puts it over his head while peering down street level, Meehan gently pushes the sisters toward the foot of the coffin in the middle of the room.

"Four o' ya come wit' me, rest stay here," The Swede says and instead of naming his followers, points to each as they shoulder toward the kitchen door.

"Just a broken shoe," I whisper to Vincent Maher.

"Whad ya say? Kid, whad ya say?" Meehan answers for Maher.

Shaken by the room's attention, I look down.

"Say it, what did you say?"

"I . . . heard it coming up here, broken shoe on the horse. Like glass, I heard it on the cobbles before we come up."

Dinny Meehan walks over to me with his eyebrows pushed down, interested. "How you know it's broke? Was it broke when you walked past?"

"Not yet."

"Did ya hear it break?"

"I didn't, but . . ."

"Go look then, go look out the window," he says, rushing me over.

"Is it broke?" Vincent Maher asks.

"Looks so . . . it is. It shattered off the hoof. I can see it did. That man has another shoe hanging out of his back pocket. Hoof knife and pincers too. He's a horsefarrier," I say looking back.

"Not a gangman?"

"I . . . I don't know that, but I can tell you he's no blacksmith, that's for sure."

Dinny Meehan turns to Maher, "Tell 'em all to come back up. It's nothin'."

"Yeah," Maher agrees and shoulders around the mother and crowd toward the door, then thumps down the stairs.

Meehan puts his hands in his pockets, looks me over. His handsome face built around the pose of a chieftain's stolid stance. Under dark brown brows and hairline, his green eyes shone like archaic stones in the window room's dull shine.

"You from Ireland?"

I nod.

"Farm boy?"

Nod.

"How do you get stronger shoes? So they don' break so easy?"

I shrug. The room had lost interest and some of the men itch their faces nervously while the widow stares out the window. Her tiny daughter stands between her and the coffin with uncombed hair partially covering her eyes, ears stuck out of the light blond strings like a gnome with pursed, wet lips and large eyes. She seems smaller than a normal five-year-old.

"G'on, say it," Meehan presses, putting his full attention on me.

I look around but only Meehan's face waits. "Well, to break down the iron ore you have to smelt off the rock and slag to keep the iron. Flux it," I gulp.

"Like potash?"

"Potash is a flux, it is. Or charcoal even. So, you have to scrape off the gangue or turn it to gas in the heat. Then you have to forge it. Bend it to your need when it turns orange but if there's too much carbon in it, it won't bend . . . too brittle. It'll just snap off, doesn't connect to anything either but you can cut away the iron in the shape of a shoe or if you have a mold. It's lesser quality and it makes bad shoes, especially cobble-walkers like you have here. Muscular perch-erons have too much weight for bad shoes. You need wrought for them, cast iron won't make it. Sounds like glass on the pavestones, that's what I heard downstairs."

Dinny Meehan watches me speak. Not so much to listen to what I say, but to see me.

"You ever worked with iron?" I asked.

"No . . . my father worked in a soap factory in Manhatt'n, off Washington Street. He was from Ireland. Uncle was a gang leader. Ruffians, back in them days."

I didn't know how to answer that, but managed to ask him what year his father came over.

"1847, when he was a babe."

Without answering I look at him again and put it together in my mind all those stories I heard of how bad a year it was in Ireland, 1847.

"Your father works with horses?" he asked.

"Some, he does a lot of things. Sells peat too. Mends thatch, carpentry."

"You Joe Garrity's nephew?"

"I am."

Looking at Maher, "He tells me ya still fourteen."

I nod.

Over the next two hours some four or five hundred men, women, and children wait their turn to give respect to the dead. Snaking up the stairwell, they keep as quiet as they can while the neighbors downstairs and next door stand in their doorways smoking, watching. A woman with a great scar on one side of her face appears with many children and strides out from the line to shake Dinny's hand. Mary Lonergan then grabs hold of the mother of the dead, and with a great and awkward bawling, wails for her. Mother McGowan is patient, though I can feel that Mrs. Lonergan is seen as the lowest of the neighborhood mothers. Still in line are her children, some fifteen of them in line along the wall sniffling and digging in their dirty noses. The five at the end though are teen boys from the neighborhood led by their limp-legged leader, the eldest Lonergan. The shortest is Petey Behan of the Flatbush orphanage who still wears my coat.

A large man who walked quickly passed everyone in the stairwell elbows in through the kitchen with his bowler cap in hand and a fitted, gentleman's suit over his paunchy midsection. I couldn't have known who he was, but later I would. He was Mr. McCooey from the Madison Club who handed out favors for Democratic votes at the Elks Club down in Prospect Heights where all the Democratic backslappers entertain themselves with violin players and operatic arias and such. He gave respects to Mother McGowan and the widow, shook Dinny's hand without planting his feet, and quickly made his way back from where he'd come. The boys in the gang called their like "Lace Curtains." While they called the gangs on the docks "Famine Irish." And looking back over at the Lonergan clan, I could see why.

After McCooey is gone, a beautiful woman in a plain dress and a small boy on her hip exits the line after crossing herself over the dead man. She drops her shawl behind her head and comes to Dinny Meehan's side with a kiss on his cheek, then looks upon myself with warmth. He whispers to her from above and she smiles at me while the boy stares in silence, then crawls up her shoulder in a sudden fit of discomfort.

When the crowd has gone entirely, an unlabeled whiskey bottle has somehow made its way onto the top of the coffin and is passed from mouth to mouth. A story about the dead man was at first muttered, then turned to a round of laughs. The dockers become animated and John Gibney's face turns red while Big Dick Morissey flicks him in the back of the head.

"Ya lucky ya dead, you," Gibney points down into the dead man's face. "'Cause I was gonna get even wit' ya when ya got outter the Sing Sing, ya fookin' arsehole."

The mother laughs at Gibney, then cries again. I see Maher talking to the youngest sister of the dead man as she sits on the arm of the sofa. She looks up at him, nervously enjoying his attention, and notices how honorable the wife of Dinny Meehan is treated. And the widow still stares out through the window while the gnome child taps on her knees.

Dinny nods, then points to the coffin with his lips to a few of the guys after The Swede came back in. When they make for moving it off the chairs the mother explodes, dives onto the top of it as it is lifted. The dead man's sisters begin their chorus and the small children stop their running to stare upon the spectacle.

"Nah, nah, nah!" the mother keens and wails. "Nah, let'm stay here den! Not to take'm 'way from me! Not to! My bhoy, my bhoy! Nah . . ."

Meehan reasons with her, though not expecting to persuade. He tries faintly to block her from the yellow pine and whispers.

"Open it up!" she cries. "I want to see him one last time . . ."

Meehan whispers.

"Not wert' a shite to me, I wanna see'm. Don' care how bad he looks. Haven't seen me own bhoy's face since they sent'm up in the stir six month ago. Open it up! Open!"

"Ma, please be . . ." the eldest daughter attempts.

"Not!" She stamps and shrieks, leaving a stern and shaking silence. "Open it!"

Placing it back on the chairs, a crowbar is summoned. Soon the sound of spliced nails being ripped from deep in the pine rings slices through the parlor air and the gray glim of dancing dust by the window swirls around the mother's face and blue and red shining eyes.

The head is dented on one side, the darkened hair matted with a dried fluid, eyes swollen but shut. The shock of death still painted on the face though the crust of blood has been wiped away. Silently the mother bends. The eldest daughter holding the back of her sack dress so as not to allow the breasts to show in the eye of men. She kisses the dead man, her only son. Kisses his swollen cheek and smells him. Smells him deep in her. To remember him. As the babe inside her twenty-three years ago. As the smell of hope as he toddled around the barren, one-room tenement as a child. As the smell of the household's provider as a teenager running with the gangs.

"He t'ought of us first," she said aloud, teeth clenched. "Became a man before his time. Found earnings the only way there is out there for it to be found."

She crosses herself as she rises. Immediately the men push forth with the lid and again she wails, pushes them back.

"Dinny Meehan."

"Yes."

"Knife."

Harry Reynolds hands Meehan a blade, who then comes to the side of the mother. The Swede bends down and pulls back the lifeless wrist. Vincent Maher holds a small broken-handled English tea cup below as Meehan slices. The blue vein opens to drip a mixture of coagulated redness into the cup. Filling it up to the top, it is handed to the mother whereupon she drinks a proud swig, then closes her eyes and tears under the gray shine from the window, over her son. She then hands it to Dinny Meehan. "Drink fer your bhoys. Fer me son's strength."

Dinny Meehan offers his palm for her to place the handleless cup and gulps down the rest with a slow toss of his head. The mother watches his face to see if he will grimace. He does not. Dinny comes again to the side of the mother and places one hand on the back of her wrist, his other hand draped over her shoulder and whispers. She nods and leans into him, then Dinny nods toward Cinders Connolly and Maher and they begin to untie the boots from the dead man and pull them off carefully. The lid is then dropped and the men line up the nails, passing the hammer around to punch them back in place. The mother falls to her knees as it is lifted away. She bows her head among the empty chairs, takes a deep breath, and sings a song never sung before. A melody made by a mother. Then it evaporates in the dusty air.

Soon enough all the men are gathered in the dank stairwell with the coffin pointed downward. It too has no handles and takes five men to negotiate the angles in the thin, steep steps. Outside a priest appears by the morgue dray, Father Larkin from St. Ann's.

"I t'ought t'was 2 p.m. dat McGowan's wake was to begin, I was told so?" He grouses, Gibney and Morissey laugh, and me thinking that here in America the priest is lied to and his power over minds brushed aside.

The coffin is put in the back of the dray as Father Larkin blesses it in a rush. Moans can be heard from the third-floor window above. Out from the small mouth and thin lips I can see the priest's breath in the air as he looks high, rushes up to their aid.

We follow the morgue dray through the slush of melting snow and up ahead of me are men fanned out unevenly in their sulky trench coats and wool caps. The moving guard is a motley army and instead of the soldier's crack of polished boots on the cobbles I hear the squish of wet peasant footwear. A bell jingles in the distance from an old China clipper in the harbor. The procession of slum soldiers stare in the windows above and down the street ahead and looking over at Maher with his slyly tilted cap and strutting march I see a thin, long pistol move from his coat pocket to his belt where his trench coat obscures it. I notice too the shine of a long knife in the palm of Harry Reynolds and a cudgel somewhat longer than a hurling stick at the end of Gibney's arm.

For me, I stare at the halved carrots the driver has in a linen cloth for the nag and swallow my own spit into the emptiness as the snow gently rains in our faces, the wind against the guard and the dray. The silence on the street is fantastic. Out on the water, barges dump their horns in the air like moaning dinosaurs and the trolley bells and clacking elevated tracks play beyond our clearing. But where we walk the onlookers honor the dead and the mourning. This man's memory is known here by one and all as hats are taken down generously, crosses made from forehead to chest, mouths kept closed. Shopkeeps, grocers, and tenement-window dwellers above nod sullenly. Factory workers and warehousemen open their iron shudders to pay respects in the cold air. Some children and grown men toss flowers on the coffin, shake Meehan's hand honorably. Too among us are The Swede and Big Dick Morissey and Connolly and the one they call Red Donnelly and Tuohey the tinker and many others. We stride between the brick walls and wooden shacks icily through the neighborhoods from cobblestone to sidewalk until a few large policemen come from the side of us and attack Cinders Connolly, hold him by his arms.

The dray stops in the middle of the street and Meehan walks sternly in front of me, "What's ya purpose arrestin' a man here, Brosnan? I've got . . ."

"Better to go along wid it, Dinny," I hear the policeman's lilt as that of a jackeen from Dublin. "Four immigrants was beaten to a pulp up by the Fulton Terminal sometime ago and one of'm died the other day from his injuries. There's answers that's wanted here."

Maher spoke up, "Ya know just where to find us too, don't ya? Puttin' our dead to rest."

"Would ye like to come wid us too, Vincent? I'll bet ye'll be havin' more than just a lead pipe in yer pocket, like Connolly here."

"Let it go," Meehan said to his men, then turned around.

"What's he got to do with it?" The Swede mumbles to Meehan. "Ain' even his business."

"He don' have a choice himself," he mumbles back. "Be out in a day o' two."

I see Brosnan light a black cigar and look angrily at The Swede. He stashes the matches in his blue tunic and disappears with his own gang of men through the snow and the unkempt street.

We continue together, surrounding the clopping horse and the coffin. Eventually we reach the funeral home, which is not much more than the basement of another tenement with only a makeshift sign above to make it an official place.

"Hungry?" Meehan slows up to ask me.

I nod sheepishly.

Free of the morgue dray, the men walk with a mighty pace through the streets. Taking shortcuts between buildings, under fences, and around lean-tos we are soon on Warren Street. When it is seen that Meehan and myself are walked to the front door on the third floor of a brownstone safely, the others begin to retreat back down the stoops. Maher at the tail end of them winks to me as Meehan and I go up.

"Sadie!" Dinny Meehan bellows as we walk in the warm parlor room where the child I saw on his mother's hip at the wake sits with his chubby fist in his mouth on a round carpet in front of the fireplace, staring up at us in a happy surprise.

"Shikaaaah?" the dote says, pulling his hands from his mouth and opening his palm to us.

"Yes?" come a voice from the kitchen.

"We got a visitor from the ol' country, see to it he gets some soup or porridge or whatever ya got on that Quincy, yeah?"

"Aye, the choild from the wake?" She comes rushing out. "My, my youngsta, yu look bea'en by da cold an' God 'imself, don't yu? Come, come and put yu 'ands by the foire and I'll fetch yu some'in' dat'll warm the marrow. Yu so fin, must be sta'vin', sweet choild. 'ow old are ye any'ow? Yu look about twelve yea's long, yu do."

"Still fourteen," Dinny bellows from a back room.

"Stiw fou'een?" Sadie looks at me and smiles. "Not quoite fif'een yet, aye?"

"Not yet," I manage.

"An' whe's yu muva?"

I didn't answer. Didn't understand what she said.

"Ya mother!" Dinny yells again.

"Back home, Ireland."

"No fam'ly? 'At's a odd way'a live in New Yook, innit?"

"His uncle turned'm out!" Dinny calls.

"An Oirish 'at come over durin' da war's got'a be desp'rate. An' wha' of ya fava?"

"Fenian," Dinny answers as he emerges from the bathroom drying his hands. "Isn't he?"

I nod, though it's an outdated term by then as my da always saw himself as a legitimate soldier.

"From Clare," he again speaks for me.

"Clare? 'At's whe' Dinny's fam'ly come from 'riginally, 'e tol' yu dat roight?"

I look over at Dinny who stands emotionlessly in a small shirt that reveals his round muscles and scarred forearm, then turns back to the bathroom.

Confused by Sadie's accent, I know of it only as that cruel sound from the landlord's paytaker and the stewards and all the terrible stories, though hers was in fact the cockney Irish which I had not then heard much of yet. She was kind though. So kind. I stared into the warmth of the heater and was mellowed by the rubbing palms she spread along my back. As she encouraged me, I began bubbling up. Bubbling with hidden tears, I could barely constrain myself from the happiness the fire gives me and the finality of finding someone in Brooklyn that is thoughtful of my pitiful state.

"What would ye loike 'en, I 'ave pea soup or meat pie?"

I look at her.

"Bof it is 'en!" she laughs and drapes a blanket over my shoulders, then looks me in the face and whispers as Dinny watches from behind, "'Appy Christmas, choild. Welcome 'ome."

CHAPTER 7

Upstairs, Under the Bridge

THE DOCK LOADERS' CLUB, THE GANG'S headquarters under the bridge they and their fathers built, never had electricity. Though it was true that much of Brooklyn by 1915 either had gas lighting or electricity, along the waterfront where the White Hand ruled there was no such thing. Most of the slums along the rim of the docks from the Navy Yard down to Red Hook where the poorest of the poor lived among the elevated tracks and the factories and within earshot of the barge horns and the pier house whistles lit their faces and their one-room apartments with candles made of paraffin wax or animal fat.

There were some things in "Auld Irishtown" that never changed. That included an absolute and obstinate disbelief in law, for it was law that forced their parents and grandparents from the homeland during the Great Hunger. No one blamed the blight of the tuber. All blamed the law and saw it as foreign to them. And so, change came slowest by the Brooklyn dock neighborhoods where the Famine Irish settled. And when I arrived in October, there was no electricity and no change and too, there was no law but the clan ways and the gypsy sways of the old days. A place caught in the time of archaic codes, bard-told lores and bare-knuckled rites. The only place in New York where a gang could still rule the streets in 1915, was where the ancient candle lit the darkened diddicoy faces under the bridges and along the Brooklyn waterfront here, and where back when their faces were lit in the dark of cave and cover, hiding their religion and their language too. Some say things never change, like these boys. Some say some things change, while other things stay the same, and yet more say with a whisper, like Beat McGarry in my ear, that some don't want things to change.

Mick Gilligan sits among a few immigrants at the Dock Loaders' Club. He cracks his knuckles, presses them against his forehead above two fearful eyes. He can't think about anything more than what is on his head: he's a bad person. Bad people exist, he thinks. That's what happens in this world. Bad things happen. He doesn't blame his wife for wandering. Isn't her fault. He always knew she deserved more than him.

Mick gritted through the thoughts of her whining in pleasure with Joey Behan atop her flayed thighs while the man of the house is gone looking for work. Behan's pants are on the floor and he is smoking cigarettes while she kisses his ear and smiles at him with her breast filling his palm, children in the backroom. Mick Gilligan presses his knuckles again, but won't pop this time. Even with admitting he feels it's his fault she has cheated him, what turns his face red and makes him shake in fits is the embarrassment of his name's suffering. Angers him to a rage that only blood can salvage so that his honor will again be redeemed among the men of the Bridge District. Only blood. Nothing more matters now to him and he looks up to the door with phobic eyes when he hears the *chu-chum, chu-chum, chu-chum* of the trains on the Manhattan Bridge above. Still no Bill Lovett.

"Must be fookin' six by now," he mumbles as Ragtime Howard levels a stare at him from the side.

Mick runs his fingers roughly over the rim of his whiskey. Pushes his knuckles against his forehead and looks over again at the opening door and the screeching streetcar shoeclamps grating against the rails like iron-piped banshees calling for him as they slow for the connections over Flatbush Avenue. With the saloon opened, the brine of the East River churns in his nose with the rust and the January freeze too. And the candles are

wincing and jerking on the wicks and the ceiling lanterns rat-
tling above from the cold doorwinds like the answers to prayers
from kneeling, black-shawled peasant women in a city church.
Gilligan jumps when he sees Non Connors and Frankie Byrne
enter looking everyone over. Lovett emerges from behind,
shorter and thinner than most, cold eyes ugly and fixed and with
a childish brutality in them underscored by bright pink lips and
cauliflower ears like immature cherub wings.

"Bill!" Gilligan announces, then reaches back to finish off his
drink. The tender Paddy Keenan peers up knowingly from
behind the bar. Non Connors steps up and pushes Gilligan to the
side with an elbow and Byrne measures the head of him with a
leaning back of his right fist, biting his lip from behind Connors's
shoulder. The two men wall themselves between Gilligan and
Lovett by the crook in the bar as the door slams behind.

"I jus' wanna talk to 'ems all."

"No ya don't," Connors said, keeping him at distance with a
straightened arm.

"It's personal, Non," Gilligan whined.

"What'll it be, fellas?" Keenan asks in his brogue. "Beer Bill?"

"Fill it to the top. No foam," Lovett answers elbowing himself up, loosening his black tie. "Gimme two 'o dem yokes."

"You got it, Bill."

"Gimme a bat an' a ball," Connors nipped.

Byrne nods for the same.

Behind the front door of the Dock Loaders' Club, in a corner
wall leans a wooden coatrack with a gaggle of picks and shovels,
bale hooks and tool belts, mortar-hods and the like. The weapons
of the working class. No music rings out. No entertainment
makes the air, just stories from old-timers like Beat McGarry, the
saloon's resident storygiver. McGarry has many stories. Knows
them all and is oft to articulate his knowing that 25 Bridge Street
was once the home of the Brooklyn decisionmakers, political or
non, back when the area was known as Irishtown where the
famine-runners settled and where the ships unloaded them. The
survivors of the Great Hunger, *An Gorta Mor*. Tough years. Lean

years back then before Jews and Italians and Scandinavians and Poles and Russians came to the waterfront of Brooklyn. Back when Brooklyn was a city separate from Manhattan and the rest of the boroughs and where the alderman had 25 Bridge Street as his official place.

Back too Beat McGarry witnessed himself, well before Dinny Meehan brought all the wild gangs together somewhere round 1912, so the Black Hand couldn't rake the rackets from the old locals. Now he, Dinny Meehan, the young man who honors the aged and rules from above the saloon upstairs where he can overlook his territory, the Bridge District of the largest port city in the world.

And when Mick Gilligan makes his way to Bill Lovett, old McGarry gave a knowing look upon the tender Paddy Keenan who always listens to everything said when the truth serum makes the men of the docks say things they know they shouldn't.

"Bill, ya know I ain' gonna ask for nothin' stupit, Bill," Gilligan called over the shoulders of Connors and Byrne. "Listen Bill, can I come talk at ya? Can I?"

Staring into his beers, Lovett picks the one on the right and ate it down, fists the glass on the mahogany and wipes it off his face.

"Listen Bill, I can't ask Dinny for somethin' I know he won' do. I only come to you. Ya gotter help me. I spend all day lookin' for work and Joey Behan's in on checkin' wit' my wife. I can't be there to defend my home and go out and work at the same time, Bill. Ya know?"

Before Lovett grabs for his second beer, Keenan plops a replacement in front of him, filled to the top, no foam.

"Bill, listen to me. Ya gotter listen. I need that fuck taken out, Joey Behan. You think Dinny's gonna do that for me? No, he ain't."

"What'd he say?" Lovett spoke, unconcerned if Gilligan hears.

"I didn' ask him. But Bill, ya know he ain' like that. I need a man with your talents, Bill. Ya gotta future, Bill, Dinny's got no reason . . ."

"Shaddup," Connors pushes.

"I'll pay ya. I don' care what it cost. I pay. And I do. This Joey Behan? He's gonna die and I'm gonna get my name back. Thing is, he knows I want blood, so I can't do it. Anyway, I ain' got that kinda talent like you got, Bill."

"Maybe if ya didn' talk so much, ya'd get hired more, then ya could spend more time with ya wife," Lovett said without turning his head. "Ain' Dinny sent ya a ham on Christmas?"

"Yeah," Gilligan remembers.

"Den why don' ya go home and beg ya wife to forgive ya, Mick, she ain' slept wit' no Joey Behan. And I ain' for sale."

"Bill, I . . ."

Connors puts down his rye whiskey, reaches across and grabs Gilligan by the back of the jacket, and slings him to the floor down by the feet of immigrants and patrons. Pushing him off balance, Byrne kicks Gilligan with an outstretched boot. A few men laugh, but silence follows.

"I want justice, Bill," Gilligan yells from the floor. "I don' go to the tunics, I go to you and this is what I get? Huh? Where's Darby Leighton, Bill? Huh?"

"Shaddup, Mick," Connors warns him away from the topic.

It is there that everyone listening knows that Mick Gilligan is almost dead. Paddy Keenan takes a step back from behind the bar and Beat McGarry haults his banterings. Ragtime Howard holds his liquor for a moment before swallowing, Connors and Byrne stand stone silent, immigrants and other labormen listen closely. Someone mumbles, "Man's scareder of his own thoughts than another's consequence."

"Where is he, Bill? Darby?" Gilligan demands. "Who proved Darby's brother Pickles kilt McGowen up in the stir, huh? No one! And still Darby gets eighty-sixt? And why? 'Cause Dinny says so? That ain' like you, Bill. You takin' orders now, Bill? Darby's one o' yours from the old gang on Jay Street, an' y'ain' got nuttin' to say fa dat?"

"Ya jus' stupit, Mick," Connors said moving in.

"G'ahead an' kill me! A man ain' a man wit'out his honor! He ain' nothin'! Ya kill me wit'out my honor and they'll bury me at your doorstep!" The crowd of men at the bar, along the wall and in between stare quietly. "If he can't find it, he goes'n gets it! Honor's all and all! It is too! And I'm gonner get mine!"

Connors pushes Gilligan through the crowd and against the wall while Byrne jumps over him and grabs Gilligan's head, yanking it down by the neck to the floor where the two can rip at him, fists and boots. Gilligan yelps as blood appears at his nose and through the crowd pushes The Swede with his long hands and dangling height, "A'right, a'right. Ain't you're saloon to make corpses in Connors, go'n! Go'n! Both o' yas."

As The Swede separates Connors and Byrne from the prostrate Gilligan, Vincent Maher and a group of others support him.

"Ya ain' got the right to stop me from my business," says Connors to The Swede as he backs away.

"I'll do as I see fit, Non!" The Swede bellows, then speaks toward Lovett's back, as he hadn't moved from his beers at the bar. "Nothin' personal, Bill, jus' don' want any corpses in here. No tunics."

Lovett nodded but never looked in The Swede's direction.

"Thanks for nothin', Swede," Gilligan says looking up. "No one'll say it except me, why don' ya let Darby back in the Red Hook? His brother didn' do nothin' to McGowen. It was the screw that got'em, not Pickles Leighton! Right, Bill?"

With a swoop The Swede backhands Gilligan who again falls to the floor as the patrons grunt and fall back to the drink.

Out of the corner of Lovett's eye moves a vagabond tomcat out the front of the saloon looking for him as he had every day around the same time. Lovett orders another beer and a piece of bread and makes his way through the din of the saloon and outside to the sidewalk. The matted cat hid in the alley next to the saloon behind some paint cans and crates when the door opens, then peers out to see Lovett kneeling down, leaning on the facade among the saloon's garbage while placing his glass of beer next to him.

"*Spspspspsps*," the fawn-eared gangster cooed to the cat while reaching out with the bread in his hand.

The tomcat appears, pretending not to be interested, then looks Lovett square and then away disinterested while tossing his tail in the air.

"Come 'ere, boyo," Lovett said gently whispering. "I know ya hungry, ol' boy. I won' hurt ya, promise. Ya know who I am, come and smell my fingers."

With a decisive turn of feline philosophy, the tomcat walks directly to Bill without fear and takes a quick sniff of his knuckles, pulls from the bread with a showing of his teeth and a yank of his neck. Both of Bill's arms rest on his knees pointing toward the cat while he squats. Smiling at the critter's ignorance, Bill calms in the tough's presence. He enjoys seeing the cat feel welcome. After a few bites it let Bill pet him slowly across the back, then dove its head into Bill's shins in a sign of trust and lay down on his back daring Bill to touch his flea-strewn belly. When he does, the cat bites down and kicks up with his clawed hinds, then jumps up quickly again, looks down Bridge Street at something that seemed important, and then falls into a deep purr.

The sloping cobbles below them eventually halts at the water along a great brick structural warehousing reach where men begin closing the big double-doored shutter windows where goods are hoisted from ship hulls. No ice accumulates on the muddy cobbles, but the sidewalk has long slippery stretches of it and the wind seems to ricochet into Lovett's face with a great slicing and drying of his lips. Afterward the thin air around them begins to retract and as darkness takes over the waterfront with the Manhattan lights across the river, a light flurry shimmers with flat crystals that disappear into watery specks on the brick-brown and yellowed cobblestones. A wind then again swoops into his face and ears as he looks down at the tom that hunches his shoulders and bends his little legs at the gust as it unfurls his matted mane.

Lovett cracks a pensive smile and with it moves his ears on the sides of his head sadly. His stomach aches in emptiness as he hadn't eaten a thing all day but instead of tearing from the bread in his left hand, he bites from the beer in his right, gritting his teeth afterward as the fluid flushes through him.

And out of a sudden the door of the saloon is cranked open. Mick Gilligan appears and the tomcat scatters in a frantic sprint down the alley, galloping gently when he finds himself at a safe distance.

"Bill," says Gilligan spilling a few drops of whiskey on his shoes. "Bill, ya gotter help me, ol' friend. I heard what ya said in front o' the others, now hear me out would ya? Can we work somethin' out? I gotter family to protect. You know Joey Behan, right? Been checkin' it at my home when here I am tryin' to . . ."

"I heard y'already," Bill mumbled while standing up, then drank down his beer and looked Mick in the eye close-like, feeling the drink in him mingle and ferment a disgust from somewhere old in him. "I know you. I know ya good. I don' know who sends ya, Dinny or tunics or what, but I know ya better'n ya think, yeah? Ya fuck. Ya testin' me. You're a tout, I know you."

"Whatta ya talkin' about, Bill?" Gilligan begged as Bill opens the saloon door against another freezing gust and a train clickety-clacking above. "Bill? Whatta hell is ya talkin' about, tunics an' Dinny? I'm tryin' no more than to protect . . ."

"Shaddup," as the door banged shut.

Men step from Bill Lovett's path when the look comes across his face as it does now. And as he come to the bar with an empty glass Paddy Keenan dumps another in front of him. In exchange Bill pushes forward coinage through the whiskey and beer-puddled mahogany. Taking the frothless drink and barking it straight down, Keenan has yet another on the ready after slicing the head off it with a butter knife onto the floor with a *fap*. Non Connors and Frankie Byrne stand close to Lovett with drinks in their hands too, Connors double-fisting it; a shot in one hand, thin glass of beer in the other.

Elbowing back up to the mahogany, Bill begins to transform. The stories of Bill Lovett's drinking are not just mine. All knew him as a hard worker when sober and a ferocious fighter after drinking. As I see him, he sits on the stool after work at the Dock Loaders' Club, staring into his drink angrily. His face now wearing the wounded staring of the drunk. And as the drink takes his reason, he sees all those round him as traitors and touts. His eyebrows pushing downward over the untrusting orbs, lips thrust outward as if he has just waken, fists clenched, he closes himself in.

Listening to the conversations of dockbosses lit by the ancient yellow of candlelight, he moves his dulling eyes. Hears all the voices as one. He looks back and into the darkness beyond the bar to the guarded stairwell that leads to Dinny Meehan's office above, where the authority of the gang resides with all his protectorates around him counting the day's tribute. Bill knows Dinny is always listening for plots, and plants silent men around him, like Paddy Keenan the tender. Paddy Keenan is known to one and all as Dinny's minister of education because he listens to stories told under the serum of truth at the bar, then debriefs Dinny upstairs. He is a tout, Paddy Keenan is, but a tout for Dinny Meehan is no crime at all within 25 Bridge Street. But Bill sees a tout as a tout, no matter whose side you're on. And as they used to say in this neighborhood years ago when it was only Irish that lived here, "T'is clouts for the touts." Which vaguely translates to "A hit on the head for the informer," except it rhymes, as you can see.

Along the stretch of the bar, and highest among the low-going men are the dockbosses and their right handers; Gibney the Lark and his cohort Big Dick Morissey take up a large part of the trough across Bill with wide-shouldered necks like bison propped on elbows. Boxheaded Red Donnelly is there next them, known too as Cute Charlie since he is so ugly and red. The lean smiler Jimmy "Cinders" Connolly sits with his big paws hanging over the bar like a long hound with his fool-mute right hander behind him, Philip Large. And Harry "the Shiv" Reynolds too casts a subtle eye at Bill here and there. Behind them all, Tommy Tuohey the pavee boxer stands at his post in the back by the rear room with his fists folded, guarding the stairwell.

These men are the dockbosses who have their own terminals and report directly to Dinny Meehan each day. Down in the Red Hook, Bill is boss, just as the others are up in the Navy

Yard, under the bridges at the Fulton and Jay terminals, and down Brooklyn Heights at the docks that terminate on Baltic Street and Atlantic Avenue. Except Tuohey, who just likes to fight on a challenge. But Bill is the youngest and newest of the bosses, just only months earlier took over with Dinny's nod after McGowan had been sentenced to Sing Sing and then had the life beaten from him by a screw. Again Harry gives Bill a silent lookover, then looks away. McGowen was well-liked and Bill can see it on the faces of Dinny's dockbosses. But Bill has no regard for those men, Dinny's men. And they know it. See in that lack of honor, blame for the death of one of them and their own.

"Bill," Connors leaned into his ear. "Mick's still onto ya, whadda ya say?"

"Gentle when stroked, fierce when provoked," Bill threatened like a cornered animal as Mick Gilligan strained to hear him.

Just behind Mick the saloon door opens and the sounds of the screeching city enter again, candles wincing, lanterns tilting, and under the stiff wind a lilting call came out. "Look what I got for dinner!" A man shouts heartily while a cat being held by its tail upside down is at its hissing and making its wicked sounds abound, scratching into the air. Wobbling and warbling like a man on the gibbetnoose.

Wild Bill Lovett turns round, faces the laborer with a sporting smile and tomcat in grasp, immediately pulls the .45 out from his jacket, and claps the hammer with an explosion that sends shoulders flinching, silencing the saloon. Mick Gilligan thought certain the blast was meant for himself, though it was not to be. The power of the bullet knocks the fool Scandanavian cat abuser back into the picks and shovels and coatrack and the old tom sent a flying out of his grasp, flapping across the front glass window and scraping off the edge of a table.

Confused by the scene and out of his element, the tom darts from one side of the saloon to the other as a stampede of gangsters, soused sailors, laborers, and immigrants elbow for the exit but not before they pull their coats from beneath the man with a bullet in his chest behind the door. The dockbosses barely move however, and instead watch Bill while keeping a palm over their own weapons.

With fear sunk into him and honor forgotten, Mick Gilligan gapes upon Bill who holds the metal canon in his small hand and a butcher's stare in his eye among the flying elbows and the heavy tide of patrons frantically swimming and bottlenecked at the front door. At this emptying of order, Bill awakes, and shoving his .45 into the back of his trousers, storms upon Mick without effort like a man finally in his comfort only when chaos churls around him and with the horrid grates of streetcar stoppers screeching through the spliced January air. As Mick sees the intention on Bill he pushes and shoves within the crowd and yelps to get through for the exit, never mind the coat.

Jumping over three men, Bill yanks at the back of Mick Gilligan's shirt with a strength uncommon to men his size and with him go three others to the ground. At the lash of his downthrusting fists Bill squeezes and grits to break the head off the coward until the crowd unintentionally throws him off balance in their rushing for the door. Standing up with his left hand still holding Mick, Bill swings at any face behind him he can see, then plows into the back of the head of Mick with a feral man's intent.

After losing his grip on Mick, Bill then turns his attention to the tom that has splayed himself across the flooring in a toothy hissing and a ridge of crazed hair standing on-end over his raised back, tiptoeing sideways in a miniature menace. Hoping to coax the poor animal into his arms, the tomcat continues thrashing at the mouth until finally the saloon empties entirely.

As the dockbosses look him over with unemotional stares, Bill busies himself at his own mind's taking. With one hand he keeps the door open while pushing the injured man deeper into the corner, the other hand again holding the .45 across his knee for someone to question him. Ignoring Non Connors's urging until the tom has made its way out of the saloon safely, Bill whispers gentle assurances, "G'on boy, it's right here. No worries, really. No worries, everythin's over now. Everythin's fine."

CHAPTER 8

The Souper

THE DOOR SWINGS OPEN AND BANGS against the legs of the dying man. Head Patrolman William Brosnan looks behind it as Paddy Keenan and Patrolman Culkin turn to his entrance. A great barrel-chested man of a powerful build and the height of some three inches above six feet, Brosnan's dark blue copper's tunic and tilted cap contrasts the gray in his short-haired cut above the ear.

"Jaysus," he booms, then looks to his son-in-law. "Who done this? Ambulance on the way?"

Culkin steps away from Keenan and comes close to Brosnan whispering, "I called for a doctor, but this feller won't talk, won't say nothin'."

Dropping his hat on the back of his head and wiping the snow from his face, Brosnan walks toward the bar with his hand extended, "Paddy Keenan, is it?"

Keenan looks at the large policeman and lays a hand out for greeting, "'Tis."

"From what part are ye then?" Brosnan offers while pulling a pack of cigars from his tunic that reads "Na Bocklish."

"Kilmenagh."

"Sure, sure, over Kilkenny way," Brosnan agrees. "Why not give us a drop o' the pure when ye're ready, eh Mr. Keenan?"

Keenan nods.

"That'll be the cure of it," Brosnan says as Keenan pushes forward the home brewed poteen. "Might as well take the drop while the life is still in ye. I've known me quite a few from them parts. Kind people they are, from Kilmenagh. I'm from Dooblin meself."

"I know," Keenan answers not so cordially.

"But Kilkenny! Oh my, lovely place it be. Seat of our ancestors beyond the pale, but close in our hearts still today."

"'Tis, 'tis," Keenan agrees.

Leaning across the bar and whispering, "Is Dinny h'opstairs?"

Keenan looks up toward the dark, empty stairwell at the end of the bar, then back to Brosnan, "I wouldn't go up, sir."

Brosnan though, he only hears a challenge from Keenan's advice. He grinds his teeth inside his mouth, but doesn't show it on his face. Instead Brosnan smiles and takes off his hat, begins to sing where quickly Keenan joins along, Culkin watching by the door and the injured man.

> *"There once were two cats liv'd in Kilkenny*
> *Each t'ought dere was one cat too many*
> *So dey fought and dey hiss't*
> *An' dey scratched and dey bit*
> *'Til instead o' two cats dere weren' t'any!"*

Laughing along, Brosnan pronounces, "only good t'ings come from Kilkenny, ye must be a good man Paddy Keenan! How long ye been on for Dinny now?"

"Wisha, I just tend bar sir, nothin' more."

"Ye know what," say Brosnan, pounding his hand on the bar and pulling the Na Bocklish out of his head. "I believe that! There's a lotta gobshite round here, I'll be the first to reco'nize it. But I believe ye, Paddy. Ye know, we that come from the auld lanes aren't as violent as them that dragged up round the waterfront here."

"I see it that way too," Keenan agreed.

"Do ye?"

"I do."

"Kilkenny cats, Mr. Keenan," Brosnan said smiling with a finger in the air, Keenan listening quietly and without offering his own opinion either. "Dinny's got 'is day t'day, but these bhoys got the nature to bring down their king. And what a king he be, yeah? King of the Diddicoys, if ye believe them larrikins are wert' presidin' over. Watch 'em, Paddy Keenan! I seen it many time in this neighborhood. Ye t'ink Lovett's got loyalty fer the king? Do ye? Those ol' Jay Street hooligans and their knavery: Lovett, Connors, Frankie Byrne and his boyos, the Leighton brothers and others. They're Dinny's now? Ha! Are they, Paddy? Even with Dinny's gift fer arganizin', ye can't break some, ye can't. These bhoys down by the docks, I seen over many years. Here me," Brosnan said leaning across the mahogany for a whisper. "They're the Kilkenny cats themselves."

"Are they?"

"They are! Bill Lovett?" Brosnan announced while staring at Keenan's face. "Wild Bill Lovett?"

Keenan wrinkles his nose but for a moment.

"They'll fight each other outta existence, they will. . . . If I don't take Dinny down meself, as a matther o' fact," Brosnan warns before blasting down a shot, then looks up the stairwell angrily. "I've done it before, take that Dinny down I did too! Back when he was a tyke and runnin' with that no-good scootch who was nottin' but a fluke, Coohoo Cosgrave before he took to the groundsweat by drinkin' down oxalic acid after he gone off the deep end. That's right. I sent Dinny and McGowan up to Elmira's Reformatory for a stint, and I'll do it again!" Brosnan boasted and blaguarded, then looked upstairs thinking. "Must've been 1905. . . . Then again I sent'm up in 1912 when the yegg Christie Maroney was shot 'tween the eyeballs. . . . Dinny Meehan . . . hmm. Sitting up there like he don't exist like. Too many enemies to keep happy, ye know. Now he's got Thos Carmody and the ILA in his neighborhood over on Sackett Street? And Bill Lovett in the chicken coup? Matther o' time, Paddy Keenan. Time's all. Dinny Meehan huh? King of a class o' low-breedin' diddicoys, he is. Put'em away before and I'll do it again too!"

Keenan smiles.

Brosnan raises a finger again as Keenan pushes another poteen in front of him, "Time," then turns to Culkin. "Get me Bill Lovett, son." Turning back, "Thank you Mr. Keenan," he bellows, drops the shot down his face.

"Not sayin' a t'ing to ye did I."

"Didn't have to," Brosnan mumbles then yells for Culkin to come to his side.

The cold enters the saloon again and with it the screeching sounds of the Manhattan Bridge trains above. In with it rushes the ambulancemen finally arrived to tend to the health of the victim who now lies motionless in the corner of the room behind the door.

"Son," Brosnan stops Culkin with a hand on his forearm, looking away from Keenan. "Ask 'em nicely first, don' go jumpin' in on Lovett. Ye gotta family to care fer."

"Yes'r."

"Ye doin' jus' fine son," Brosnan said pulling the black cigar out from his mouth. "Jus' fine so far. No thug's wert' yer wife's tears. Get Ferris and at least t'ree others to go with ye."

"A'right."

"Good lad."

As Culkin walks away and the deadman in the corner is covered, Brosnan looks at Paddy Keenan and points upstairs, "Ye tell'm. The law will have him, t'will. New Yark won't be run by a band of culchies and diddicoys, mixed blooded tinkers."

"You and yours sipped the soup didn't ye, ye jackeen ye? Yeer a Protestant are ye not?"

"No, American!" Brosnan thumps.

"Not a Souper, so ye're not? Still nothin' from ye to offer but a law that can't feed a poor gorsoon runnin' shoeless in yer own path!" Keenan yelled as Brosnan opened the door to allow the city sounds over Keenan's voice, closing it as he walks out.

CHAPTER 9

Eating Meat

UNDER THE KIND NURTURINGS OF SADIE Meehan and her soups, I begin to gain weight again. Even more appreciable than her care for the rounding of my pointy bones and the filling of my tight skin is her nursing of my person back to health. The way she accepts me so quickly and seems to know how best to comfort a homeless child when the greatest distrust was blossoming in me like a cancer or a virus, well, she made me back into the good. I not being the type to request food without earning it, she calms my guilt and says only that it'll be far from her to wait for a humble, starving child to ask.

"No, no Liam, s'not a way to live loike 'at. A boy's gota ate. An'e 'asta ate a lot'a catch up on los'toime!"

And me feeling bad for hearing her cockney and thinking that anyone with such an accent can't be trusted.

"Yu've such a good way 'bout yu Liam. Yu'll turn out oo'roight, sure o' it!"

To make me feel better though, she sends me downstairs on minor missions such as the baker's or Mr. Cohnheim's the butcher.

"Don't let'm sell yu the meat's already been grounded, aye Liam," she points at me. "We'll pay de extra for a flank, den tell'em to groind i'up in front o' yu, got 'it' en?"

"Alright."

"But be noice wif'em, 'e's always been good t'us since even before Dinny was 'ooy is now, but God only knows what 'ey put in'at stuff to cut a profit."

Full of energy, I stomp down the stairway hall skipping steps
as I go as she wishes me not fall in my hurries.

"Where ya goin'?" Vincent Maher asks as he stands on the
stoops outside the Warren Street brownstone smoking and
watching out.

"Cohnheim's!" I yell, running along the sidewalk of the row-
house stoops on my mission.

I sit at the table in the middle of the afternoon eating meat.
Eating carrots. Eating potatoes and eating stews with meat,
potatoes and carrots too. A young man in his heaven has meat
all day long, right and left. And with a beautiful woman serving
it up and her smile and a pat on the head. And so I was, a young
man in his heaven. Chewing and chewing and with my mouth
bursting with the pinched taste of salt-cured meats and the brine
of fish sautéed with butters and the tenderest chicken and onions
and peppers and garlic and corn and peas and gravy! Gravy!
Where did gravy come from? Some genius for certain. Brown
gravy poured over a potato and heaving unrelentlessly onto the
steak which barely complains and who'd have thought gravy and
potatoes and meat and carrots and corn would mix so well like
an orgy of lovers overcome with the passion and the satisfying of
each other's inner needs without a hint of jealousy?

"Deeblooooga," L'il Dinny says as he watches my concentra-
tion from his highchair.

"I know it," I say playing along.

"Chikanongkaya?"

"It sure is," says I as Sadie laughs.

Grasping a fat-fingered gob of mish-mashed foodstuffs and
offering me a bite he asks, "Blabligruandikkka?"

"Thanks but no thanks," I say to him respectfully.

"'E loikes yu Liam."

And just when I'm feeling so fat I can hardly breathe Sadie
strikes up a match and a song, "'Appy Birfday to yu, 'Appy
Birfday to yu . . ."

I can't believe my happiness and I can't believe it's true.
Sadie there standing over me and L'il Dinny with a real cake

and with icing too. Fifteen candles swayed as she swung around in the sunlit kitchen and dropped it proudly in the center of the table.

"Bababababaaa, baaa," L'il Dinny tries to keep along with the song while staring at us wonderingly from his highchair throne. Though I can't possibly fit another piece of food in my belly, Sadie slices a grand piece and plops it in front of me. Even L'il Dinny is impressed with the size of it and within five minutes he is wearing more of it on his face than he's able to swallow.

And it's L'il Dinny who's a miniature monster in his own right. If only this world was smaller he would have us all at his will, he would. Smashing his toys to the ground and tossing them across the room menacingly with his big head and bright eyes and round shoulders and full belly protruding over the cloth around his savage legs. Loving the attack, I let him win and knock me to the ground because I want him to feel strong and confident just like Sadie makes me feel.

But Dinny, the man who Sadie calls her husband and the man I barely remember as the leader of the dock gang hardly shows his face. Leaving so early in the morning that the court-yard roosters on Bond Street are caught unawares as he walks past them, and returns so late at night when I'm already fat'n happy that I put a lid on the day in the back room with L'il Dinny in the crib next to me snoozing away.

Sundays and we're off to St. Ann's Roman Catholic Church on Gold Street back up in the Bridge District with merchant marines and deckhands and sailors of all stripes strewn across the pavement from a long Saturday night with the drink. We take the trolleys like everyone else, Sadie and L'il Dinny with his head out the window and me too, all of us dressed like country charmers. The swoon of Father Larkin's prayers echoing off the arches sadly, I stare up at the columns and rows of the gentle people on the balcony who find God even in a place like Brooklyn where once I thought for sure there was none.

"Ave Maria, gratia plena, Dominus tecum. Benedicta tu in mulieribus, et benedictus fructus ventris tui . . ."

And though I am trying to think of God and all that he's brought me, there's only one thing I can think of and that's the purity of the American girls that are sitting, kneeling and standing all around me. (Kneeling I think is my favorite.) They sit close with their mother and closer to their father and I don't know exactly what I'd like to do with them, but I'm willing to feel my way through it together if they'd like. I pretend that Sadie is my wife and I have loads of experience. Proof being the young child between us, but that's all blather, yet still I have to hold the bible over my lap to hide my excitement, though the guilt of it touching me is too much so I exchange it with the songbook.

"Where ya goin'?" Vincent Maher asks me from the stoops outside the Meehan brownstone.

"Cohnheim's," I say.

"Shit kid, when ya gonna get ya fill, huh?"

And that's when I start to think. Start to think that it must mean something I am in the grand Meehan home. Of all people in this new world, to be sitting in such great comfort and care as this. Can't be just luck and it was true I allow myself believe good things are in store for me because of it. That good things for me are coming here in America. But my childhood was spent earning what I keep and at this third-floor flat where the man of the family is rarely home and his wife is serving a stranger, I can no longer go on accepting charity. My father had worked off land, and his father too before him and back many moons. Every generation that our plot got smaller, my family had to work harder to keep up. In such poverty, we become humble in our humiliation and we gave great thanks for everything we had. More thankful than any king could ever be. And as I'd find out soon Brooklyn is full of kings, but I'd make a terrible one, for a king can't show so much thanks, as he'd soon be seen as filled with the weakness.

"Is Dinny holding me here for some reason?"

"'E's always got'a plan, loove," Sadie said opening the window in the kitchen.

There'd always be something in the peaceful for me at that brownstone. It was set off far enough from the waterfront and the

elevated trains so the city noises were set to a low hum. Every now
and then could be heard the dinging of a trolley in the distance
and gentle clopping of Boru, Mr. Campbell's old horse from the
stablehouse across the street who washed him with a handbrush
and a wooden bucket below our fire escape. The appreciation I
feel for Sadie, and in a distant kind of way for Dinny too, is something I haven't felt since I left home with my mother standing in
the doorway with wet and blazen eyes. After seeing a bit of the
world I am beginning to place her in it. And although her place in
the world is not such a dignified one, being ignorant and being a
peasant, she still stands in my mind as the most dignified woman
in the world. Sadie too, even if she does live in the slums of a city.

Sadie leans on the window with her palms on the sill, arms
straightened. L'il Dinny napping in the backroom and the
dishes washed after lunch.

"Why not go'n 'elp Mr. Campbell scrub Boru, I know yu
loove 'orses. 'Ere, bring'em 'tatoes for us."

"I will," I said looking down as she pulled a few potatoes
from a pan. "Did you know that when I was out there, you
know, wandering around the city . . . One day I came across a
dead horse on the street? Just dead and left there. Some kids
played around it and one of them told me the butcher was on
the way. It looked certain that poor old girl had been mis-
treated. Real bad. The people here . . . why are people so cruel?
To each other. To everyone."

"It's a tough toime s'all," Sadie started to softly cry by the
breeze in the window. "People just tryin' to get by enough, to
feed 'emselves."

"Why did you leave London?"

"Can't live in London, the Irish, for at the start in England
we're not wanted."

"And here we are? New York?"

"It's the labor 'at's needed, innit? Labor, aye? New Yook's
growin' fast innit? Needs men to build it."

"How did Dinny know my father was a Fenian? How could
he have known that?"

She stood from the window, "Dinny knows a lot'a 'fings 'bout people just by listenin' to'em. Watchin'em. 'E's a good card to 'ave in ya pocket, Dinny Mee'an. A good 'and indeed."

"Hmmm . . . What was McGowen like?"

"McGowen? The man 'oo just died?"

"He was killed."

"Aye," she admitted without wanting too. "Well . . . Ol' frienda Dinny's. Ran the Red 'ook 'til they sent'm upstate. . . ."

"I mean what was he like? I saw him dead there in his coffin."

"Some fings we don'talk on much, Liam. But'e was a good young man, suppo'ted his fam'ly loike'e should," It was the first time I saw her uncomfortable.

"Who killed him?"

"G'on an' 'elp wif Boru 'en, Liam. G'on 'en."

I just looked at her, unknown to me that I was pushing and pestering her.

"Where ya goin'?" say Maher.

"Help wash Boru."

"Hey!"

I turned round.

"You been two months up dere, ya freeloadin'?"

"Well . . ."

"Ya like girls o' what?"

I raised my eyebrows at that.

"Any time ya wanna girl, just ask me. I know a lotta'em. See . . ."

"Vincent!" We heard from above.

Vincent Maher looked up.

"Don't be fillin' the poor boy's moind up wif yu buggerin, leave'm be. Liam g'on now, 'elp wif Boru."

"Ya gonna come out from unda dat skirt soon, kid," Maher mumbled as I was backing away.

Up above Sadie looked at me and Vincent. Closed the window.

CHAPTER 10

NY Dock Co.

THE NEXT MORNING I AM AWOKEN at 4 a.m.

"Liam," the deep voice in the room opens my eyes to the surprise of Dinny Meehan above me in the dark, fully dressed in vest and coat and tie and ready for work.

"C'mon, time to wake up. Let's go."

I raise myself from the bed and move to slip on my shoes when Dinny drops a pair of boots next to me, then walks from the room in the dark. I knew without asking that these were the boots of McGowan.

"'Ave some bu'a an' bread, boys," Sadie said.

"No thanks," Dinny says.

Sadie takes my hand and forces two pieces of buttered bread in it, closes my fist. And that was that. As we close the front door, I look back on Sadie who quickly turns round back toward the kitchen so as not to allow me to see her. And so, out of the nest.

Vincent Maher on the stoops looks up, smiles. Half a block away The Swede appears from the crowds of morning travelers and joins us. Another block and Cinders Connolly is there and as we stand on Atlantic Avenue underneath the Fifth Avenue El, Red Donnelly and Harry Reynolds and John Gibney and Big Dick Morissey walk up. It is early March and the morning bites into us, and as the men begin noticing me, they nod under the *chu-chumming* of the train passing over us. Connolly shakes my hand generously and with a smile and Gibney comes upon me with a quick shake too though his hand feels strange in mine. As I look down at our hands grasping each other's I notice Gibney has no fingers other than a pinky and a ring finger on his right hand. When I look up at his face he smiles a great toothy grin, so sarcastic is the cemetery smile lined with astray and amiss stones and the goofy bulging eyes on him that I can see why they call him the Lark.

"Some say he's got more fingers dan he do tooths," Morissey jokes in a baritone voice.

"You don' like my handshake?" Gibney demands angrily, pulling me close to him, face on face.

"It's only that . . ."

"Don' listen to that fookin' yoke of man, kid," Connolly offers. "He'll lark ya all day long if ya let'm."

Tommy Tuohey then came on.

"This is Liam Garrity, he's gonna be wit' us for a while," Dinny said. "He's from Clare."

"Clareyeah?" Tuohey mumbles.

"What part was you born in, Tommy?" Gibney asked knowing the answer before asking.

"Born-under-da-big-blue-sky-is-where," Tuohey said so fast that Gibney and Morissey laugh.

"Coulda been anywhere, eh Tommy?" Morissey says.

"Giverteek, moraless."

Back in those days most men dressed the same as the next and in a place like Brooklyn it was hard to tell the difference between he who was well-to-do and he who is half-starved. The poorest and most destitute man still presenting himself with honor because of the pride, for no one wanted to look poor. And because of all this sameness no one can tell the difference between a gangman and an everyday laborman. Except maybe the way he acts. Walking toward the piers and waterfront, the Lark and Big Dick goof it up, bouncing off each other and pretending to brawl. Running in to passersby and knocking over metal garbage cans in the process. Dinny stops and tells them to pick up their messes and "make 'em neat, just like they was before ya tumbled 'em."

Older men bent by many lean years look upon us and steady themselves on the stoops and metal stair rails, chewing the fat with neighbors while pulling from cuddy pipes under their graying walrus moustaches. Thin women who've lost their warmth and were hollowed out by giving all they had for so long a time appear in the windows above whipping faded clothes in the cool March air, then pinning them on pulley lines that cross the street above us to the other tenements across them.

"Tommy," Big Dick calls over as we stride along. "How do ya say 'Kiss my ass' the old way?"

"Kiss-me-arse, the-auld-way?"

"Nah, just kiss my ass."

"Kiss-me-arse?"

"Yeah, how do ya say it?"

"Pug-mahone, ye-feckin'-sausage-ye," Tommy answered.

"Wha'?"

"Pug-ma-hone, I-say," to which I confirm when Dinny looks over to me.

"Pug mahone?" Big Dick laughed. "I killed a man named Pug Mahone once."

"Nah," Gibney giggled. "That yoke was Pug McCarthy, the pugilist."

"Oh yeah," Big Dick mumbles under his breath, then yells out with a booming voice up to the third and fourth floors. "Pug mahone! Pug mahone! All ya's!"

Next thing I know the flabby one they call Lumpy, Eddie Gilchrist the accountant shows. And then a few moments later peeling off toward their territories were Gibney, Big Dick, Donnelly, Reynolds, and Connolly while Dinny, Maher, Gilchrist, Tuohey and The Swede, and I walk across Atlantic Avenue to the Columbia Street piers. Then taking a left while walking with a quick pace as the sun struggles through the morning dark we go. So quick a pace I can barely keep up.

I am unable to stop myself from watching The Swede walk with his great strides, meaty hands and long head. Others on the street notice too, but it seems most have seen him regularly and so the shock of his dangling height and gaunt scowl has mingled into commonality though he looks a circus traveler or a hovering apparition to my eyes with his thin face, white hair, and shouldery span.

We pass shopowners unloading trucks for the day's selling, the poor in their homeless morning routine of scratching the scruff off their heads, and the ladies scurrying about perfectly ignoring everyone around her. They all stand at attention when the like of Dinny Meehan and The Swede leading a pack of gamey-looking larrikins like ourselves amble by. They all seem to know the gang, but are trained to look the other way as we pass.

Vincent Maher winks at the younger lasses and tips his cloth cap like the sarcastic nuisance of a gentleman he is. Tommy Tuohey in his chummy seriousness spitting on the sidewalk and not taking a notice of the citizenry jumping to the stoops to allow our passing respectfully. And me with the floppy boots and Eddie Gilchrist trying to keep up with his lumpy limp and breaking into a jog to catch our heels with the foolish charm he has and the open-mouthed stare. But I don't know why I walk with them, though I am not inclined to question things as I am in no place in life to be thinking I know better. So I go then without a peep from me.

But for The Swede, he can't stay calm too long and yells at a man sneaking and peeking inside the back of a truck after the men unloading it disappeared inside the retailer it was parked in front of. The man jumps out of his shoes in fright, looks angrily to the ground while pulling his cap over his eyes. Maher laughs as it seems a lot of the other boys think him funny, but I don't see him that way myself in his bally-ragging ways.

"Where are we going?" I whisper to Maher.

He laughs, "Cohnheim's! Nah, we're jus' goin' down to see a stevedorin' man about the Red Hook. See, been three different dockbosses runnin' things over the past few mont's an' he ain' happy," Maher counted on his fingers as we walked. "McGowen who's dead, Lovett who's in the workhouse right now, and Tuohey now that he's been fillin' in since Bill shot a man for pullin' a cat's tail."

"Workhouse?"

"Not-what-yer-t'inkin'-bhoy,"Tuohey said."Here-in-the-states-a-workhouse-is-like-a-jail."

"Oh," I agreed, barely understanding him.

"What's a workhouse in Ireland?" Maher asks.

"Where they used to send people to die of the famine fever," I answer.

As we come upon our destination I am amazed at the size of the building we are walking into. It isn't so tall, but the width is massive and made almost entirely of cinder blocks. It must have been as wide as twelve streets. Overlooking the water on its back side, the New York Dock Company's main building off Imlay Street was a sign of Brooklyn's dominance in importing for the entire Northeast, not to mention its heavy exporting from the manufacturer's and factories that produce goods in the neighborhood and sent to Europe or up the Hudson River to the Erie Canal for the west.

We are rushed through the lobby and onto an elevator, then frisked by two large men. I look over at Gilchrist, who is not at as much unease as myself. It all seems normal, so I allow the men to search my private areas without a fight. They are called Wisniewski and Silverman. Neither are as tall as The Swede, but pretty close. Wisnewski just looks like a piece of meat, but Silverman watches us closely through his sunken eyes. Staring at me for a moment, I'm sure he quickly learns that I'm a harmless one.

"Well, well," a fat man who holds the majority of his weight in his midsection and is dressed like a London banker from the previous century welcomes us into his grand office. "Ol' Dinny Meehan and his band of miscreants. Welcome then, yes. Come on in. Would you like a drink, boys?"

"No, we wouldn't," Dinny said, "But thanks for askin'."

"Sure, sure," the fat man says, then points at me with limp wrist and an uncomfortable, sardonic smile. "Who's the stranger?"

"He's wit' me, not to worry," Dinny answers.

I quickly learn that a handshake is not needed for my intro-
duction and though he has an Englishman's accent, I can see
that he pretends to be more of a snob than his American background suggests.

"Jolly good then, let's have a seat, shall we? And how are
you, Mr. Gilchrist, still counting those numbers in your head?"
he asked at first with a genuine smile, then finished his sentence
in a mocking tone.

"Yeah," Lumpy says innocently.

"Have you ever seen one of these, Edward?"

The fat man points with ruling class pride to a machine sitting on a table behind his large desk, "It is a thing of the future,
surely. It is called a Dalton Adding Machine, Edward. It does
all the work for you. All you have to do is type in the numbers
and it regurgitates the answer for you. Isn't it a smash?"

Gilchrist looks with interest at the machine's black and green
body where thirteen little push-button fingers stick out with
black and red pads on them. He then looks up at the fat man as
if he's been spooked.

"Don't be scared of it Edward, it couldn't harm a fly," the fat
man then points to the seat he wants Gilchrist to sit in. "Good,
then," he bellows while rubbing his soft fingers together. "Mr.
Swede, how are you, sir?"

No answer.

"Always a delight, how about you, Vincent?"

"I'm fine, thank you, sir," Maher replies.

"How does a Mick get a name like Vincent anyhow, can you
say?" The fat man laughs aloud. "I am kidding, you know.
Surely you do. . . . Must have something to do with being a
papist, how would I know anyhow?"

Vincent's face turned from respectful to confused, but the
man walked right past him and continues his talking.

"Come sit down fellows. Over here, we have some chairs for
everyone."

Behind the fat man is a large window with a view of the
Atlantic Basin and masses of ships docked next to each other on

the piers. Behind the basin in the distance across the Buttermilk
Channel is Governor's Island where warships dock. At the front
and center of his desk among neatly organized and polished
trinkets I notice a gold-rimmed rectangular name plate:

JONATHAN G. WOLCOTT VI
VICE PRESIDENT, WAGE AND LABOR
NEW YORK DOCK CO.

"Mr. Meehan, is there truth to the rumor that you no longer
will allow cranes to operate in some territories?" Wolcott asked.
"There is a lot of money in those cranes. I will have you know."
"I've seen men get kill't," Dinny said. "A man got kill't at the
Baltic Terminal not long ago 'cause the boom hit 'em in the
head. As far as I see it, men need jobs. Not cranes. Cranes don'
have kids."

"Mr. Meehan," Wolcott said, sitting forward. "I have always
seen you as a man of some intelligence. You know that. Mr.
Swede? He knows that, doesn't he, Mr. Swede? But I think you
may have a touch of the Luddite in you."

"What the hell is that?" The Swede demanded.

"Luddite? It means he doesn't approve of change, Mr. Swede.
New things? Technology?"

"The more things change, the more they stay the same,"
Dinny mumbled.

"Oh, how dreadfully obvious an allusion. And I shall say,
that mentality is going to get you in trouble, dear sir," Wolcott
said, then leaned back and showed a sarcastic frustration. "Oh,
the whole lot of you then too, I dare say. May I tell you of a trip
I only just weeks ago made? To a place called Japan, have you
heard of it Mr. Meehan?"

Dinny refused to answer.

"Well then, I promise to make it brief, while at holiday on
that most intriguing island nation, I noticed there lived a subgroup among them . . . Below the very dignified culture of the
Japanese. Yes, subgroup we can call them. They are considered
clever thieves. And I may venture, that's what you are as well,

Mr. Meehan and here is what so reminded me of your own, eh
. . . community I suppose one could name it. Stealing from those
who work and earn for their livings. From people like me. Living
off the hard work of others, they do. With a great cunning. Just
like you and your band of tinkers, Mr. Meehan. So clever you
are, in fact, I allow myself to indulge in some sort of friendship
ritual with you, don't I? Yes. Even paying you for services, hither
and yon. For services you should be doing on your own. Very
clever indeed. This Japanese subgroup are violent too. And
unbearably fertile, as similarities go. For the Japanese ruling
class, they too have a similar fate as the American, eh . . . 'swells,'
to use your diction. True it is impossible to even consider any
form of eradication. Not only due to the disgusting fertility rates,
but because people are infatuated, even fascinated with your evil
practices and trickery and transience. Fascinated why? Oh I
believe people appreciate the base in all of us as entertaining."

"What type o' yokes are they?" Vincent Maher asked,
interested.

"The Saru."

"Saru?"

"Yes, Saru. Thieving bands of primates. They are better
known as macaques."

The Swede looked at Dinny, then back at Wolcott. "You're
tryin' to be like that on purpose. Why don' ya talk straight'n
quit wastin' time."

"Well Mr. Swede, I will speak bluntly then. They are not
human at all, this subgroup. Have I not clarified this already?
My mistake then. Snow monkeys! My dear Mr. Swede," Wolcott
boomed with a snide turning of the nose. "They are commonly
known as snow monkeys. Now, may I ask a rather important
question? Mr. Meehan? Have you ever heard of a man named
Thos Carmody?"

No answer.

"I am certain you have," Wolcott said, sitting back in his
chair. "Mr. Carmody . . . well. May I speak frankly? I will. Mr.
Carmody is a man I would like dead. Will you, please Mr.

Meehan, will you look at my face? Thank you then. I would like him dead, is that at all unclear?"

"Who's Thos Carmody?" Maher asked dumbly.

"Thos Carmody is antibusiness," Mr. Wolcott answered quickly. "He does not want stevedoring companies to supply jobs to you and your people, Mr. Meehan. He wants to tell us how to run our business. Indeed, he aspires to put you out of business, Mr. Meehan. I can promise you that. A promise. But still, Thos Carmody is alive."

"Yeah, and?" The Swede said.

"You were born on the West Side of Manhattan, is this true, Mr. Meehan?"

Dinny nodded as he watched Wolcott weave through his strategic presentation.

"Why don't you ask your people over there who Thos Carmody is?"

"Why don' you save us a trip?" The Swede barked.

"Thos Carmody is the muscle behind the International Longshoreman's Association, Local 856. He struts up and down Chelsea and the Hell's Kitchen docks behind the likes of King Joe Ryan with a big stick, Dinny. He kills morale, he kills strike-breakers, he kills profits, and he kills business, and guess where my people saw him just three days ago, Mr. Meehan? Would you care to guess?"

"Where?" Maher asked.

"Sackett Street, here in Brooklyn," Wolcott said, leaning back in his chair and fingering a long cigar from a wooden box at the end of his desk, then lighting it slowly, allowing the imagination of all those watching him to overtake them.

"In your neighborhood," Mr. Wolcott exclaimed.

Dinny sat unfazed at the pitch.

"In our neighborhood," The Swede repeated who stood up and began pacing. "A union guy in our neighborhood?"

Dinny smiled when he saw The Swede become undone.

"Yes," Wolcott said. "And I'm sure you are well aware of the topic of conversation. Aren't you Dinny? If you won't answer, I'll say . . . Huns!"

"What about 'em?" The Swede asked.

"One million dollars to the ILA."

"Wha?" The Swede tilted his head.

"For a general strike," Wolcott said. "You think Thos Carmody's just comin' around Brooklyn for St. Patrick's Day? No, he is organizing the German plot. Mr. Swede? Have you ever been run out of your own neighborhood? Hmm? Have you? By your own people, no less. Another Catholic, but with a much different agenda. The Irish union's will take power with this strike and you and your's will be left as waterfront scabs, nothin' more. How does that sound, Mr. Swede? A general strike for guaranteed salaries, limited hours, better working conditions, sick days even! Worker representation . . . union cards! All these promises to the very men that work for you currently. Who could deny them their right to better their conditions, Mr. Swede? What laborer would deny such gentrification and luxury? All paid for by the Hun, America's enemy! Why Mr. Swede, maybe you could get a job in crowd control when Mr. Eugene V. Debbs comes for a speaking engagement! That is your line of work, is it not? Crowd control? Security?"

The room was taken by the story.

"Mr. Meehan?" Wolcott asked, addressing us all. "Do you know how many piers the New York Dock Company owns?"

"Yes."

"I will tell you then," Wolcott ignored. "Thirty-five piers from the Brooklyn Bridge down to the bottom of Red Hook. That is close to three miles of waterfront property. More than one-hundred-fifty storehouses. Close to six million square footage of covered storage area. Four large terminals at Fulton, Atlantic, Baltic, and right here where we're sitting on Imlay. Every day we employ thousands and thousands of laborers. You, Mr. Meehan," Wolcott pointed, raising his voice. "Represent about ten percent of our workforce, which are nothing more than stevedores. Not counting the warehouses you extract premiums from, for which I am not in the least in agreement, though that is a topic for another discussion entirely," Wolcott turned his back and paced in front of the large window, "Mr. Meehan, can I ask you a question?"

"Mmm," Meehan mumbled patiently.

"Do you need help? Are you losing your grip? I'm sorry I have to ask you these questions, but it doesn't change the fact that I have to ask these questions. Is Mr. Lovett pressuring you? You know he has an exquisite reputation. Has he taken over Red Hook? Is he coming back?"

"I sent 'em down here," Dinny said, playing the game. "He works for me. He'll be back."

"But not in the same sense as Mr. McGowan, am I right? I mean, Mr. McGowan was loyal to you. Is Mr. Lovett equally as loyal as Mr. McGowan was before death came knocking on his cell wearing police blue?"

Dinny didn't answer.

"You see the two gentlemen standing at the door behind you?" Wolcott requested.

"I know them."

"Those two men work tirelessly to control ninety percent of our work-force from even uttering a single word concerning unions. Those men are not allowed to pass wind without us knowing it ahead of time. That's two men. We have succeeded in controlling thousands with only two men. We have utterly closed the ranks on any possibility of worker organization. And you know where our company's weak spot is, Mr. Meehan? Our weak spot is in the ten percent you watch over."

"That's easy for you to say, not easy to prove," Meehan said. "I've seen union guys in their midst. The warehousing units? They're union, a lot of 'em are. You can't prove nothin'."

"Thos Carmody is making my case for me," Wolcott again turned his back.

I watched Dinny. There he was, sitting solemnly in his chair and taking such a verbal beating without so much as a word in return. The Swede ready for murder, Maher and Gilchrist confused by the wordiness of it all, I sat behind with only pity for Dinny and what does he do but slowly turn in his chair and look upon me and my shocked face. Why, I couldn't know but it would be soon I'd be finding out.

"When's the last time ya went down to Florider, Wolcott?" Dinny asked abruptly.

Standing high over his desk now after he had created his tension like a chess player, Wolcott paused before answering the question. Then started to laugh. "Why do you ask, Mr. Meehan?"

"To me, Florider don' suit ya. The heat and the dirt roads. I don' think you like Florider."

"Alright then," Wolcott started to secede, then sat down at his desk, held his hands together, then opened them to Dinny. "Tell me about Florida, Mr. Meehan."

"Who gave you them cigars?"

"What, these?" Wolcott said, pointing to the box on his desk.

"The box says they came from Ybor City," Dinny said. "That's I-talian territory."

Wolcott knew that if he lied, Dinny would know it. Instead, he calculated that letting Dinny know the truth would be to his advantage, "What? Can a man refuse a gift?"

"A couple guinea stinkers' from Frankie Yale s'all it takes for you to listen to'm, is it?" The Swede said, pointing to the box.

Dinny stared at Wolcott, and then looked up at The Swede who had stopped his pensive pacing.

Dinny's hands were weather worn and tan. They were also very muscular. They told a story. They sat evenly on the arms of the chair in front of Wolcott's desk. In fact, Dinny's posture, his head, eyes, and shoulders all sat evenly. Directed toward Wolcott, you could say. While staring ahead at the fat man with a watch hanging from his breast and his thinning pate greased back like a Wall Street big shot, Dinny called out to me, "Kid?"

Gilchrist, sitting next to me, looked in my direction. Then so did Maher and The Swede. I became nervous, "G'ahead Liam," Maher said.

I looked up.

"Tell the man your first and last name."

"William Garrity," I replied.

"Now, Wolcott," Dinny continued. "Do you know the name of the man Thos Carmody was visitin' last week?"

Wolcott cracked a smile. His smile then turned into a laugh and then the laugh turned into a howl and as he began opening up I noticed his English accent had faded away, "I don't know about you, Dennis Meehan, you old son of a bitch you. To answer your question Mr. Meehan, yes, I do know the name of that man. How could I have ever doubted you wouldn't know something? I apologize, Dinny. From the deepest part of my cold heart! I didn't mean disrespect. Doubt you? That was my mistake and you have played your hand well, I should say so! I see you have a plan in place then and I will trust that plan will be carried out successfully. To make sure," Wolcott snapped his fingers toward Wisniewski and Silverman. "To make sure we are together in our thinking, I have assembled a nice little package. . . ."

"How much?" Dinny asked.

"Oh, well considering . . ."

"How much?"

"Five hundred dollars . . ."

"Fine, give it to Gilchrist," Dinny said.

As we all stood up to leave, Dinny then looked back at Wolcott. "Frankie Yale?"

"What about Mr. Yale?" Wolcott suddenly became defensive. "Oh, am I going to work with those gentlemen? Is that what you are intoning? No, I can't work with those fucking animals," Wolcott said, while enjoying the hand-rolled he drew under his nose. "Unless I can . . . that is. You know Dinny, a man can only work so hard and stay happy. It's the pleasurable things in life that make it all worth living for."

Vincent Maher nodded his head slowly in agreement.

"That's funny," The Swede started berating the fat Wolcott. "I thought we was the reason ya able to enjoy dose pleasures. I can't wait to see the day when ya gotta bunch o' fookin' dagos tellin' ya how to run the docks and when ya disagree with 'em, ya find ya family in danger. That's the way dem guineas do. And you know dat. You walk wit' dem, we'll burn this place to da ground."

"They send me presents. You send me threats," Wolcott said for the first time showing his frustration. "Dinny! If I was you? If I was Dinny Meehan? Nah, I wouldn't worry about me making a deal with those fucking ginzos. If I was Dinny Meehan? I'd worry more about a deal with Bill Lovett."

And after retaliating with his own threat as we began to walk toward the door where Wisniewski and Silverman stood guard, Wolcott's forehead and upper lip drenched in sweat from his sudden anger, he then mocked Dinny's Brooklyn accent, "Take care o' ya nayba'hood, would ya. I wanna see Thos Carmody's name in the obits within two months! Two fookin' months, Dinny Meehan!"

CHAPTER 11

The Code

IT WASN'T FOR ME TO KNOW at the time, but The Swede was at his his wit's end and in Dinny's ear on a Saturday night along the stretch of a pier below the Arbuckle warehousing stores.

"Lovett's gotta go," he yells while pacing around Dinny, rubbing his head agitatedly. "He'll deceit us as soon as he can! Soon as he's outta the workhouse. Fuck Lovett! Fuck Non Connors, I'll run Red Hook, me and Dance will. We give them too much string and it's all o' us that'll lose out, Dinny."

Dinny listens as its The Swede who thinks more about the angles than any other. Aside from himself.

"And Brosnan? Fookin' tunics in the Dock Loaders' Club? Thos Carmody and the ILA in our neighborhoods recruitin' an' talkin' strike and millions o' dollars from the Germans? Frankie Yale and them pinchin' in on us. And Wolcott givin' us orders? Us? Dinny, the fuck we doin'? We're losin' it, Dinny. We're losin' control and ya know we can't afford to ease up, not even for a second. . . ."

"Lovett's valuable," Dinny said, folding his arms. "He can be swayed. He's only twenny one. But the man can run Red Hook with fire on his side. That's our border, the Red Hook. You know that. We need only the best down there, but I need you wit' me and available up and down the territories. I can turn Lovett around, just need to control those whisperin' in his ear."

"Connors," The Swede said. "They take McGowan, we take Connors. . . . Me or Vincent."

"Just wait."

"Why? Why, why, why . . ."

"Because I don' jump before I know where I'm gonna land, that's why. Don' touch 'em just yet. Hands off. Death is a message to the livin', the only message we'll send by killin' either of 'em now is that they scared us. They don' scare me. They scare you, Lovett, an' Connors. Frankie Byrne an' them?"

"No."

"Let's do some maneuverin' in the Red Hook. That don' work, we'll show everyone that we gave 'em a chance. Show 'em that we tried and that we'll try for them too. But when we try and we don' get the response we're lookin' for . . . that's when ya send ya messages."

"And this kid? Joe Garrity's nephew?"

Dinny nodded. "Still early on him."

"Yeah, but he's dangerous now," The Swede said.

Dinny smiled. "Dangerous, yeah, I guess so then."

The next morning and it's Sadie and L'il Dinny and I off to St. Ann's again. The trolley we board slides on the tracks through the tenement halls with a motorcar here and there scuttling by us on the left, keeping up on the right. Pedestrians dodge opposing traffic and look behind us as they run ahead of the trolley or wait in the middle of the street for us to pass. Apple carts and potato shays and one-horse drays park along the sidewalk for the morning markets under the awning of laundry wires and elbows and faces pouring out from the window ledges above, staring lazily at the scenery movements. And along the rooftops are flocks of pigeons pecking at simple flecks and pooping on bald spots below as if they are targets. Ladies dressed to the nines, or as best they can, have the big hats that flop in the breeze of the trolley air with ruffles on their sleeves and squeezed between many a stranger who thinks long and hard on her curving thighs and heart-shaped hips hugged by the make of her church gown.

Inside Father Larkin blesses the tabernacle and just before the baskets are sent round for the offering, there is a clamor behind us all as the church door swings open with a fling and a bang against the back wall. Two men storm down opposing aisles like soldiers through a prisoner's camp looking through the crowd for the wanted. Ignoring wholly, even desecrating the vaunted rituals adhered to by the flock of prisoners and true, the rituals of most millions too.

"Ya see'm?" One of the rebels yells across the flock.

"And who might ye be lookin' fer, bhoys?" Father Larkin echoes angrily over St. Ann's hall. "What on eart' is it that gets in ye so impartently s'mornin' that ye feel overcome wit' yer inclinations as to interrupt this service. . . ."

"Dere he is! Dere's da yoke, I see'm," Tommy Tuohey yells over Father Larkin's complaints.

I can tell by the accent it's Tommy Tuohey and by the time I see him, Vincent Maher has come behind me and begun his pulling me out of the pew by the underarms.

"Let's go, kid," Maher mumbles, then signals at Sadie. "Don' ya dare say my name out loud. Don' do it."

"Oop-ye-go-bhoy." Tuohey lifts on my legs and together they carry me over the heads of the faithful of the aisle.

"I can walk on my own," I yelp with embarrassment. "Let me down, let me down. I'll go on my own!"

"Ye're not to hert the bhoy," Father Larkin cautions in echo form with all his summoning.

"Clouts for touts!" Maher yells back.

Father Larkin doubles his tone, "Don' let me see dis bhoy hert in the slightest, I say! I'll have the justice upon ye! For heaven's sake, let the bhoy down and be off wit' yerselves den!"

By then the flock has all but stared at my sequestering and is beguiled and betwixt by the treachery and the tragedy and the blasphemy in it. L'il Dinny has begun crying and grabbing through the air for me to come back while Sadie has turned her attention to his soothing. I unwrinkle myself angrily next to Maher in the aisle and blush at the attention. Father Larkin continues with his celestial scorn and instead of answering back in kind with snide remarks, Maher pulls out two bills from his pocket and drops it in the offering basket, then starts his pushing me toward the door with Tommy Tuohey in tow like two trench-coated rebels marching their informer to his execution. The people mumble and they gasp and Sadie has turned red in anger, though a few of the older men giggle happily being as it reminds them of their own brash youths in the place they used to call Irishtown.

Following us from behind is Cinders Connolly who is a churchgoer himself and who assures his wife all is well as he leaves his family to be with his boys. Outside we are, and with a crash of the door Maher and Tuohey push me up Gold Street until a left we take on Plymouth.

"Real tough now, ain' ya kid?" Maher taunts.

"I don't think I'm tough."

"Yeah well, ya know things now, don' ya?"

"What do I know?"

"T'ings!" Tuohey yells in my face, then pushes me again.

I look over at Connolly hoping he will help me out since I know from the look on his face that he is kinder than most, but he keeps distant and nods toward me to go along with it all.

"We'll find out whatcha know, won't we?" Maher says.

"Sure will, givertake moraless," says Tuohey.

When we turn on Bridge Street and enter a saloon I had yet never seen before, Paddy Keenan stands behind the bar and looks upon us as we enter. On the end of the bar is Ragtime Howard with a small glass sitting ahead of him, though he hadn't moved when the door opens nor gave us a glance, and finally the old storyteller Beat McGarry comes from the rear room with a big smile at our entrance. These men reside day and night in the saloon, even on a Sunday morning as this.

I am pushed to the middle of the saloon as McGarry begins clearing the stools away and putting them in the rear room.

Menacingly, Maher motions in my face as Tuohey walks around the back of me and pushes me closer to Maher.

"What, ya wanna fight me?" Maher asks since I came upon him so close.

"I don't."

"Then why ya gettin' so close on me?"

Connolly comes around to my side when the front door opens again, this time the two large figures of Gibney the Lark and Big Dick Morissey enter and seem to know from the look on their faces what the situation is. Together, they form a circle and push me not so gently from one side to the other.

"Tell me what ya know," Maher says to me. "What did ya hear the other day?"

"What are you talking about?"

"Don' play stupit, kid. I was there and I wanna know what ya hoid and and what ya didn't."

"How can I tell you what I didn't hear?"

"Shaddup and start singin'!"

"About what?"

"That fat bastard Wolcott, whad he say that ya hoid?"

A range of thoughts run through me. Gibney kicks me in the seat of my pants and Morissey laughs in his baritone. Connolly pushes me to the center of the circle again as a matter of routine and McGarrity seems to be enjoying the whole scene like an oldtimer would.

"Let's pull his trousers down and cut off them barnacles," says the Lark. "Then we'll send 'm back to church where he can't do no one no harm."

"Join the choir," Morissey laughs, then shoves me to the ground at Maher's feet who then puts a boot on my shoulder. "We'll get it out o' him one way or da other."

"Get up! Get up ya fookin' yella coward," Maher pushes through to get to my face. "Ya think ya better'n the rest o' us, don't ya? Don't ya? I seen ya over there at Dinny's pretendin' to be so important. Pretendin' like ya gonna live for free forever! Get up! Now ya gonna find somethin' out, get up!"

So I did.

"Lie down!" Gibney yells and kicks the legs from under me and I slam to the ground on my elbow and back.

"I said get up!" Maher hoots.

By then the room has started spinning on me and next thing I know the box head of Red Donnelly is jabbing me in the kidneys and Harry Reynolds too has somehow appeared while old man McGarry laughs it up.

"Are ya gonna kill 'em?" McGarry asks.

"No let's torture 'em first," Red offers.

Suddenly a terrible smashing sound came to my ears and it took me a moment to realize I'd been boxed with a hand across the side of my head and ear. Then Gibney grabs me by the tie and jacket and pushes me backward where Donnelly had gotten on all fours behind. As I tumble over top of him and onto my back again, my head hits the cement flooring. Someone drags me from behind and throws me into some chairs and a table and then all men are over me yelling one after the other, so much so that all of their angered voices mix together and I can't do anything or return a word so I decide only to stare at them with the strongest scowl I can muster. Slaps come across my head and face and then a fist splits my lip and I can taste the blood but instead of spitting it out, I swallow and all I can think about is Father Larkin and his warning, which had fallen on deaf ears.

"Ya're the most dangerous man in Brooklyn right now, kid!" Maher yells over them all. "The most dangerous man 'cause ya weak and ya know things! That's the most dangerous combination! Now ya gonna tell me what ya hoid Wolcott say to ya or we're gonna beat it outta ya!"

"What? He didn't say anything to me that you didn't hear."

A knuckled crack came thumping on the top of my head and my ears got boxed again as I lay in the corner among the shambles of the toppled tables and chairs.

"Where's ya pride!"

"Why don' ya fight back!"

"Tell me what ya hoid!" Maher shouts in my face, his toothpick flying out of his mouth with the spittle too. "Whad Wolcott say and how much did he give us!"

By that time I am so upset and angered that I refuse to say a thing since already I know that Maher was there too at the big building on Imlay Street in Red Hook. There was nothing I was going to say to him that he doesn't already know. Nothing. But to stop the beating and the yelling, all I have to do is say the words. That's all I have to do. But something obstinate wells in me, walls them off in my eyes. Something so strong and so overwhelming is culled that I simply refuse, no matter the consequence.

In the saloon we hear the *chu-chum-chu-chumming* of the train come running overhead as the door has been opened again. In ducks a man of great height and white hairs. A man so long and slow in his strides that he seems to ride in like the swoop of an apparition. Something from the past that haunts us more in imagination than reality. A darkness so old and ancient that shanachies in all their trying could never bring the death-scare that the face of The Swede could summon as it does with me then and there.

"Where is 'e?" He bawls.

Everyone steps from his way and with the length and strength of a long moving crane, he crinkled his fists into my jacket at the chest and picked me up over his white-haired head, slams me up on my duff at the bar with a bang so hard that the bottles sang in their shock and in their shimmering.

"Ya gonna tell me how much Wolcott offered!" The Swede blasts into my face like a flung open furnace door. "Ya gonna talk an' sing. Then I'm gonna make ya dance like a little choich goil too! Sadie Meehan ain' hear to save ya now, is she! Dinny ain' here neither, now start chirpin'! How much was it?"

Tears streaming from my eyes in anger and my face red and ready to burst, ears ringing and body shaking in a shock and fear eclipsed not even by the horror I felt of drowning in the Atlantic by a U-Boat's will, I scream as loud as I can, "I don't know any Wolcott!"

The Swede throws me across the bar where I fall to the floor on my neck and my back. Connolly half-catches me there and tries helping me stand back up on my own.

"Let'm go!" The Swede yells, then grapples me again by the jacket and flings me into the arms of another.

"Hold'em, Philip," The Swede bellows. "Send'em to his heaven, that's where he wants to go, see! Get ya hooks in him Philip!"

Shorter than I, Philip Large grabs me from behind obediently as Connolly whispers into his ear. I can hear the whisper and know that he won't allow Large to break my back. But I also know that the only reason Large won't snap me in half is because of Connolly's influence. Connolly's whispering. And if The Swede or anyone else orders Connolly to shut up, I'll not walk again. Large fells me to the ground, and as we go back, he wraps his stout legs round my torso and pulls my arms yet over my head, choking me in his stubby grasp. Next to us on the floor below the crowd of larrikins is Connolly who continues whispering in Large's dumb ears and I can feel that Large yearns to squeeze the life from me. Yearns like a snake to break the will from its victim or the yearning a man feels to stay inside his woman instead of pulling out when the sensation overcomes his reason. Above me I can only see Harry Reynolds's face as the air is squeezed from my lungs. He looks on me with a businesslike stare. Looks to see if I will succumb and this look of his gives me the knowledge. Lets me know that giving the information these men are after will mean death. Not giving them their information will mean more torture, but it will also equal something else entirely. Something I hadn't much experience with yet. Those things in life that men are entranced by.

Suddenly in my view is Vincent Maher after he has pulled a .38 from the back of his pants, then leans over me with his legs opened around us.

"This is ya last chance, kid. Last chance to walk outta this place alive! Ya gonna answer this question or else we're gonna dump the remains of ya in the river."

He pushes the gun on my nose and on my cheek enough so that I can see it on my face.

"Who does Wolcott want dead! Answer me! Answer me!"

More tears running down and into my ears, the anger builds in me so high and terribly that the obstinate feeling makes me happier than the relief giving way could ever achieve. I look at his face through the lack of breath and tremble to answer. Large's hold is so strong now that even if I want to answer, I can't. My back is beginning to bend and the more I try to muscle it back into a normal position, the more yearning I can feel from Large to squash it. Then I hear Connolly whisper and Large's grip slackens a bit.

"Who's he want dead?" Maher yells, gun to face.

"Your mother!"

The room burst in excitement and laughs. Large lets me loose at Connolly's request and the whole lot of them pull me up and backslap me with big broad smiles. The congratulations come like the way men used to congratulate others back in those days, with a simple shake of clasping hands and a proud look in the eye. To be happy for me. That's how it was back then. To be happy to see me enter a new place with them under the crushing force of a world that turns its back on people in the low, as we are.

Then from the stairwell I hear footsteps and we all look up at the slow figures coming down. It is Dinny Meehan upstairs all along and as he calmly swung to our direction, he looks at me in my pitiful state with Eddie Gilchrist behind him.

"Ya know what honor is? Honor?"

"I think so."

"Paddy, get the man a drink, can ya?"

Keenan pulls down a bottle from behind the rudimentary shelf and fills a small glass of whiskey, pushes it in front of me.

"Have a sip, den," says Dinny Meehan confidently as he sits next to me while the others stand behind.

I did so.

"Wipe off those tears from ya face, kid. . . . There ya go. Don' let me see 'em again. Just self pity. Do ya pity ya'self? Do ya? Sure ya do. We all do. It's alright to do that, of course, but it don' help ya for nothin'. As long as ya know that. Honor is knowin' things ain't right. But still needin' to survive, ya make what ya can wit' it. Make the best for the people you care about. Go to the end o' the earth for just a single moment of happiness for 'em. Honor is goin' through hell, never talkin' about it to ya wife an' fam'ly. To ya mother. Honor's feelin' empowered by listenin' to others complain about things, then fixin' it wit'out even bein' asked to fix it. These men here? Us? We don' need a fire to bring back the blood of life in us. We are the blood of life. We're made for struggle, that's what we are. We are the struggle, dig? It's a code and those that don't know the code will never know it. Because the code's ingrained in ya, locked in the blood, can't be taught. You know who Patrick Kelly is?"

I looked at Dinny, then looked away. Then looked back. "I am."

Dinny nodded his head and looked at the others in pride of my knowing the answer, "Everybody's Patrick Kelly in here."

The Swede stood over us, still not convinced. Never convinced. The others smiled however.

"Ya think this country's here for ya? The police? The gov'ment? The businesses? They here to help ya? They're not. Don' give a fuck for ya. These men," Dinny waved his arm. "They care about ya. I care about ya. The only way we can survive, carin' about each other. Been like that for a long time here. We survive because we make survival out of it. Not because o' fate or coincidence, nah. To believe in fate is a sickness. We make our survival by the power of will. And what we talk about ain' no one else's business. No one's. Death or starvation can't break that from us. Torture either. Nothin' break's the code. That means silence is all they get from us. Ya understand? Ain' nothin' stronger in this world than the silence. Ya understand? What is it?"

"Silence."

"I don' know any Wolcott," Dinny said. "Who's Dinny Meehan?"

"Never heard of him."

"Gibney the Lark?"

"Don't know him."

"Tommy Tuohey the tinker?"

"I don't know any tinkers."

"Vincent Maher?"

"Can't recall that name."

"The Swede?"

"Plenty of them around, Danes too. Norway, Germany, Finland . . ."

"He already knows," says Maher happily. "We all thought you was soft since ya didn' grow up around here. Like maybe ya'd turn a tout on us 'r somethin'."

"Nah," Dinny said. "He grew up in a place teaches ya from the day ya break ground. They don' even teach it, it just is. It's in the soil and the songs. Seven hundred years of it."

"And counting," say I, and wipe blood from my chin to coat.

I wanted to say something. Held it in tight. I wanted to say it, though it wasn't the right time. Why did you flaunt my name to Wolcott? Like I was a trophy. Thos Carmody? My uncle Joseph? Why have I been taken in like a king? But it wasn't the right time. Not yet. I lifted the whiskey to my mouth and bit at it again. It spread like fire in my mouth and as I swallowed the heat down through the chest, my lip burned where it had been split and the whiskey and the blood mingled in the grit of my mouth as I tapped the empty glass down on the mahogany.

CHAPTER 12

The Runner

STARTING NEXT DAY DINNY IS AGAIN urging me to wake with his deep voice in the peaceful morning coos of L'il Dinny's breathing. Sadie patches me up a bit and out the door we are. Maher is again at the stoops and again men come from behind tenements and under elevated stairwells to meet us here and there. Plans are made for the day and when completed, they all go in different directions except Gibney and Morissey who always seem to go in the same direction.

Bill Lovett appears too while his right-hand, Non Connors, waits a block away and acts as if he were a stranger to us with his hat over his eyes and his hands dug into trench pockets. The Swede stands, staring down the road at him for they are mortal enemies, The Swede and Non Connors, for reasons I was not to know yet. Eddie Gilchrist mumbles to himself waiting for his orders, I stand next to Maher and Tuohey.

"Welcome back," Dinny says to Bill.

The small man with the cherub face just wavered around and nodded, staring firmly ahead.

"I'm only gonna say this in a nice way, Bill," Dinny said. "You can respect my home. You can not respect my home. That's ya choice."

"You went to see Wolcott?"

"Yeah, he's worried about unionizin'. Recruits and whatnot. You hear o' anyone tryin' to recruit down in Red Hook, that needs to be taken care of?"

"I don' speak I-talian," Lovett sneered.

"These are Irish too, ILA."

"Yeah?"

"Some Chelsea, Hell's Kitchen feller testin' the water. I'm gonna go see some people in Manhattan soon and see what's the deal wid' it."

"What's the name o' him?"

Dinny looked away discouragingly. "Thos Carmody. Ya know'em?"

"Nah."

"ILA's talkin' about a big strike, funded by the Germans. Wolcott thinks Thos Carmody's the point man. You see or here of 'em, you say somethin'?"

"Sure."

"See ya back at the Loaders' Club."

From there we go straight to the Jay Street Terminal where a ship is awaiting us. Ragtag soldiers in floppy hats and coats that got too big for them due to the loss of weight stand as best they know how when Dinny walks up. Tuohey goes straight for the ship's captain and Gilchrist for the stevedoring table.

"Not even a thanks for Tommy fillin' in like he did," The Swede grumbles about Lovett.

"Dat's alright, look where we are, Jay Street," Maher says happily. "If it was his gang, he'd be here. Not stuck down in the shit wit' all them guineas."

The Swede turns to me. "Liam, go down to Atlantic and ask Reynolds if he's got fifteen men to send up here. Only the good ones. Ask him which ones the best are."

I look up at The Swede who hadn't spoken a single word to me since he threw me off a bar.

"G'on!" he says.

"Which way is it?"

"That way, keep runnin' 'til ya see Atlantic Avenue. Take a right to the water. Ya remember what Reynolds looks like?"

"I do."

"Don' say his name, though. Run!"

I run under the bridges and everything barely seems recognizable. After the bridges I see the train yard by the Sands Street Station and keep along the waterfront. Middagh, Cranberry, Orange, Pineapple, Clark, and I am concerned that I may have taken a wrong turn. Pierrepont, Montague, Ramsen and I really start to worry. Grace and then Joralemon streets come and I can't even see the next crossroad so I'm surely lost, and my head is tingling and I'm throwing doubtful curses left and right so I'm forced to ask a stranger, "Where's Atlantic?"

The man hears my brogue and wonders if I'm looking for the ocean.

"I'm not," says I. "The street."

"Atlantic Avenue?"

"Oh yeah, Avenue."

"Keep goin' south."

Finally I see Atlantic Avenue and a relief comes over me that I feel like I won't be demolished by The Swede for getting lost. Then I can't find Harry Reynolds and the worry comes over me again until a black man with sharp features comes upon me.

"Kid, what ya lookin' for?"

"Nothin'."

"Hey," he says as I'm walking away. "You're the new kid, come're."

I don't remember any black in the gang, but there he was shaking my hand and congratulating me and telling me not to worry, he knows where Harry is and his own name is Dance, Dance Gillen, "just ask aroun', everyone knows me. C'mon, I'll take ya to Harry."

Harry says calmly, "Sure I got fifteen, go wit'em, Dance."

"Wait," I say to Harry. "Which ones are the best?"

Harry Reynolds looks at me strangely, but with a great and distant sense of dignity.

"Make sure the kid only gets the best o' the best, Dance. Very important, no spalpeens. We don' want him to look bad."

"Uhright," Dance says, and he and I and fifteen happy laborers walk in a pack back toward Jay Street under the bridges and when I arrive, The Swede sends me to the Navy Yard to check on Red Donnelly and if he needs anything.

"Run!"

"Which way is it?"

"That way." The Swede points in the opposite direction as he had last time. "When ya see Hudson Avenue, keep goin'. If ya find yaself on Navy Street, turn around."

"What's on Navy Street?"

"Ginzos."

I don't know what ginzos are, but they sound like a menace.

"If ya find yaself on Grand Avenue, turn around."

"What's on Grand?"

"Sheenies."

Don't know what those are neither, though I should because it's an Irish word but it only sounds like a tribe of cannibals or savages of some sort, so I steer clear of those places carefully. Next thing I know I've been to the Baltic Street Terminal twice and the Navy Yard three times and the Dock Loaders' Club four times running messages back and forth all day long and somewhere along the line I hear someone call me a runner. That's what I am, then. A runner. And I don't mind being a runner because at the end of the day Dinny gives me money, which I give to Sadie since I don't know where to put it or what to spend it on.

"Why not ask yu muva if she wants to come to New Yook?" Sadie says, stashing it away on a high ledge in the kitchen.

That's when I tell her that I've been waiting for responses from my mother, father, brother, and two sisters back in Clare, but because all my letters had my uncle Joseph's return address, I'm not sure if they ever responded. Only three weeks earlier I sent a new letter with 452 Warren Street as the return address and I don't even know if that has arrived in Ireland yet.

"Where's the closest post office to them in Clare?"

"Tulla town, about a twenty-minute walk, but a postman comes by bicycle to the farm when letters come in."

"Well, wif as much as yu makin', yu'll 'ave'm 'ere in no toime. Yu know Liam, yu make f'ree toimes as much as a fact'ry

worka wif fif'een yea's sperience, yu know. Yu lucky, yu know.
I've a cousin oo works as manager at a fact'ry. Shameful wages!
Dat's why so many people 'ave to live togeva 'round 'ere. Not
enough work o' not enough wages when they do work. O' bof!
Yu lucky, Liam."
    "I know," I say.
    As February turns to March of the year 1916, my role with
the boys on the docks evolves. The more I run, the more I work,
the more I get to know things. Every morning at 4 a.m. I am
down the stoops with Dinny and Vincent waking the roosters
on Bond Street that always anger at our passing. Sometimes
there are requests for The Swede's assistance up in the Navy
Yard or Jay Street or Baltic Street and sometimes they request
Vincent Maher, so I run back toward 25 Bridge Street. The
messages are often cryptic, encoded, and rightly so since it is
often that I run by the Poplar Street Police Station where Head
Patrolman William Brosnan keeps a blind eye on us and then I
run by the Adams Street Courthouse where Judge Denzinger's
harsh sentences are known far and wide.
    "No talkin," Vincent reminds me. "What's ya name?"
    "Patrick Kelly," I say.
    "That's right, you know what Patrick Kelly means, right?
Shut ya face the fuck up. No touts around here or ya'll get the
clouts. Everybody's Patrick Kelly, now go'n take this envelope
to Mrs. McGowan's home. Let'er open it in front o' ya and after
she's done readin' it, ask'er if there's anything else Dinny can do
for'er, dig?"
    I nod my head.
    "Then tell'er everything's gonna be all righted now."
    "Everything's gonna be all righted now?"
    "Go."
    I can't help but read what's in the envelope and as soon as I
get around the corner, I pull out a letter and twenty ten-dollar
bills inside. All three of the McGowan girls and the widow are
to show up Monday morning for jobs at the new clock-tower
building on Main Street between the bridges, fifth floor.

"Do you have any questions for Dinny?" I ask the mother who is surrounded by her girls.

"I don't believe so," says Mrs. McGowan smiling, the eldest daughter kissing her wrinkled cheek. "Can ye tell the man many t'anks from us?"

"Everything will be all righted now Mrs. McGowan," I assure her as she looks at me with only the pride holding back her tears.

And so I run, and all that food I'm eating in Sadie's kitchen is turning to lean muscle. And then when I'm working on the docks as needed, I feel like the muscles are getting bigger but Vincent says it's in my head, "Shaddup'n keep runnin'," he says. From one dock to the next I send messages back and forth but it's to the Red Hook I'm never sent, and I don't know why except maybe the danger, for it's the Italians that live in the neighborhoods inland of it. I hear things from different men, but Vincent tells me a lot of things. He talks all the time, in fact, but I don't always know if I should believe him.

"I-talians on Navy Street," he explains as he struts downhill on Fulton Street toward the old rundown Union Ferry Company dwarfed by the Brooklyn Bridge's brick tower above. "They're different on Navy Street. They're Camorra. In Red Hook, they're Black Hand, Sicilian."

"Oh," I say, pretending to understand.

"Most people hate I-talians, but they love me. They think me a classy feller. Most people do, as you know. 'Specially the lasses, as you know."

"Yeah," I agree.

Loaded with the moon-faced Italians, Sackett, Degraw, and Union Streets in Red Hook are dangerous places for a kid like me to wander among. So I don't complain about not being sent to Red Hook as I avoid all Italians at any cost since they eat their own babies, Vincent tells me, and if you cross them, they'll chop up your mother ten years later (because they have the memory of elephants) and make meatballs out of her and serve her up with pasta and red sauce down in Bay Ridge because

"they're all a bunch o' pagan Catholics, fookin' animals,"
Vincent says.

In the Navy Yard, men build ships paid for by the government contracts and this is wartime, so business is good. England
is buying and as far as the manufacturers in Brooklyn are concerned, there should always be wars. All day and night long
steam hammers slam down on hot iron slabs in the Navy Yard
foundries. And you can hear the pound of them all the way over
at 25 Bridge Street, even making ripples in Ragtime Howard's
whiskey glass. When I yell up to Red Donnelly to ask if he needs
any messages sent, he just waves his hat in the air revealing his
red hair and fat head atop a barge where he directs cranes and
bellows at his boyos.

The floating piers and pier houses at the terminals under the
bridges like Jay Street and Fulton Street have industrial freight
tracks dug into the Belgian brick that runs along the waterfront. Cargo is hauled from ships to floating piers to railcars
that amble in their clicking and their clacking through the
neighborhood and pull up at warehousing units where the train
cars butt against the platforms and where men with suit and tie
and hats of all sort unload them by hand or by bale hook in the
morning sun. It is there, under the bridges, that Cinders
Connolly always shakes my hand and speaks to me like a man,
smiling humbly as he is known to and with a mean set of
crooked teeth and scabbing knuckles.

The terminals at Atlantic and Baltic take in shipments that
mostly go onto automobile trucks to be driven over the bridges
to Manhattan or east toward Queens or Long Island and wherever else, as it's New York's piers and the piers only that all
goods are shipped since it is well before roads connect the cities
to the farms and also before planes are to fill the skies. And
everyone knows that it's New York that is the center of the
industrial world, now surpassing even old London town with
the completion of the Erie Canal years ago.

At Baltic, Gibney the Lark speaks with me in a serious tone
and I never seem to realize that it's all a front as Big Dick comes

behind me and picks me up. Spinning me upside down, he dumps me in a garbage can so everyone can have a laugh. But when he's not looking, I punch him in the stomach as hard as I can, though I'm never able to knock the wind from him.

"See, ya don' wanna go to Red Hook anyhow," Vincent says. "Il Maschio is down there. That's trouble. Real trouble."

It interests me greatly though, Red Hook, and so I ask around about it. In fact, asking questions becomes what I am known for and it is more than once I am told to "shaddup." But because I have the hunger for knowing things, I never take it the wrong way. Beat McGarry tells me it's the incumbent Irish that have run Red Hook for many years, but is now overflowing with immigrant Italians. Frankie Yale knows the value of the area and so he often sends in Il Maschio to remind the pier house supers and the stevedoring managers that it's only a matter of time until the Black Hand takes over.

"Who is Il Maschio?" I ask, but nobody knows. No one. If he's a man or a group of men, no one can answer me since it, or they, slink in the shadows and when the clean-shaven Irish show up he, or they, vanish like they never existed, or he never existed. Maybe like they exist everywhere, or he does maybe.

"What's the Black Hand and what does Frankie Yale have to do with black hands and Il Maschio?" I ask Cinders Connolly, but he won't say.

"What does Il Maschio mean in Italian?" No one's sure, but Dago Tom tells me it means "the mail."

"Like sending letters, like?" I ask. "The postal service?"

"No, like man. Or boy. Male, ya know? *Male?*"

"Oh, that kind of male."

Somewhere I learn that Il Maschio is Frankie Yale's wing of Italian thugs, or thug, who work on the docks and believe in something called "the Sicilian code" and that if they can't reach your mother, they'll kidnap your child for ransom. And if you talk to the police or anyone else, the child will end up in a barrel at the bottom of the Gowanus Canal. And I learn too that Il Maschio only appears when the Irish fight amongst themselves, which happens often or when the dockboss is sent to Sing Sing or the workhouse, which also happens often. And since I can't get straight answers about Italians, and I'm filled with strange stories I sense that there is mystery around their ways, even if they are Catholics like us. They are a mysterious people and since they show up only when we are fighting among ourselves, I sense that they must be in cahoots with the pookas from the stories of my childhood. But then, I am starting to get to the age where the validity of the old stories become questionable and that only confuses me more.

I think of my father and his quips, and though he was speaking of the British being preoccupied with the German, he used to say, "With your enemy's turmoil come opportunities," and so it is in Brooklyn with the Italians. Before being sent up to Sing Sing, McGowen had long been charged with controlling Red Hook for Dinny. But a couple months after McGowen was sent up, Dinny came under great pressure to take the area by force as it had been coming under the influence of Il Maschio in McGowen's absence, since that's when the Whitehanders are most vulnerable.

Wolcott of the Dock Company also was to use the turmoil like a stoic card player and was not so reluctant to refuse Yale's offerings as a way of improving his hand with Dinny and the Irishers. But I don't blink when I hear Wolcott takes advantage of other people's disadvantage because he's a capitalist and that's what that means; to capitalize.

But that's where Bill Lovett comes in. Only twenty-one years of age, the leader of the Jay Street Gang was brought under the umbrella of Dinny's White Hand and immediately sent into the border at the Red Hook. It was a legendary combination because previously the two gangs were enemies. Even though Lovett's young crew was smaller and less experienced, they were seen as the future. But it was a bloodless coup. Dinny was accommodating and courting and respectful, and offered Bill both security and a stable income, not to mention the two fierce gangs wouldn't have to go to war, which Dinny reminded

Lovett could only end in the Jay Street Gang's demise since the
Whitehanders had so many more men. The other factors in
Lovett's gang joining Dinny's were twofold: the notion of honor
and Bill's hatred of the Italian.

"Them ginzos," Dinny said to Bill. "Let'em have the prosti-
tution and gamblin', no honor in that. You know that Bill. You
know that like I do. Not in our neighborhoods they don't."

Bill Lovett was a lot of things, but a pimp and a numbers guy
he was not. Dinny was at his best in persuading and as a way of
reminding Bill of his honor, he asked this question out from the
blue, "Ya parents, ain't they from County Kerry?"

And of course Bill Lovett could never face his mother again,
if and when it ever got back to her that he was making money
off the beauty and purity and sanctity of a woman's body that
was formed from the innocence of Eve and embodied by the
Virgin Mary, holy mother of Jesus himself. Since it was his
mother that tried to steer the young William Lovett into the lay,
until she found out he was more influenced by the Peck's Bad
Boys of Catherine Street than by the homilies at Mass.

But in those days, living from the streets was not seen as so
terrible a thing since there weren't enough jobs for as many
people needed them in New York. If you did get a job, it didn't
pay enough. It was in the blood of the Irish American, working
on the docks. The famine families that came over and certainly
any Irish American back then could see that dock tribute was
not as bad as enslaving the female body for sinful pleasure and
gain, surely.

So the deal was done then, Dinny Meehan's White Hand
enveloped Bill Lovett's Jay Street Gang and everyone in the
waterfront neighborhoods sighed a big relief for there would be
no war between the gangs that dominated the Bridge District
from the two main arteries, Jay and Bridge Streets. Lovett and
Non Connors, Darby Leighton and Frankie Byrne's boys were
all in now and decided to make a legitimate go of it and work
the Irish-Italian border at the Red Hook and as far as Lovett
and his men were concerned, if killing Italians came with the

job, the job wasn't so bad for them.

Tommy Tuohey told me, over by the stairwell at the Dock Loaders' Club, that although Bill was the smallest in his gang, he was always the leader. When drunk he was as ruthless a murderer as Brooklyn has ever seen, but when sober he had an intelligence about him, and in joining the White Hand, "Well, he-has-his-own-motives-o'-course, giverteek, moraless," Tommy said.

Anyhow, Lovett and his boys drove out Il Maschio from the Red Hook in a matter of weeks, but it was his force of will and cold ferocity that came back to bite Dinny when McGowen was murdered in his cell up in Sing Sing. "Rumors-a-flyin'," Tommy explained, that when McGowen was to return, Bill and his boys would be "off-the-trolley." With Pickles Leighton (Darby's brother), already serving a sentence, and with Bill Lovett as the beneficiary, Dinny and the Whitehanders knew from where the order came.

Up in the Navy Yard, Red Donnelly muttered to me under his breath that "Instead o' hitting Lovett back tit-for-tat, Dinny expelled Darby Leighton from the gang altogedder as a way o' showin' his power." Which the rest of the gang approved of.

"Most at least," Dance Gillen told me. "The Swede wanted blood and war of course."

But Dinny was not one to go to war with his own kind. And as far as the Red Hook goes now, it's a war front of a different stripe. The Black Hand is still rising, the International Longshoreman's Union still demands worker rights and Wolcott's duplicity is just as snide as always, but Lovett had done well to clear the way for the old Irish method of running things, gaining complete and despotic control over Red Hook in just weeks.

"Can't argue wit' facts," Harry Reynolds said. "Lovett's a man and he's to be honored. Killin' Lovett?" Shaking his head. "Can't kill a man wit' honor. Not right."

So to the Red Hook I was not sent, and for the better.

CHAPTER 13

The Divvy

ONE EARLY APRIL EVENING AFTER A day's running, I walk in the door at the Dock Loaders' Club as all the other Brooklyn workingmen do this time of day, and like one of them I feel. So many of the familiar faces are there and look up from the thundering of the giant Manhattan Bridge behind me and above the saloon. It brings me back to the place and to the time. And just thinking of it brings the nostalgia of the good old years as men's personalities were wholly shaped by the circumstance for which they were thrown. They didn't know how much things would change in just twenty, thirty years. They lived in their time. Lived for the moment and to survive in their day.

Along the mahogany stretch are the dockbosses with monikers that either the police give them or they somehow earn: Gibney the Lark, Big Dick Morissey, Cute Charlie Red Donnelly, Harry the Shiv, and Wild Bill Lovett by the crook in the bar with Non Connors and Frankie Byrne behind him and quickly sitting among them is Cinders Connolly, named Cinders because that's what he turns a ship into if a captain refuses White Hand authority. Behind them are the men I get to know so much better during my time. Men who don't lead, or can't. Men who are loyal to the gang for the most part, or at least are strong workers or have specific talents. So many names I scarcely believe I remember them, but they exist. Oh yes, they are the children and grandchildren of our people that survived the Great Hunger and evictions before and after the Land Acts or the general lack of any hope at all in the place where all our hearts still hang, Ireland. Men of America now, like the half-black, half-Irish Dance Gillen, King of the Pan Dance as he is known for stomping another's face with his boots.

There are loads of kings in Kings County, as I've mentioned. Proud ones too like long-nosed Chisel MaGuire, the Craps King of Ballyhoo for his talent of introducing pugilists at prize fights and fanning the odds too. I never knew his first name, but all call him Chisel since he's always at work on some sort of scam or skim or dealing craps or faro, looking for an angle to put the screws on someone, smiling sly when he gets in trouble. But I'm ignorant to usurers and schemers and such. I only see the dated vest and dusty tails on his coat that he wears like royalty as being odd. And the beat top hat too, as if he were some sort of London theater-goer from a hundred years previous, patchy beard and all. He seems to find happiness in his own wit and gives a stately bow when a dockboss loses patience with his badgering them. Everyone knows he longs to be a shylock or a craps dealer or a policy wheeler, but the Whitehanders don't deal in numbers, as mentioned. Though he's not to have much luck talking Dinny into his double-deals, there are no other groups for a chiseler to hang on to as he's a low-goer, even though he acts like he's among the high-regals and the old Dutch aristocrats of the county of Kings.

Some of the men shake my hand out of interest as Dinny's new mascot, while others avoid me coldly like Garry Barry and his crony from the old Red Onion Gang, James Cleary. Others greet me kindly while they stand behind the dockbosses like flat-faced Philip Large and Dago Tom, the half-breed Italian Irish that grew up in the shadows of the Benjamin Moore Paint Factory and the spire of St. Ann's in the Water Street rowhouses of Vinegar Hill. Best friends Eddie and Freddie; Eddie Hughes and Freddie Cuneen are there too. And so too are the Simpson brothers Baron and Whitey, the dust sniffer Needles Ferry, the fair scrapper Mickey Kane, buddies Happy Maloney and

Gimpy Kafferty, the old Frankie Byrne Gang members Jidge Seaman and Sean Healy, the desperate Mick Gilligan is there too and Ragtime Howard who sits in front of his enabler Paddy Keenan who keeps everyone at the bar happy, listening to the day's stories and replacing empty glasses with full ones.

Other than the old-timer Beat McGarry, Paddy Keenan, and a few immigrants, there is not a man beyond the age of twenty-six in the entire saloon, though most have many years, experience and have been working or in gangs since the age of ten, even younger. Lacking the self-importance of the better classes, the gangs in Brooklyn are always filled with the young who can't see much farther than the cheapness they hold for life itself, as does a soldier ready to die, and see honor and respectability in it and the songs they sing in the Dock Loaders' Club shows it to be true:

> *Oh, a soldier he leads a very fine life*
> *And's always a-blessed with a charmin' young wife*
> *Payin' all o' his debts without sorrow or strife*
> *And always lives pleasant and charmin',*
> *Yes a soldier he always is decent and clean*
> *In the finest of clothin' he's constantly seen*
> *While other poor fellers go dirty and mean*
> *And sup on thin gruel in the mornin'. . . .*

There are many others too, but not wanting to confuse, we'll leave them out for now. But it is in those names that this story owes much. Old clan names, most of them; evidence of the people driven down so low by the oppression and by the hunger and by the flight. On their leave to America in such a state their parents, maybe grandparents having no money or means to continue their journeys, settle in the neighborhoods that berth them: along the waterfront here in Brooklyn. And these young men in the Dock Loaders' Club are haunted by the reason for their arrivals here in America, though most don't even know they are haunted. But haunted they are. I can see it now all the more clearly, of course, as I have outlived the times. Found it in myself too, I did. Haunted

by a great distrust passed down for many generations, these new
Americans gave to what come of their lives. Lived in their time
and from what they knew only, their wild eyes a window into
their persecuted souls, yet hidden in the dress of the modern man
in ties and jackets like savages dressed with zoo bars.

Among the crowd, Paddy Keenan reaches across the bar to
give me a cherished beer.

"Enjoy, kiddo," Cinders says as Beat McGarry smiles and
pays for it with the click of a coin.

Tommy Tuohey walks over from the stairwell for a shake.
"Dere he is, da yoke! Fine broth of a lad, is he. Young slacaire
o' County Clare show'n up fer da divvy."

Other than some candles on the bar, a few lanterns hanging
from the ceiling beams and some wooden chairs and small
tables, the saloon is not dressed with accessories or decorations
of any sort, which I'm certain is the reason the lone framed
picture on the wall by the front door grabs my attention. On
the top of the frame is dust many ages old and at some point the
glass that once covered the portrait had been broken, exposing
the man in it who had a proud beard while his mustache was
shaven away entirely. Below the man's face was an old yellowed
newspaper clipping. "When Lilacs Last in the Dooryard Bloom'd,"
I read aloud. "What's that mean?"

"Hellifino," says Tommy.

"It sounds so beautiful," says I.

"Beautyful, he says," Cinders laughs. "It's beautyful, Beat."

"Sure it is," Beat McGarry smiles.

"I mean the way the words are put together, it's poetic. Isn't
that what poetic means?"

"Is it a poet ye wish on bein'? A poet?" Paddy Keenan asks.

"Regula' Eddie Allen Poe," Ragtime Howard mutters, the
only words I ever heard from him.

"I don't know," I say thinking on it. "Who's the man in the
picture above the words?"

"That is Abraham Lincoln," Beat McGarry claims proudly.

"What'd he do?"

"Freed the slaves."

"Wow, what a feat. How did he accomplish it?"

"Well, he was president back den."

"What party line was he?"

"Republican."

"I want to be a Republican then, freeing slaves is honorable."

"Jaysus," says Paddy Keenan.

"*Phphphph*," Ragtime chuckles under his breath.

"No ya don't," Cinders interrupts kindly. "You're a Democrat. We all are here."

"I'm a Republican in Ireland, why can't I be one here too?"

"*Phphphphph*."

"What's Democrats got over freeing slaves?" I say.

"Well," thinks Beat McGarry good and hard. "We got Tammany across the bridge, the Madison Club here in Brooklyn."

"What's that? Tammany?"

"The old wigwam in Manhatt'n."

"What's a wigwam?"

"Like a Indian hut."

I look at him, confused.

"Tammany is the Democratic machine, named for the Lenape Indians."

"Are there really Indians in Manhattan?"

"*Phphphph*."

"Jaysus," says Paddy Keenan. "He's got questions."

"I want to see th em, can I see them?"

"No kid, it's where all the New York Democrats call home now," says Beat.

"Did they free the Indians?" I ask, still confused.

"Jaysus."

"*Phphphph*."

"No," says Beat McGarry. "They represent the workin' man and the unions."

"Oh, and we hate the unions right?"

"Sure we do."

"And who do the Communists represent?"

"Unions."

"They sure are well represented. I think I'd want to start my own independent party if I can't be a Republican and if I were a politician here in America."

"They already have that party," says Beat McGarry.

"What party?"

"Independent."

"Who do they represent then?"

"No one."

Scratching my head, "Maybe they should represent the Irish, we've got no one to represent us, so say my da."

"*Phphphphph.*"

"True for you, child," Paddy Keenan calls out. "Spoken well too."

"Except for the Irish Parliamentary Party who are nothing but a bunch of jackeens, my da says."

"He's right too," Paddy Keenan agrees while Tommy Tuohey rolls his eyes since he couldn't give a care about one government over another.

"Ya're a good kid, Garrity," Beat McGarry says to me while Paddy Keenan smiles from the other side of the mahogany.

I look back at the picture of the stately man, Lincoln. He's a gentleman, I can see. But my eyes are brought again down to the words that sound so light and airy, "When Lilacs Last in the Dooryard Bloom'd." And I care about the way the words sound together. Reminds me of the shanachies that used to wander the country lanes or tell stories by the fire in the inns of Ennis coaxed by the wondering eyes of the children listeners. "When Lilacs Last in the Dooryard Bloom'd." It sounds so nice the way they work together, but since I'm uneducated I don't know what else to call it, but I think its poetry. And I wonder if it's better to be uneducated so that things remain mysterious because it's in mystery that I find beauty and, not to mention, all the men I am beginning to love are all uneducated too, even Sadie is. My da didn't allow his family to go to the schools in Clare that were dominated by the Catholic Church, which was

bribed by British parliamentary funds and where each child
was made to recite,

I thank the goodness and the grace,
That on my birth have smiled,
And made me in those Christian days,
A happy English child.

But I did go to a hedge school when I was back home and
learned arithmetic and reading and writing and about pookas
and Cuchulainn and the Irish language too, so maybe I could
be as gentlemanly as Mr. Lincoln looking so proud and smart
and caring in the picture. But then I look around, and at myself
too wearing the floppy boots of a dead man and remember that
I won't be much of anything since I'm not only Catholic, but
I'm Irish and the son of an IRB man and an immigrant and
anyway, maybe I'd just end up like Mr. Wolcott if I did go to get
schooling, who I hate more than anyone else. "When Lilacs
Last in the Dooryard Bloom'd," but at least I know what sounds
beautiful.

"Tommy!" A voice yells from upstairs, so he ambles over to
hear. A few seconds later Tommy the tinker waves me over.
"Dinny's h'opstairs dere, just knock ona daar two time and weet
fer da bellow. Migh' t'ave to weet a minute er two fer an answer,
giver teek, mora less," and it seems the more I hear Tommy in
his pavee speed, the better I understand him.

So up the stairs I go, two-by-two and knocking on the door.
After a moment I hear a bellow and the door opens just a sliver
to reveal the half face of Vincent Maher, who then closes the
door to undo the chain, and then opens it wide.

"Kid!" Vincent smiles gallantly while holding a paper cigarette in the doorway like some would point a dart. "Come on
in, yeah."

Along the back wall are rows of dirty, curtainless windows
that light the second floor. Eddie Gilchrist sits in a corner below
them and is engrossed in his numbers, a squat pencil and a collection of envelopes scattered on his small table. The pencil
looks snug in Gilchrist's hand. As snug as some men feel a gun

in their grip or the handling of a spade in my father's hard hands under my window back home in Clare, or the bale hook of a longshoreman's grasp even. I want the pencil in Gilchrist's hand for myself. I want it in my own hand and I can feel it there, snug. But somehow I have already gathered that in the gang a pencil and paper is a most dangerous collection of weapons. There is more suspicion surrounding the pencil and the paper in fact, than there is in a gun or a bale hook.

Behind a large makeshift desk that looks as though it was left there some forty years previous, Dinny sits back with one leg crossed over the other while speaking with The Swede, who stands behind him to his right, leaning against the long window sill, arms crossed. Closing the door behind me I hear Vincent lock it and take a seat in a lone chair by the entrance.

Other than the few things that I've mentioned, Dinny's office is surprisingly barren. Emptiness seems to be the point of it. In front of his desk is another chair, which he motions for me to sit in. So I do while continuing to look around.

"So," Dinny says. "Whadda ya think so far?"

"About what in particular?" I ask cautiously.

"About anythin'."

The Swede scowls at me, Gilchrist hasn't noticed a thing, and I look back to Vincent.

"He's speechless, Dinny," Vincent says laughing. "First time he stops talkin' since I met'em."

"Well," I struggle. "I'm very grateful. . . . Thankful for how you've helped me so much. . . ."

"No worries, anythin' I can do for ya?"

"For me? I don't think so. You've already done so much."

"Ya good people," Dinny says. "We need good people. Good people that can help us."

"How can I help?"

Dinny smiles, looks passed me to Vincent, then back at me in front of him, "Have ya talked wit' ya fam'ly since ya come over?"

"I haven't, the letters I sent to them had the address of . . ."

"Was ya uncle Joseph's."

I nod.

"He moved, ya know."

"Yes, but I don't know . . ."

"Down to Red Hook," Dinny confirms.

"Oh."

"Safer for'em down there."

I don't answer that because I am confused, but only a little.
The Swede bends down and mumbles something in Dinny's
ear. Dinny nods without looking up at him, then looks to me. "I
want ya to know somethin' Liam. Ya ever need anythin', ya
come to me. Your mother, your family . . . I can help ya get
them here. Done it many times. When the time comes, you ask,
okay?"

"Okay."

"We're like a family here too. Families work together, ya
know? I help you, you help me."

Of course, I am too green and young to understand the
gravity of that agreement, so agree I do. I am impressed by
Dinny for he is the most powerful man I've yet known, and for
as much as he had already helped me, I feel indebted even
without him asking a favor. But a favor in New York is not in
the same class as a favor back home. And as I look at Dinny
Meehan with the Manhattan Bridge reaching across the East
River behind him, I am unable to imagine the sheer weight of
things just yet.

The city is a vast place, and all its movements confuse me and
its loyalties and calculated deceits and underground agreements
and entire sects and strains of livelihoods based on an illegal
society that gives more to the needy than the legal system has
even thought of yet. Beyond the bridge behind Dinny is the misty
skyline that seems to fill up every open window in the second
floor room, stretching from left to right and just like the angles
people have to take in order to survive in the city, the massing of
step-stone buildings never seem to stop filling out the distance.

"Ya ever been there?"

"Manhattan? I haven't."

"I got a friend I gotta visit over there," he says looking behind him. "Maybe you and me can go see'em. He's a West Side feller, I grew up wit' him. Taught me a lot. Ya come wit'?"

"Okay."

Dinny looks at me and smiles and the silence feels strange, so I say, "When I first moved here I thought St. Louis was on the other side of the bridges."

"Yeah?" Dinny smiles, then looks at The Swede. "St. Louis, he says."

Vincent laughs, but The Swede's face just looks pensive and his forehead wrinkly under the white hairs.

"Eddie," Dinny calls out. "Give'em his envelope for the day's work."

"Lumpy!" The Swede yells at a startled Eddie Gilchrist who hadn't heard Dinny.

"Wha?" Gilchrist looks up with his round glasses at the end of his sweaty nose.

"Give the kid 'is envelope."

Gilchrist looks at me as if he has never seen me before, then stands up and sifts anxiously through the envelopes spread out on his table. He has spent the past two hours preparing them and seems completely surprised when the time comes for him to hand them out.

"Fookin' eejit," The Swede mumbles under his breath.

"Come stand here," Dinny motions to me. "I want ya watch this."

As my envelope is passed over to me at the side of Dinny, he motions to Maher. "Connolly."

Vincent opens the door as far as the latch allows it and yells down to Tommy Tuohey, "Connolly!"

In a moment a double knock comes.

"Who is it?" Vincent asks the door.

"Connolly."

Vincent opens the door, looks out, then closes and unlocks it for the entrance of Cinders Connolly and behind him wobbles the stout Philip Large.

"Gimme one o' dem yokes," Connolly says to Maher, who hands over a cigarette. Cinders then flashes his wide, humble smile, tucks the cigarette behind his ear, and strides across the room reaching over Dinny's desk for a shake. "What's doin', boss?"

"Yep," Dinny responds.

For me, Connolly is a likable docker. Light brown hair, long on top, cropped on the sides and a sledge-head jawline with a clamp to it. His back and shoulders are long and broad, strong as a weathered Celtic cross. I always find him smiling. They say he came from the Lower East Side of Manhattan, an old gang named the Swamp Angels that called the rookeries of Gotham Court their home. Beneath Gotham Court, they made the sewers their hangout and mode of business. Stealing through them to the docks, they pilfered ships in the middle of the night and sold the booty inland at cheap prices, but once the Strong Arm Squad posted snipers, they were out of business. So he came across the bridge where the old ways were kept alive since many of the Manhattan gangs were being broken up by the Strong Arm Squad and all their touts and stoolies. In Manhattan, many of the gangs were being rooted out, and either snitched on one another to save their own skins, or were forced to go legitimate. But in Brooklyn, things mostly stayed the same. Especially in the Bridge District where the silence was kept silent by quiet enforcement, long stares. In Brooklyn, when a man is shot and no one knows why, it is said he broke the silence between the White Hand Gang and the world.

"How goes it wit' ya by the Fulton an' Jay?" Dinny asks Connolly.

"Yeah," Cinders says, sitting down in the chair in front of the desk while Large sits quietly behind him in another chair. "Things are fine, the day went without a hitch after ya left in the mornin'. Had some Polacks hittin' the vodker half-way t'rough da day, but Philip scared 'em off."

Eddie Gilchrist again walks up and stands over Dinny's shoulder after dropping three envelopes on the desk in front of him. Dinny then explains "the Divvy," though it is probably for my own benefit: there is the payment from the shipowner, Connolly, and Large's hourly wage through the stevedoring company, and finally the percentage of the tribute they extracted from each laborer, the ship captain, and the pier house manager. It's up to the dockboss to give his right-hand man what he feels is sufficient and anyone else that helps him during the day is often given a stipend, if not bought drinks on top of it. That includes The Swede for the help he gives and Vincent Maher too, if summoned. The rest of the tribute apparently goes to Dinny and the gang or whatever he does with it is not to my knowledge, of course.

"Anythin' I can do for ya Jimmy?" he asks Cinders.

"All's well boss, thanks."

After another shaking of hands, Cinders stands up and walks toward the door Vincent has opened for them. Large wobbling behind obediently, staring at the floor. I look up at Vincent who smiles.

"Good job Philip," Vincent says sarcastically, then pats him on the shoulder.

Philip looks at Vincent's chest dumbly, moans something in the air innocently, and walks through the door.

"Send in Gibney," Dinny calls out in a scolding tone.

"Tommy! Send in Gibney," Vincent yells down the stairwell and again with the routine:

The double knock, the "Who is it?" the peering through the chained door, the closing of the door, the undoing of the chain, the opening again, and finally the entrance.

John Gibney is a large man with some girth in his chest and legs. At six foot tall with big shoulders and a powerful lower back and legs, Gibney waltzes in as the perfect specimen of the physical demands of a dockworker. But at his side was a hulk that carries the same build as Gibney, though two inches taller and thicker too. With a full head of black hair, short at the sides, long on top and the voice of a barge horn, Big Dick Morissey is known far and wide as a man who enjoys abusing immigrants as much as he does having good times. The only person that likes good times more than Big Dick is John Gibney, and that's why they call him the Lark.

The bulky pair both wear suits three sizes too small, torn at the seams, and on top of that they smell of stale beer and the sort of sweat that seeps into cheap fabric over a very long period of time. After Gibney and Big Dick shake hands with Dinny, Gibney sends a facetious hello to Gilchrist in the corner, who returns a distrustful sneer.

"Hey Lumpy? Gullet feelin' a little better is it?" Big Dick offers as Gibney giggles silently in front of the desk.

Maher laughs too from his spot by the door and Gilchrist tries to ignore the goons and instead looks at The Swede who then points angrily at the two rascals, "Just so ya's know, there'll be no fartin' in here."

"No, no," Gibney gets serious while waving his palms and looking up at Dinny. "I know dat."

"Thanks for that too," Gilchrist says under his breath, referring to the prank the two pulled on him by passing horrific wind in the water closet, then locking him in it. "Dis-Gusting."

Big Dick giggles also, though deeper, while Gibney mentions, "We wouldn't want ya da have da spring for another suit, dere. Dem yokes're expensive, yeah?"

In front of Dinny's desk the two goons whisper to each other and snicker again. Giggling like overgrown children in outgrown attire. When The Swede demands to know what they are laughing for, Gibney the Lark speaks up.

"Garrity?" he says as his cohort giggles, then both look my way, "We was wonderin', Dick and me, since ya from the country an' all," more giggles. "What's it feel like to stuff ya pud in an unsuspectin' sheep?"

"I don't know the answer to that," I say, which only succeeds in making them laugh harder and frolic in their chairs until they calm themselves under the patient stare of their boss when finally things are quiet on the second floor.

"What about a cow den?" Big Dick says, overcome with the giggles while Gibney holds his hand over his mouth, laughing through it until Dinny interrupts, "So how goes it at the Baltic Terminal fellers, all's well? What?"

"Sure boss," Gibney answers, still blushed. "Fine exceptin'
that we had to deal with the Reds today and yesterday. Forty
t'ousand pounds o' rugs, twenny pounds at a time and they
wanna do two men to a rug, fa Chrissake. Big Dick over here
laced 'em for bein' so stupit as to assume that's how the gig was
gonna shake and then they send a emissary to lobby me, Dinny."
he continues, pointing knowingly to him, "Ya know who I'm
talkin' about, Dinny. You know."

"You can say the man's name here," Dinny assures.

"Garrity," Gibney answers looking toward me while Big
Dick nods. "Joe Garrity, sorry, kid. He came up all the way
from Red Hook just to talk wit' us like some politician'r
somethin'."

"Don' worry, Liam. We'll talk about it, okay? I wanna talk
about it later," Dinny says.

"I ain' even seen no Thos Carmody in weeks," Gibney continues. "But this Joe? With the accent and the labor lingo? I
know ya don' want me to do nothin' to'em, Dinny, but this guy's
gotta mouth on'em, and he does!"

"Well," The Swede speaks up. "Leave it up to me and . . ."

"It ain't," Dinny flatly states as The Swede leaned against
the window with his arms crossed, staring forward.

"Yeah well, other'n that, all's good Dinny," Gibney leans
forward, his right hand leaning on his left leg where only the
pinky and ring finger remain.

After the goons get their envelopes and stroll for the door,
Gibney kisses his lone left fingers and winks at Lumpy. Morissey
laughs and pushes Gibney from behind.

Next was Red Donnelly who stammers in with a guilty look
on the gob of his box head. He seems to have a different right-
hander each day, sometimes it's Mickey Kane, sometimes Dago
Tom, maybe even Chisel MaGuire or sometimes he'll take in
Eddie and Freddie, but on this day it is Dance Gillen that sits
next to him in front of Dinny.

"How's things in the Navy Yard, Red?"

"Good, Dinny. Good."

"Ya know, Tim at the Wheeling warehousing units keeps tellin' me that they're missing cargo. Inventory's off. The numbers counted on the ships never match with the numbers in the warehouse."

"Well, I guess we oughter lend 'em Gilchrist, eh? He'll get it right . . . if they can't."

Dinny calmly looks over Red's shoulder at Dance Gillen, who doesn't know how to show guilt on his face in any case, though guilt seems to suit the two of them well, like charity does a nun. As far as Red Donnelly is concerned, missing cargo is part of an old tradition. A tradition his father defended, and a tradition he continues as a matter of familial rights. Like a generational trade secret. Like what they call "benefits" nowadays, instead of getting stock options on Wall Street, Donnelly gets booty in the Bridge District.

"I'll make sure my guys keep they hands in pockets, Dinny," Red gives in. "I'll make 'em act properly like."

"Alright Red," Dinny nods. "Eddie, give 'em their shares for the day."

"Lumpy!" The Swede yelps.

As Red and Dance walk out with Red counting his bills slowly, Dinny looks up to Maher. "Reynolds."

Maher opens the door and yells to Tommy and after a minute or two comes the knocks, the "Who is it?" the look, the unlock, the close, and the entrance.

Harry Reynolds walks in alone. Looks around the room not too obviously and sits down in front of Dinny's desk quietly, but with a calming confidence.

"Things?" Dinny asks while searching a drawer in his empty desk.

"Good," Reynolds nods, folding his hands together and looking away.

"Anythin' I can do for ya?"

"Nah, I'm good," Reynolds says with a bored stare, pretending to look out the window behind Dinny.

"Give 'em his money," says Dinny.

"Lumpy!" The Swede startles Eddie Gilchrist again.

Cordially, Harry Reynolds again nods when handed his envelope. He quickly counts the money and while getting up, nods again, this time to The Swede, and was out the door and walking down the stairwell.

I look over at Maher who closes his eyes and shrugs his shoulders quietly by the door.

Before Dinny has a chance to call the next dockboss, a commotion outside comes to our ears. The Swede notices first and turns around to look down the open windows. As the others notice too, The Swede is opening a shudder and sticks his head out.

"What is it?"

I look over Gilchrist's shoulder as everyone in the room is moving to the windows to see what gives. Down in the alley and looking up to us is a middle-aged woman with a broken paving stone in her hand threatening us with her next move while a whole schoolyard full of children swarm around her.

"Put the rock down, woman," The Swede instructs. "Ya can't throw this far up anyhow."

"Divil I can't!" she scorns with legs apart under her wash dress in a daring stance. "I'll t'row it up at yer mug and make ye a grand improvement, ye oogly sonuva bitch, ye!"

I am watching her from above and even Gilchrist notices her, the half-Brooklyn, half-Irish accent billowing in anger upon the second floor, threatening us with stones and surrounded by shorn-headed, shoeless children in the alley. I look closer and recognize the scar as that of the woman from McGowan's wake, the one who stepped so oddly out of line and groped Ms. McGowan for attention. On the one side of her face there is a pale hue that of a terrible burn and on the same side as this is a large bald patch over a disfigured, crumpled ear. One eye is closed too, though I believe it is because she is aiming the paving stone at us. Winding it behind her head, it falls short and thumps off the wooden facade harmlessly.

"I'll get anodder fer ye!"

At her side and looking up at us is a flaxen-haired girl a bit younger than myself with a toddler on her hip. Hair falling over her soft shoulders elegantly and reaching behind toward a slightly curved and immature waist, I was taken by the natural beauty that was still growing in her. The skin on her arms is soft and I can only imagine the grace in her legs as they were covered by a drab, oversized dress missing one sleeve. Lacking in attention, I see that her allure and the finesse of the natural femininity in her is not to be spoiled by a childhood in peasantry. Not even by malnutrition and it is remarkable, this beauty, growing out of the darkness. Blossoming out in great color from the depths like a great remembrance of an ancient glory.

"That's Anna Lonergan," Vincent says to me from the next window, pointing down at her with his paper cigarette.

"Who, the woman?"

"Not that ol' yoke," says Vincent smiling. "The girl ya starin' at."

"Oh, yeah," I admit. "But she's just a wee lackeen."

"Well, that ain' her moppet on'er hip."

"But she's too young for . . ."

"Oh yeah? You wouldn' ride'er?"

I look down at her again, then back at him.

"Another year or two an' that tomato'll be ripe," Vincent says bouncing his head up and down.

"Why's the woman so mad?"

"Ah, that's Mary Lonergan. That biddy ol' flab. Ol' Man Lonergan burnt her face off one time 'cause she's such a heckler. She comes here all the time askin' for favors. She wants her eldest son to open a bike shop, but of course she don' have the money for it. So she wants Dinny's help."

I look down on her again; her peasant manners, her missing a front tooth, and the dirty hands from pulling up paving stones aimed at us. The Swede scowls and Vincent laughs cruelly.

"Dinny Meehan!" Mrs. Lonergan scolds. "Why won't ye let me climb up and spake at ye 'bout it."

"No! Women! Allowed!" The Swede yells over her. "You and ya brood needa go for a long walk on a . . ."

"I'll sit on yer doorstep then!" She yells up. "The lot of us will, and we'll die starvin' 'till ye come to yer senses, Dinny Meehan! And if ye let me starve to death on yer own doorstep, then the whole neighborhood'll look on ye badly, Dinny Meehan. I'm ready to die for it! I'll die on yer doorstep, how's that? Think I won't?"

Vincent snuffed through his nose in frustration at her, but when I look over to Dinny I see him smiling.

"She's gonna kill herself to make us look bad?" Vincent asks.

"It's an old tradition," I say. "They call it the *troscadh*, it goes a long, long way back."

Dinny still smiling, tilts his head as he hears me speak.

"Let me son come an' spake of it then," she demands, thickening the accent for the occasion. "What harm can a bhoy do ye's? I know ye let'em bhoys in thare, Oi've seen it! Let the bhoy come oop, Dinny. He's a good kid, so he is!"

"No kids either, woman," The Swede bellows angrily. "Why don' ya take them scrounges, and ya'self too! Take'em home an' wash'em, ya ol' . . ."

"Send the boy up," Dinny cups his hand over the side of his mouth, then sits calmly in his chair.

Gilchrist looks over to Dinny with an interested look. Vincent raises an eyebrow, squiggles his mouth.

"Dinny?" The Swede pleads. "Ya know who that kid is, he's the same griftin' punk of a . . ."

"I know who he is."

I look over at Vincent, "Pegleg," he whispers in my ear.

Dinny then waves for Vincent to let the kid in downstairs through the bar. As Vincent walks toward the door I look over at Dinny with a shock of hair falling to his temple, cut real close on the back and sides and sitting deep in his chair behind the desk. The muscles in his neck and shoulders are evident even as he is covered by a jacket and tie, but I see in him also that he has weaknesses uncommon from the others. He looks over at me with his green eyes concentrated on his occupation. Unaffected completely by my watching him or that he could in any way alter his approach because of it. It's somewhat difficult to explain, but Dinny Meehan knows that the world is not watching him. Knows the world doesn't care about him. Even disapproves of him. Still, it appears to me sitting next him, there are many men and families that rely on his hand and his maneuvering. The weaknesses that Dinny Meehan has are of a nature that men like The Swede are unaware exist, yet it is these weaknesses that summon the truest sense of honor I have yet to see among these men. The weakness of caring.

Upstairs a few minutes later and a wild-eyed, windswept, floppy-booted, dirty-blond-haired fifteen-year-old limps in the room like some forgotten, defective cur on a prison ship. Almost as skinny as myself, but with a much tougher look on his face. I immediately spot the fake half leg and foot. The nailed boot at the end of it looks empty for the fact that it's sunken in and bent upward at the toe. It drags behind him menacingly and the blank look in his eyes is a cold one. Very cold. His hands are dirty with grease from the sprockets of his trade and the grease has migrated to the side of his bone-cheeked face and along his ragged coat. His tie is fraying and leans to the left carelessly, but it's the eyes that stand out. A pair of mean things earned from beating the coinage out of drunkards and sleeping outside with the aching emptiness in his belly that causes it.

Dinny still sitting behind his desk, looks at the wild child in front of him. Then at Vincent.

"He's clean."

"He's scum," The Swede growls, his lip curling up on one side. "Trashy scum underbelly of the fookin' slums and the lowest . . ."

"That's good," Dinny says, then looks upon the boy. "What brings ya to the headquarters o' the White Hand?"

Lonergan stares for a moment. Keeps staring. Doesn't answer and it seems a minute has passed in the quiet room when he finally mutters, "My Ma."

"And all her other weans too," The Swede admonishes.

Lonergan never breaks from the stare of Dinny and is then asked, "There somethin' ya want? Somethin' I can do for ya?"

"Nah."

"Ya from Cath'rine Street, right?"

"Yeah."

"John Lonergan's ya father?"

"Yeah."

"Mary Lonergan's ya mother? Yakey Yake Brady's sister?" Dinny nods his head back as if pointing down behind the windows at Mrs. Lonergan.

"Yeah."

"Why ya in my neighborhood? Cath'rine Street's across the Manhatt'n Bridge."

"I been livin' in Brooklyn since I'm six, on Johnson Street."

The Swede jumps in, "Yeah, the Lonergans and the Lovetts. Two peas in a pod."

"Ya family's close wit' the Lovetts, right?" Dinny asks interested.

"Kinda."

"Ya know Bill Lovett works for me now? We ate up the Jay Street boys and good thing too. Might as well work together instead o' fightin' each other. A fellow Irish American ain't ya enemy, is it?"

"Nah."

"Ya wanna work for me?"

"Nah," without a sign of interest.

Dinny smiles, "I guess ya got ya own gang and ya own gimmicks, eh?"

"Yeah."

"This our neighborhood," The Swede demands. "Time'll come that ya'll pay tribute. Real soon too . . ."

"Hey?" Dinny asks the boy.

"Yeah."

"Ya ever hear what a king lion does when he takes over a pride?"

"What's that. A pride," he asks without the inflection of a question in his tone.

"A pride's a group o' female lions that're loyal to the king. Kinda like the businesses and the ships around here. Longshoremen, they're my pride, dig?"

"Oh."

"So, lemme ask y'again, Richie. . . Ya know what a male lion does when he takes over another male lion's pride?"

"What?"

"He eats the younglings."

The room became quiet. The Swede crosses his spider arms. Vincent smiles from the side of his head and lowers his eyes. Lumpy isn't listening again. Dinny is relaxed. Leans on his elbows while pointing his attention at the boy.

"How'd ya know my name?" the boy asks.

The Swede jumps in again, "Ya think we don' know ya been jackrollin' sailors and beatin' on drunken laborers and holdin' up shops around here? Cutpursin' and pickin' pockets at Sands Street station? Eh, kid? You and ya cullies Abe Harms and Matty Martin and Petey Behan and Tim Quilty? Ya think we don' know everything? Everybody? Shit, Dinny, this fookin' guy thinks we's dumb, Dinny. Dumb like dumb. He ain't . . ."

"How ya gonna operate a business without knowing what the competitors're thinkin', Richie?" Dinny says.

Richie looks over at The Swede for a moment, then back at Dinny. His head tilts slightly to the side, then back and he lowers his eyes while his mouth remains open. This is his way of defense. I could tell this is his way of both calming himself down so he doesn't explode, and still looking mean at the same time.

"Ya don' wanna open a bike shop? Do ya Richie?" Dinny asks in a fatherly tone.

"My Ma wants me to."

"Why don' ya open the shop and let ya Ma run it, then?"

"I don' have that kinda money."

"What happen't wit' all that money ya got from the trolley company for the accident?" Dinny says, looking down toward Richie's leg.

Everyone knew that money, something close to $6,000, was spent by his fool father almost as soon as he took possession of it.

"Ya come work for me and I'll do ya Ma the favor."

Lonergan stares at Dinny while The Swede stands up from the ledge apparently unaware that Dinny was interested in engulfing Lonergan's gang too.

"Eddie," Dinny announces just before The Swede was about to start complaining. "Give the kid two hundret dollar. That should be enough, right, kid?"

"Keep the jack," Lonergan says standing up.

"Vincent," Dinny says. "Let the kid out, but give 'em the terms."

"Right," Vincent says, who then stands up in front of Richie and walks with him to the door.

"And tell Lovett to step away from the moanin' of Mick Gilligan and come up here," Dinny gives an order, directing the last part to Richie Lonergan's back. "Bill Lovett! My dockboss!"

As Vincent opens the door I hear him whispering feverishly to Richie, then yell down to Tuohey to bring in Lovett. The door closes but I can still hear Maher talking. Asking questions and then coming to conclusions on his own without Richie's response. Only about five years older than Richie, Vincent advises and warns all in the same sentence, then laughs at his own jokes too.

Meanwhile, another brutal mug walks in the door. This time it's Bill Lovett who carries a full beer in his right hand. He walks in the room looking in a different direction, then sits his beer on the floor and folds his hands in his lap. Behind him is the scowl of the one known as Non Connors, Lovett's right-hand.

The Swede immediately starts in, "I don' know why ya let this fookin' yella-larrikin-spalpeen Connors enjoy the light o' day in this neighborhood . . ."

"Shut the fuck up," Connors snarls. "Least I ain't fook't my own sister! Ya fookin' mongrel . . ."

I tilt my head at that accusation.

"Yeah?" The Swede says jumping toward him with his eyes popped open wide.

The room is quickly filled with the temper of wild dogs. Full grown males barking at one another's faces in warning while a few chairs fall to the ground behind. The Swede and Connors are screaming and Dinny gets between them. Vincent Maher comes flying in the door, a pistol hidden behind his hip at the end of his arm while Lonergan leans up against the frame in the background unaffected. Vincent grabs Connors's right wrist before a punch can be thrown and Dinny whispers up into the ear of The Swede. Bill Lovett then begins warning Vincent to let loose Connors's arm. Increasingly agitated, Lovett opens his jacket to reveal his own piece, "Let go of 'em! Let it go now!"

And I'm unsure if I should hide under a table or sprint for the door where Lonergan stands uncaringly and at peace. The Swede and Connors continue at the extent of their lungs, straining to let loose their grievances as their heads turn a bloody hue in the excitement. Tommy Tuohey then runs into the room, pushing Lonergan out of the way and standing in a boxer's stance in front of Connors and Lovett and ready to throw until finally Dinny yells at the top of his lungs above every other voice and blasts down his fist on the desk, leaving a wound in it.

"You take your place!" He spits into the face of The Swede, pointing toward the window sill. "Pick up the chair!" he yells at Connors. "I won't have this old war between you two!"

And I have never seen Dinny lose his cool before this, but he is so alight that I believe for certain someone is going to get killed.

"I don' wanna hear a word from the either of yas!" Dinny says as they slowly back in to their places holding their stares on each other, The Swede and Connors. "Yas think ya can walk in and turn this place upside down? All we have here? No ya won't! Too many good men worked too hard to get us where we're at. Too many men died for ya small rivalries to disown it now!"

The Swede leans against the windowsill with his arms crossed and looking away. Non Connors sits down with Bill Lovett across Dinny's desk.

"G'on, Vincent," Dinny says with a wave of his hand. "Go Tommy, downstairs."

Slowly, Dinny walks around the side of his desk while looking back and forth at each man, then looks at The Swede. "Not a word!"

Sitting down, he looks across the desk, "Now, what ya find out about this I-talian feller, what is it? Majio?"

"Maschio," Lovett returns, then remembers the beer he put on the floor by his feet, picks it up and takes a long slug from it. "Yeah well . . . You know Strickland? The pier house super down there?"

"Yeah."

"I got 'em to talk."

"Fookin' coward," Connors mumbles.

"He's weak in the brain," Lovett continues. "He tells me Maschio's been talkin' wit' Wolcott, but he ain' all that involved wit' Yale. Yale pays him, though. For information."

"Information about what?"

"The ILA, the New York Dock Company and . . . the White Hand."

"An' how long's Strickland known about this fookin' guy?" The Swede demands.

Dinny holds up his palm to The Swede, then looks to Bill. "How ya know what this Maschio looks like?"

Lovett finishes off the beer. "He's gotta white streak a hair over his forehead, like an albino thing in his hair. All black except that one white part."

Dinny nods his head while thinking. "Thanks, Bill, that's damn good work."

The Swede wrinkles his nose.

"Anythin' I can do for ya?"

"I need Darby Leighton," Lovett says.

The Swede jumps in, "That scally's been eighty-sixt, y'ain't gonna . . ."

"Shaddup!" Dinny yells without looking at him. "I'm sending ya Mickey Kane, Bill. He's got plenty o' experience and he's a fighter."

"I already got my second in command, Dinny. Non's my right-hand. I need another guy who's got more to 'em than Kane. Every day we fight. Every day them fookin' guineas jig in for a job or a whisper to the linemen or the pier houses, the captains or the stevedore companies. I need more muscle and more brains. Darby's all that an' more . . ."

"So why haven't ya called on The Swede, Bill? Or Vincent? Not once have y'asked me for help. Why don't ya let me help, Bill? That's what you pay me for."

Bill doesn't answer and I see for the first time where the line is drawn; Dinny's extended hand for help, which, if accepted, means his power then takes its grip. At the same time, Bill's silent, distant plan to cut that hand off entirely. "Kane'll work out, I'll talk to 'em. He's my cousin and he's a ready scrapper, brisk fighter, that's for fair. He'll fight for ya and wit' ya. I seen 'em, Mickey Kane'll dig in wit' ya. Darby don' work here no more, and that's the end of it."

Looking at Dinny, Lovett asks, "Why? What ya got against Darby Leighton?"

"I know he's a old friend o' your's, but I don' trust 'em."

"Why?"

"I don' trust'em 'cause I don't."

"That don't mean nothin'."

The Swede almost says something, but Dinny raises a patient finger, silencing him.

"Are you makin' demands, Bill? You sayin' I don' know what I'm doin' here? Are ya? From you? The guy who shoots a man downstairs? For what? Pullin' a fookin' cat's tail? Brings the tunics in our home? Bill? Then shows up in the office wit' a beer in his hand?"

Bill stares at Dinny unapologetically. Not giving an inch.

"Ya wanna war wit' me? You sit in front o' me wit' a gun in ya belt. Ya wanna kill me? Do ya? G'ahead. Shoot me. What'll that do for ya? For us? All these men are gonna suddenly follow you around if I'm dead? Think so?"

Bill moved in his seat.

"Frankie Yale takes over Red Hook. Navy Street Gang takes over the Navy Yard, unions take the rest, and both you and me are dead. What else? I'll tell ya, every down-and-out Irish in these neighborhoods got nowhere to turn when they need help. When the breadwinner dies, or a child needs a meal 'cause he ain't eaten in three days. Who's gonna be there for them when they need it? Coal for a winter night? Who's gonna help them, the county? The state? Them goo-goo Protestants only wanna look like they care. The company they work for'll turn their back on'em, you know that. The union? No dues today, no help tomorrow. Even McCooey and his Madison Club captains'll be happy to hand over the waterfront to I-talians and Jews for the votes."

Dinny left a silence after these words. Bill shifted his jaw in thought, but refused agreement.

"If there's anything we can agree on Bill, you'n me, it's that if we don' stick together, we're done. You know what 'done' means, Bill?"

"Yeah."

"Done means *done*," Dinny says, gently tapping his desk with a fist while The Swede agrees. "We got things to straighten out down in Red Hook, Bill. Things we gotta work together on. Soon too," then shifts the conversation. "Ya've known the Lonergan kid for a long time, yeah?"

"Yeah," Lovett agrees, remembering Lonergan talking with Vincent in the doorway.

"What's the skinny?"

"He works the Sands Street station wit' his own boys, you know that. Cutpursin', pickin' pockets'n whatnot. His dad's . . . uh," Lovett tilts his head. "Ya know what I mean? And his mother too . . . it's a burden, that family. He lives day by day, penny by penny, that kid. Why y'ask?"

After a silent moment between the two, Dinny looks over, "And his crew?"

"Good kids," Lovett says. "Rookies is all. Bunch o' teenage grifters workin' the gimmick for Richie. Abe Harms is his best friend, he's loyal to Richie. Matty Martin's a follower. Tim

Quilty's a follower, but a good boxer, and," Lovett moves his eyes over to me, "You Garrity?"

Dinny looks over to me also, then back to Lovett. "Yeah, that's his name."

Lovett smiles coolly, then speaks in my direction, "Petey Behan? Does'at ring a bell? Petey Behan?"

"I know him," I say.

"He's still got ya coat." Lovett laughs, though everyone else in the room is at a loss until Lovett explains, "They was stayin' in a building off Flatbush and Behan bulldozed ya kid's coat from 'em. Ya kid didn't even fight back," Lovett kept laughing. Connors mumbles a laugh from behind.

Dinny hadn't heard this story. I never mentioned it to him. Embarrassed, I turn red with all the attention. I even feel as though I've let Dinny down somehow. It was true, I never fought back. I was too scared. I'd never fought anyone before. Dinny looks over to me trying to understand, then finding in my shame his answer. As they continue talking, I notice The Swede again turn around and look out the window. When I look, I notice a bunch of men filing out of the bar and into the alley where the Lonergan family waited below. Just then, Vincent Maher comes running in the room.

"Dinny, Red Donnelly, and the kid are gonna fight."

"Lonergan?" Dinny sits up from his chair and looks out the window while Lovett and Connors do the same. "Wha' happened?"

"We was walking by, me and the kid, and Red cracked about how the kid showed up at the saloon wit' his mother. Some laughed, but the kid went cold on 'em. Then the kid challeng't him to say it again outside, and that's it."

Dinny looks at Lovett, who raises his eyebrows. They both smile. Below, the excitement is becoming uncontrollable. I see someone get pushed who falls into a bunch of other men in the circle. This causes a wave of falling bodies and tantrums, which then turn into minor scraps. Tommy Tuohey is ready to fight any takers, and squares off against three of them. Chisel MaGuire has taken to standing on a box with a bunch of money in his hand. He calls out the line and tries to pencil down the names on a piece of paper while collecting bills. Donnelly looks sheepish as he stretches his arms out in front of him, his red head standing out among the crowd around him. He must have sixty pounds on the kid Lonergan. Across from him stands the skinny, slightly muscular opponent staring at Donnelly, who seems unaware of the bets and yelling around him. At the outside edge of the moving circle are Mary and Anna Lonergan, trying to gather the children before they get a good stomping from the fighting men. Still, two of the brood can't be found, though I could see them walking hopelessly on the other end of the rumpus.

"Eddie, you and The Swede go down there and run the line. Chisel calls the odds, but you need to hold the money," Dinny says, pointing to Eddie, then looking at The Swede. "Make sure this goes right. The house gets ten percent. And don' let Chisel get no holder's fee. There ain' no such thing as a holder's fee. Tell 'em I said so!"

Down the stairs they go. A moment later and Lovett and Connors follow, after getting their envelopes, of course. With only myself, Dinny, and Vincent Maher left, we watch through the open window by Dinny's desk. Within the confusion, I notice Gilchrist left his pencil, so I take it and place it in my pocket slyly, like the bread I stole when hungry. I look over to Dinny, but he hadn't noticed.

"Who ya root'n for, kid?" Maher asks me lighting up a cigarette excitedly, then yells down to the circle. "Hey Lumpy, put me down a fiver on the punk!" Then looks back at me. "I seen it in his eyes when I gave'em the terms, Lonergan. Kid's got mean in'em."

Dinny looks over to Maher when he heard him.

"With one leg though," says I.

"Yeah, that's true about'em. Don' know, though. Kid's got the mean in him," he said smiling and shaking his head.

"Dinny!" a smiling Chisel MaGuire calls up as the mob calms around him and listens. "Who's your money goin' for?"

The crowd has all stopped their tussling and looks up to us at the second floor completely quiet, waiting for Dinny's response. Leaning his head out the window Dinny yells down, "My money's on Red, but if the kid wins, I'll pay the openin' expenses for his ma's bike shop outta my own pocket plus three months' rent."

I first hear the screams of Mary Lonergan, who almost collapses onto the ground when she hears Dinny Meehan announce it in front of the whole world to hear. As the rest of the crowd cheers, Richie looks over his shoulder and barely reacts to Dinny's railroading him as the circle starts to close in, becoming roudy in anticipation.

"Back-up-bhoys!" Tuohey yells from within.

And the The Swede along with Gibney the Lark, Big Dick and Philip Large make the circle bigger by pushing men backward. Standing tall above all the others, The Swede then saunters into the middle and warns every man not to push inward.

"Back-up-bhoys!" Tuohey says again.

Gibney, Big Dick, Large, and Tuohey spread their legs and arms out against the crowd and push back any time it surges. Gilchrist holds a wad of bills and furiously writes down the odds while Chisel barks the going rates. The odds are highly in the favor of Red Donnelly winning, though a few have put in a couple bucks on the kid since that's where the big money is.

I see Cinders Connolly in the crowd, and Bill Lovett and Non Connors there too. Dance Gillen is having the time of his life. There's immigrants from many countries among them too and then mixed in is the rest of the gang pushing their way to the circle for a better view. Harry Reynolds though, he had disappeared after getting his envelope.

Standing next to me, Vincent Maher is smiling away. He laughs at Chisel the chiseler, a man who was always in heaven when it came to a bet on two pugilists. I look over at Dinny, but he is staring down sternly at the events below.

After consulting with Gilchrist and The Swede that all bets are in, Chisel starts yelling into the air and twirling like a barker at a carnival, "May we have attention? May we have . . . Yes, And so here it is! Friends! A challenge!"

The crowd whoops and shoulders into one another.

"As ya know him!" Chisel continues. "He has tied down the shipyard territory for a good long spell with the reputation of thumpin' immigrants into shape and reportin' to the White Hand as was done by his own father in what we then called the great Irishtown! At six feet two, two hundred and fifteen pounds, I present Cute Charlie, *Reeeeeeeeeddd Dooooonneeeeeellyyyyyyyyy!*"

After some low applause and some comical boos, Chisel continues.

"His challenger, comin' in at the ass end of four-to-one odds! He is the one known as the leader of the Lonergan Crew that makes their home the underbelly of the Sands Street station, runnin' the gimmick as he knows how to. And other'n that, I don' know much more about'm other than he hails from Cath'rine Street across the bridges . . . at five feet, nine inches and weighin' in, oh I'd say somewhere around a measly one hundret and sixty pounds, I give you *Richiiiiiiiiieeee Loneeeeergaaaaaaan!*"

"Back-up-bhoys!"

Chisel speaks among the crowd, "One more minute to fight time fellers, ya got one minute to make ya wagerin's count. Who's gonna make it big today? Who's it gonna . . ."

Lonergan stands across from Red Donnelly with his legs opened and his fists closed. He seems impatient with the theatrics, and is ready for a fight. In the background I can hear his mother scream out loud, "My son!"

"Liam," Dinny says calmly. "See how the kid's gotta look on'em?"

"I do."

"That's a look," Dinny nods.

Someone hands Red a whiskey and he shoots it down, spilling some of it on his shirt. Then he threw the glass into the air and bellows like a moose. Next thing I know, The Swede pushes Chisel out of the way and waves off all bets. Red and Lonergan begin to circle each other. And so starts the pavee bare-knucklers, as they call the men who settle horse-pricing feuds and family honor with their fists at the country fairs where I come from; the traveler community that fight each other in the country boreens in just the same way as they do here on the cobblestones of Brooklyn.

"Get-the-feck-back, ye-feckin'-sausage!" Tuohey yelps.

"Get back now!" Big Dick booms.

Watching each other's movements with their fists up over their faces, Red and Richie circle each other. The crowd seems familiar with the process of a spontaneous fight.

"See how Red's got both fists over his face and at the ready. Both at the same time? Bouncing on the balls o' his feets?" Dinny says to me.

"I do," noticing Red's comfort in the fighting stance.

Red looks down at the empty shoe on the kid's leg and watches the limp. I can see he wants to take advantage of the weakness in his opponent. He then jumps toward Lonergan, only meaning to threaten him or see how his opponent's balance is when attacked. Richie stammers backward and his eyes light up in a sparked rage. Quickly moving in toward Red, closing in fast and cornering him, Lonergan takes a mighty swing right in front of John Gibney, who holds the crowd back. Though Lonergan misses, Red loses his balance from rushing out of the haymaker's way. Before Red can catch his own balance, Lonergan swings again and belts Red on the top of the head, then catches him in the face with a wild left.

It is the first time in a long while I hear the distinct sound of a fist landing on the face of a man. So discomforting, I tense up while next to me Vincent yells down. Again I hear the sound of animals, these human animals brawling for some sort of dominance or honor, respect like bullmales in the wild brawling for a mate in an art form of necessity and the ancient contest.

Taking the punch, Red then tries to grab and grapple but Lonergan pulls away in a crazed panic. He then throws three successive punches so quickly that Red doesn't have time to react other than raising his hands in the air to try and stop the flurry, hoping to catch Lonergan's swinging fists. Losing his balance again and falling into the crowd, Red doesn't know where Lonergan is as the circle disperses and realigns itself more into the Belgian brick road and rail tracks that curve around the corner of a building across the alley. Lonergan quickly stands over Red and hits him twice with the dull thud of fist on face again. So quick are Lonergan's swings that Red is soon only reacting to the pounding he receives. Again and again Red receives punches to the same side of his face while he is sprawled defenseless on the ground. His right arm now caught behind his back and his hands open, motionless. Even with Red completely unconscious, Lonergan swings harder and harder and keeps belting the man who sleeps on the concrete pavers inside the cheering fighter's circle.

Swooping in, The Swede picks up Lonergan who keeps swinging and kicking into the air maniacally. It must have taken a whole two minutes before Lonergan finally calms, swearing at The Swede and promising him death for holding him against his will. I look over at Dinny, though he doesn't much respond. Still though, I can see Lonergan has made his impression on him. Not only for winning, but for winning so quickly and so thoroughly.

"Fer Chrissake." Vincent looks over at Dinny. "That kid can fight!"

Dinny nods, and that was how Richie Lonergan joined the White Hand Gang.

CHAPTER 14

A Hard Pragmatist

THE WINDOWS ARE SHUT. THE NIGHT is sighing and the soft sleepy sounds of L'il Dinny soothe me deeply. My teenage body far along at its midnight resting in the back room of the Warren Street apartment, I open my eyes. Sitting in a chair across from me is Dinny. I close my eyes out of laziness. Maybe trust. Open them again remembering him there, I sit up.

"What time . . ." I can tell it's not time to get up yet.

He doesn't answer and only looks at me in a calmed, serious stare.

"We'll talk in a couple of days. Go for a walk," then stands up and leaves the room.

I roll around in bed the rest of the night. Thinking. Wondering if I'd done something wrong. Then feeling guilty for making myself so comfortable in another man's home. I was helpful to Sadie at times, but she could get on without me. I thought some more, fondly too of how I had spent that day with her and L'il Dinny as it was Easter Sunday and off to church we were on the trolleys to the Bridge District and St. Ann's. The boy had even fallen asleep on my lap during Mass and I not able to stand or kneel, which also makes me feel guilty since this is the day Jesus rose from the dead after the Jews persecuted Him and the Italians crucified Him, said Father Larkin in a big echo. And thankfully, I think, Jesus wasn't killed by the Italians in Brooklyn because someone would have to sew His arms and

His legs and His head back on His body and fish Him out of the Gowanus first, but that's blasphemy to think like that, and also beside the point. I roll around some more in bed listening to L'il Dinny's cooing and feeling guilty, but I'm happy with Sadie. She makes me feel needed, but I know that my being there for her isn't a matter of necessity. Staring at the ceiling, I make excuses for myself for being so young, for being new to the country, for being without a family. But I know that being young, new to the country, and without family is no excuse in Brooklyn.

I reach over and pull the pencil I stole from Gilchrist out of my trouser pockets and look at it in the light coming from the moon outside the window. I look up at it as I lie. Roll it around in both hands, then put it in my right hand between my finger and thumb like some men hold a tool. In the air I write the words "Abraham Lincoln." I don't know why. Maybe it's because I think of him as an educated man, since I don't know many. Or maybe because he fought for a freedom that caused him so much personal distress, which reminds me of my father who quietly longs and plots for my people's freedom, which causes his family distress. "Freedom causes distress," I write in the air. "When Lilacs Last in the Dooryard Bloom'd," I write.

On the Tuesday after Easter, I help load an engineless cargo barge that'd been pulled into port over night off Columbia Street. I keep myself as quiet as the silent Harry Reynolds who whispers orders to his men. Chewing on a lot of things, I can barely smile at the jokes of Dance Gillen. The wind runs through my hair and for once I feel like all the other men that work on the waterfront: racked by worries. My muscles are beat too, I can feel them heavy on my chest and arms, my hands are straining and my back behind my shoulders are tightened up from lifting and carrying from train to barge all morning. It's about a ninety-pace walk from the ship to the pallets by the train car. In work like this, I always count the steps to avoid thinking about the tensing muscles, burning with weight.

Along the edge of the pier I can smell the weak coffee of tug drivers lined up in rows and mouthing paper bag lunches with their backs to us. Just south of us, pointing toward the sky on a thin island, the Statue of Liberty keeps still while hundreds of boats, ships, barges, tugs, and every sort floating vessel one can think of slowly scurries around her like ants at a spring picnic. The island of Manhattan seems years away from me as it stands in the north distance. I wonder if there are people like us in Manhattan, or is it all businessmen, patricians, and theatergoers. I hear stories about the place, but they only have me wondering more.

About halfway through the day, Reynolds calls upon me from the stern of the barge. I walk across the planks back onto the ship, meander around the lines of men carrying boxes, climb the hull ladder as nets are lifting up, and out the hatch until I make it to him up on the deck. As I walk toward him he is pointing down to Dance and gives an order without saying a word. Only with his finger pointing first at Dance, then to the weak spot in the line and Dance is ordered to patch it up with a threat or removal of the laggard. From above, Reynolds and I watch as Dance barks in the tired man's ear, who immediately steps it up.

As I approach, Reynolds huffs on an apple and wipes it on his jacket while slowly walking toward the bow. I follow.

"How goes it?" he asks as he pulls out a pocketknife and with calm coordination, splits the apple up without looking.

"I'm fine."

Handing me a quarter of the apple with the same hand that holds the small blade, I thank him. Quietly, we reach the bow that stretches well beyond the floating pier. This is when Harry Reynolds told me about himself being adopted by Dinny as I am, welcomed into the Meehan brownstone.

"You're actually the third," he says. "We didn't really know it was gonna be a tradition, but now since there's three of us . . . seems like a trend, eh?"

"Who was the second?"

He looks at me as if I should already know. "Maher."

"Oh . . .That makes sense."

"There's a lot o' pressure, ya know," Harry says. "Times are changin' fast."

"What do you mean?"

"The future isn't clear. Dinny knows this better'n anyone. There's pressure from all sides. We run things here. Have for a long time too. We've never been this organized before, but we've never had to be this organized either."

I listen.

"Dinny's a good man," he says with an admitted truth in his voice. "He brought us all together like we are today. It's all due to him. Hands down. It used to be a bunch o' wildmen that shook down the ships. But before they did that, they had to fight each other for the right to force tribute on the labormen. Before the dock company got so big, before the labor movement got big too, before the police or the papers ever cared, and before the Italians came. Dinny'll never tell you all this, but he knows it's true. You need to know it." Harry looks at me, "He's been thinking about the future. Now that he's swallowin' the Lonergan crew and has Lovett holding off the I-talians down in Red Hook, he's thinking about his inner circle."

"He wants to talk to me tonight."

"Yeah? You know what you gotta do?"

I looked around thinking about it, but had no idea.

"I don't admire your situation, but ya gotta be prepared. My only family's been the nun that raised me at the boys' home, and Dinny. That's it. I can't put myself in your shoes, but I can help ya prepare."

He puts a piece of apple in his mouth and pulls a nine-inch knife out of the inside of his trousers, flips it around in the air, and hands me the butt. I take the knife gently. Let it rest in my palm and wave the large blade, wielding it the only way I know. He shows me how to get the best power into a stroke by turning it around so the long blade points to the ground, hilt on the bottom of my fist. Then in a violent stroke, yank downward and across my hips. He shows me how to use momentum as force and if I were smart, I would plan on maiming my victim as seriously as possible with the first swipe. Having to rely on a second swipe to either defend myself or finish off a guy puts my safe returns at higher risk.

I look at Harry Reynolds and he notices that I am still wondering about the knife, why he is giving me a knife. Other than for general protection, I am unsure.

"You know what I'm talking about," he assures.

I look down, not wanting to admit it.

"Your uncle's gonna have to be dealt with. He makes our way much more dangerous. Ever since Thos Carmody gave'em the reigns o' Red Hook, the laborers question us. Show up to work with weapons. Talkin' about organizin' strikes and the German plot . . . And under our noses. I know he's your uncle, he's family. I know ya don't hate him, but you can get close to him without him thinkin' we're after him. He don't know you're with us."

My stomach turns. I look out onto the water.

"Ya not talkin'," Harry says out loud. "Look, if ya think ya can't do it, then ya need to come up with another plan. No one's gonna keep ya around without somethin' bein' done about Joe Garrity. You got another plan? Another place to live? To make a livin'?"

"I don't."

"Dinny'll get ya mother and sisters here, but ya gotta do what's gotta be done. I'm not sayin' it's the right thing, but it's gotta be done. By you or somebody else. We gotta cut off the connection in Brooklyn between the ILA and this supposed plot."

I sit on the railing of the barge and run my fingers through my hair, drop the knife. Close my eyes and cover my ears, move my head back and forth. I know that Harry Reynolds understands me, but I also know he is a pragmatist. At that moment I didn't know a lot about him, but I could tell that there was something between him and Dinny that didn't connect well. At the same time, Harry was loyal to the man who gave him a chance in life. The man who took him in his home, just as had been done for me. Reached out for us when we needed it the most. In that sense, Harry Reynolds's loyalty was in stone, and it made him a hard pragmatist.

"First things first, kid," he said, making me stand and look him in the eye. "Ya got no honor. None earned at least . . . In other people's eyes. Petey Behan? He took it from ya and he owns it now. Dinny knows that and beyond anything . . . that's dangerous. This is a chance to get ya honor back. Ya gotta show'em all that ya honor ain' nothin' to fuck with. Nothin'. But ya gotta stop looking like ya scared all the time. Are ya scared?"

"Sometimes."

"No matter, ya can be scared and not look it. Squeeze the knife in ya hand, then make yourself look mean. It's easy. Only thing is ya gotta remember to keep the face firm."

I did what he said.

"That's good, now put the knife in ya trousers and keep the tough look on ya face."

I did as I was told.

"Good," Reynolds says laughing. "Now ya look tough. Think about that knife at ya side and keep yourself lookin' tough. When the deed is done, nobody crosses you. Nobody. Ever."

"But . . ." I try and hand him back the knife.

He looks at me hard, then walks back toward the stern, "You're gonna need that yoke, now get back to work."

CHAPTER 15

The Village & the Rising

LATER, AS PADDY KEENAN SATIATED THE thirst of the long-shoremen at the Dock Loaders' Club, I sat at the bar thinking. After Dinny paid out the dock bosses and walked downstairs, he tells Vincent Maher and The Swede to hold down the fort.

"Where ya goin'?" The Swede asks Dinny.

"Cohnheim's," I say under my breath, wishing myself back with Sadie Meehan and her soups.

"Manhatt'n," Dinny says. "Let's go kid. We gotta go talk to a guy on ol' Hudson Street."

At the bottom of the stairwell Tommy Tuohey shakes Dinny's hand and offers me a "Good luck on ye, slacaire. Ye're a good lad."

After that, the entire bar stands up and turns round, paying respects to the boss of the dockbosses, their king. The leader of the Whitehanders. They all wish me luck too. Even Paddy Keenan raises a glass to us as we walk by. The Swede walks ahead of us just to make sure no immigrant gets jumpy. The Lark and Big Dick tip their beat up wool caps from the mahogany trough. I even saw Richie Lonergan and a couple other punks sitting around a table with full drinks in front of them. Little Petey Behan sat across them, but doesn't pay me any attention. It is the first time I see him at the Dock Loaders' Club and I feel angered, maybe jealous about it and touch my new knife as I walk by him.

Cinders Connolly smiles and reaches with his lengthy arms all the way across a few men to shake with Dinny, while Philip Large just stares into the floor. Dance Gillen, Dago Tom, Chisel MaGuire, and many others stand behind the dockbosses and their right handers. Bill Lovett sits elbows-up at the crook of the bar with Mick Gilligan whispering into his ear, Non Connors and Frankie Byrne pulling from shot glasses on Lovett's right-hand side. Red Donnelly has a dirty bandage around his head and still looks a little disheveled after his ripe beating. Ragtime Howard looks into his drink quietly as we pass, and of course, Harry Reynolds had left as soon as he gathered his envelopes.

Vincent Maher walked with us in the spring air for a few blocks but eventually smiled and backed into the city dusk where he had his most fun, out with the young lasses of Vinegar Hill who think him a big catch. It was a Tuesday, and Dinny and I decide to take the jaunt over the Brooklyn Bridge by foot. As we start up the incline just over the abutment and toward the first tower, Dinny tells me about a time before the bridges were built when everyone had to take a ferry to Manhattan. He points down over the side of the bridge to a strange-looking gingerbread building that faces the water called the Fulton Ferry Terminal where the Fulton Avenue Elevated tracks end so people could take the ferry to Manhattan.

We couldn't quite see all of Manhattan just yet as the curvature of the bridge doesn't allow it, but the sky and the river separating the two boroughs from up high is a sight for certain.

Looking back at the sea of rooftops across old Brooklyn, I feel it more as an Irish city than any other. If Brooklyn were an ocean, it would be colored black and gray and faded brown as it appears below me now in my imagination. It is choppy, smoke slowly rises from random wounds in the cement sea as if the billows have a permanence to them. Unpainted, sooted wood-framed tenements creak in the breeze like an old coffin ship carrying dead famine families in its hulls. Sunken in time along with so many of their untold stories. Memories forgotten, remembered only in the blood like a feeling is remembered, but not articulated; memories known in the blood-feeling of so many Americans in the coming generations. Whisperings of great struggles, terrible sacrifices pitting family versus survival. Struggles and sacrifices that make life worth living for the happier children of much later days. Of all those Americans what proudly claim Irish blood.

I look down at one roof after another, then more and more until I can't distinguish where one roof ends and another starts. Layers of roofs mashed together three stories high, four stories high, five and six. Brick buildings butted against brick buildings with adjoining roofs, water towers and vents for miles and miles in every direction. Pier house roofs that line the waterfront, warehouse roofs just inland from pier houses, wooden tenement roofs just inland from the warehouses, stable house roofs in the alleys. And windows. Millions of windows. Large shuttered warehouse windows. Paint factory windows. Brownstone windows. Tobacco factory windows. Gothic windows. Arched windows. Boarded-up windows. Curtained windows. So many windows to peer into that it's a peeper's dream.

Some roofs have attics on one side of the roof with windows on them. Other roofs have laundry lines strung across them. Every here and there is a tall building such as a sooted white Robert Gair Company Paper Goods building where they make boxes to package everything made in the neighborhood to send from here to India or the war front in Europe. The same goes for the American Can Company building just down the block in the distance. At the base of the Brooklyn Bridge, I even see the roof of the stout Sands Street train station with multiple levels of elevated tracks that loop out over Fulton Street and disappear between buildings and into the neighborhood, snaking over the streets.

Smoke stacks. Flag poles. Cornices. Quoins. Fire escapes and the abutment of the Manhattan Bridge reaching into the neighborhood. The Williamsburg Bridge beyond. Flat roofs. Curved roofs. Slanted roofs with chimney pots sticking out from them. Thousands and thousands of brick chimneys and chimney pipes with smoke bubbling out from their openings. It makes me wonder why so many people would want to live this way? How is it that so many people could choose to live among so many others? Millions and millions of peoples stacked together, hemmed in by huge concrete sidewalks, muddied cobblestones, brick facings, dilapidated fencing?

I looked at Dinny with Brooklyn in the background and his eyes strong in their green stare, mouth grinning and gritting in the same motion. "A lot o' the people who live in Brooklyn grew up on farms just like you. Right outta the Middle Ages in places that haven't changed for centuries. My grandparents were tenant farmers, I heard. On both sides o' my family, but they said it was a sad place. Sad place is all. No end to the sadness, so they brought my father to the West Side o' Manhatt'n."

"That's where you were born?"

He nodded, "Hudson Street, my father's brother ran a gang back then. He raised me mostly. Streetfighters over by the soap factory. His name was Red Shay and lemme tell ya, he didn't take skin from nobody. He was the law in that area. Cops didn' do nothin' back then. It was the local gang ya went to if ya needed anythin'. Someone died, ya went to a neighborhood guy. And if he was good, he'd make a respectable grave for 'em. No pauper's graves for Red Shay's neighborhood. It was big deal back then, getting' a respectable grave 'cause where they came from so many in their family were left in shallow pits an' ditches or were thrown into the Atlantic on the way here like they didn' mean nothin', ya know what I mean?"

"I do."

"But as long as Red Shay was in charge, he paid for all expenses. It was all taken care of in the background. Kept it humble, ya know? Better to have a widow tell everyone ya paid for her husband's proper burial than to take credit for it yourself, ya know? In the background." He looked at me. "Real humble. Need a job? Ya went to him. Dudes ran the streets. Not tunics with their copper badges. If someone wrong'd 'em? No one went to jail. They took care of 'em real swift like. Left 'em hangin' by a light post. They had to stick together to survive. Just like we do now. No one else did nothin' for the people in the neighborhood. They had to stick together. No government did nothin', no companies did nothin'. . . . Nobody cared about 'em. It was a matter o' survival, gangs were. Loyalty? They didn't create gangs 'cause they wanted to. They made their gangs 'cause they needed to. The conditions called for gangs. Need. Not want. Need. The Tammany? It helped us. Nowadays everyone hates Tammany. Says it's corrupt. That may be so. But so what? Who else was gonna get us in the lawmakin' gimmick? Who? If they don' offer it to ya, ya take it. That's what ya do. Someone had to take care o' the neighborhoods. They cared. People like Red Shay cared for people, brought people together. Sent a message, ya know. Those were the good ol' days. These can be too, ya know? Good days? They can be. We just gotta stick together." Dinny stopped for a second, looked me in the face. "Like a fam'ly, a real fam'ly. And those who ain' gotta fam'ly? They got us."

I looked to the ground. A trolley passed behind us and Dinny pushed himself away from the railing, then combed his hair away from his ear with his large hand. "Let's go kid, it's gettin' dark," he turned around, I followed into the middle lane of traffic where walkers made their way over the bridge. Around us were trains and trolleys on outer tracks rushing by us while horse-pulled buggies and dray carts crept around the trolleys at the edge.

"You see that big buildin' standin' above all the rest?" Dinny said, pointing ahead. "That's the Woolworth Buildin', tallest buildin' in the world."

I looked at him.

"We'll go right by it," he says.

"In the world?"

He looked at me with a smile.

As the sun was going down and the wind got a little cooler off the water, you could see that the big city ahead was going to light the spring night. Street lights, office buildings, advertisements, and even the moving lights of automobiles illumined the darkness. A kid from the country walking over a great waterway on a mammoth bridge. Into the lighted future. That was me. My dirty, hand-me-down boots, torn-seamed jacket, my callused palms, scruffy hair . . . I was sure that I'd appear like a child from the feudal past to these educated city-goers. Grown out of the earth and working the soil like, then somehow transported into the most modernized place in the world where expensive cars pull up in front of high class restaurants and theaters or whatnot. I couldn't know what they did or how they made their riches.

As we come down the bridge and enter the Financial District, the excitement begins to show on me. There is urgency everywhere. The people walk with an importance and avoid eye contact at all costs. Choosing instead to stare in front of them only to look away at their watches or avoid a speeding automobile that overtakes a slower one. Ladies carry colorful scarves and wear narrow skirts that show their ankles and reveal the long heels on their shoes. They all seem to wear feathered hats or muffs even, but what strikes me most is some wear large, very low belts at their hips, which sway with their short strides and reveal the feminine in their very strong, forward stare. Tailored haircuts with spun curls and makeup that give their faces to look even more majestic and picturesque than they naturally are. The men have their two-piece suits so that their long jackets fit them in such a way as to accentuate their sleekness while their slacks are pleated and cuffed at the end. Older men wear single-breasted vests with a looping watch and a bow tie with an ornamental walking cane. The younger men wear striped neckties with a large collar.

I am relieved to find that no one notices me in my rags as they are all too concerned about their own destinations. The buildings are very well kept also and none of them are made of wood, only cement or brick and most with steel infrastructures. I want to sit on a bench and just watch the spectacle move around me for a while, just watch all the newness, but Dinny has other plans.

"Liam!" he yells while opening a car door. "Get in here."

Trying not to show my surprise I lower my head and jog over to him. I feel so clumsy trying to move at the pace of the environment and almost trip getting into the car. I'll never forget it, a 1909 open-air Chalmers 40. That was the first car I ever rode in and the only reason I remember the name of the car was because the driver starts gabbing us as soon as we get in. First talking on the price of the ride, then going on how this is the same luxury car that is awarded to batting champions of professional baseballers and how lucky are we to be passengers in such a fine limousine and such, and so on. Dinny listens to him doubtfully, then directs him to drive by the Woolworth Building, then go up Lafayette and left on Broome.

"Yeah?" the driver asks. "Why? Well dat's gonna change ya fare fella, you know dis?"

Building after building up high above us and in front and behind us. They pass by us like a herd of giants. I can't imagine the sort of population those buildings can support. Then finally we come upon the Woolworth Building. The grandest thing I've yet seen in my fifteen years.

"Dat's the tallest buildin' in the woild, kid," the driver yells out while pointing straight up in the air.

"I know," I say defensively.

I lean my head back and watch it wave through the air as we pass. The very top of it looks like a church. After a few minutes, the big buildings start to disappear and some familiar tenements come in to view. Italians lounge in chairs along the sidewalks and gather on the stoops to enjoy the early evening breeze. The shorter buildings are stacked next to each other for blocks and blocks. Businesses are run out of apartments with signs on balconies advertising their wares. Laundry lines cross the street from window to window and the fruit and vegetable stands pulled by bored-looking, skinny horses are heading home for the day.

"Kid," Dinny says, leaning closer to me so the driver can't hear him, then rubs his thumb across his nose. "Listen . . .

there's good neighborhoods in Brooklyn that aren't close to the docks. Ya probably don't know much about 'em, but it's true. Good working-class neighborhoods where there's no gangs or nothing like that. Not bad gangs at least, just kids. Off the waterfront, ya know? They could live there. Ya mother. Ya sisters can go to school an' whatnot."

"Church?"

"Yeah, they got churches over there, like in Bedford or something. Real good neighborhoods. Well, there are good neighborhoods among the bad, like always. The thing is kid, ya gotta work hard for something like that."

"I don't have a problem working hard."

"I know ya don't, I see that in ya. It's a good thing too. But ya gotta have ya honor. If ya don't, ya don't go nowhere, see? Honor's important here. It's all ya got as a man, ya know," Dinny continued, as the cool spring night air whisked through us in the back of the car. "People might respect your work ethic, but . . . you haven't done anything yet beyond that."

I looked at him quizzically.

"Liam," he said, sitting back. "Everyone knows now. Petey Behan stole that coat from ya and ya didn't do nothing to get it back. Nothin'. You might not realize it, but something like that can haunt a man for years. They'll hold it against ya. Cross your line everyday. Anythin' ya got. Everything. No way you can continue to live like that around here," he says assuredly. "No way. You can't let that happen. No way you can let that happen and expect to live a normal life. Ya don't got honor, ya go and get it. No one hands it out. Ya go and get it. You can't never let people do nothin' to you. Ya gotta make a stand. Draw a line and don't ever let no one cross that line again without a punch and an earful from ya. That's just the nature o' things."

I kept thinking.

"I'm here for ya though, kid. I want ya know that. I'm not ya father. I wouldn't pretend that to be. No way. But I'm here for ya. I can help you. I wanna help you. And let me tell ya, it's not easy to find someone who's willing to help you."

"I know that to be the case," I said. "And I thank you for . . ."

"Ah," Dinny said sitting back again. "All ya gotta do is draw that line. Make a big deal out of it, ya know. A big deal. Then anyone crosses that line and ya rap 'em. Hard, ya know what I'm sayin'?"

"I do."

"Take a right on Hudson," Dinny says, tapping on the driver's shoulder.

"Right, right," the driver answers waving his hand to us without looking back.

"Dinny," I say, reaching into the left side of my trousers and pulling out the nine-inch knife and keeping it low. "Harry Reynolds gave me this."

Dinny looked at the knife in my lap, then looked up into my eyes.

"He taught me a few things."

"Yeah, but ya ready to use it?"

The car stops and we get out on Hudson Street where many saloons are filled and spilling over sidewalk and cobbles. A huge bonfire is whipping in the middle of the road, blazing high while chairs and all sorts of combustibles are being thrown into it. The fire attracts onlookers from the surrounding neighborhoods: it is generally known that the Tammany Democrats often make such a commotion to rally prospective voters and cook off free chicken, pigs, and cow meats for the masses and for their votes. But it's not Tammany puts this together. Even I could see that this blaze and chaos is thrown together on a whim.

As we walk around the high fire, I hear men hooting loudly and strong congratulations being shouted into the air. No longer do we find fashionably dressed men and women. They're now replaced by the woolen sweaters and wool hats of the immigrant working class that I am so used to seeing in Brooklyn. Among the crowd I see a tall Free State Irish flag waving wildly in the air on the back of horse-drawn buggies and out of tenement windows too, and saloons. Young men carrying newspapers with the evening editions are working overtime. Bellowing

as they run through the drinking crowds of hurraying festivities. A cheering assembly has gathered around a man that
stands on the back of a hay wagon. After saying something we
can't quite hear, he throws his hat in the air and the crowd all
do the same, yelling at the top of their lungs about something
which only succeeds in scaring me almost out of my own shoes.

Sliding through the chaos, I see a shopwindow that has
something painted on it, which grabs my attention right off:
"THE COUNTY CLAREMEN'S EVICTED TENANTS PROTECTIVE AND
INDUSTRIAL ASSOCIATION." I wonder what on earth all that
means, so I stop for another read and figure it must be some
group that helps immigrants from Clare find jobs in New York
who've been evicted from their land back home.

"Come on!" Dinny yells through the cheers. "There's no
time for dilly-dallyin'. This place has gone bugs."

We come into a displaced crowd of men lined up along the
wall of a saloon. They are gathered around a barrel that fills
their glasses with beer. Some of the men have two fists full of
beer glasses. Dinny walks up to them and as they recognize
him, they jump up for greetings.

"It's a Meehan come back 'round for a drink on this finest o'
nights," says one.

"Ol' feller, welcome, welcome," says another who proudly
pats him as he walks by and yet another brings him a drink and
heartily shakes his hand.

"What's the rumpus here?"

"The Volunteers and the Citizen Army stormed Dublin,
raised the tricolor up high at the GPO. It's a fact," a man says.

"Kid," Dinny interrupts as I am thinking on what the man
just said. "This is Tanner, Tanner Smith. He's a ol' friend o'
mine that . . ."

"What happened?" I ask to Tanner, interrupting Dinny. "I
didn't quite . . ."

"The kid's from Ireland?" Tanner asks Dinny. "True thing
kid, read the papers. True thing. The IRB Volunteers and
Connolly's army took it over; the GPO, Stephen's Green,

Liberty Hall. All the fookin' British was at the races for da holiday. No one expected it."

"Are they armed?"

"Sure they are."

"But . . . what are they going to do about it? Have the British said they'll go away?"

"Nah," Tanner said. "They're condemnin' it. Gonna send troops to put it down. What part ya from, kid?"

"He's from Clare," Dinny answers for me.

"Is that right? Another Clareman, eh? Welcome to the American capital o' County Clare: Greenwich Village!" he announces with his arms in the air, a few passersby agree with him too.

"But they already took over the GPO?"

"Yeah, yeah, here. Read the papers yaself, kid," Tanner says as he hands me the paper from his back pocket. "They're sayin' it's the biggest thing since 1798."

I looked at him when those magical numbers came to his lips. "Since Wolfe Tone?"

"Dat's what they're sayin'," Tanner says, looks at Dinny. "Kid knows hist'ry, uh?"

I am reading the newspaper and I can feel the world shrinking. Pulsing. Breathing, IRISH REBELS CAPTURE DUBLIN IN STREET FIGHTING, then I skip down under the headline, "England is face to face with the Fenian element's yearning to see their Ireland freed, twelve British soldiers dead thus far." Every word seems unreal as it describes the men and their surprise rebellion as a true threat to the empire.

This threat immediately gives the rebels the pride and the honor my people have so lacked for so long. Standing up to an empire. The only pride I had ever felt in my lifetime of Ireland and our people came from the men hiding behind the drink and from the stories my father told of Emmet and Wolfe Tone, the United Irishmen and the Young Irelanders. These were never real men to me, they were like saints. Like ghosts or parts of my own self that even I didn't believe. Reading these words in the newspaper there, those men start to come alive again inside me. Make some sort of sense to me for the first time, as if I never truly believed they were real until this moment.

And when I read the proclamation these young rebels posted up at the GPO for all Dubliners to read, some of the words glow in my imagination, like "dead generations," and "summons her children to her flag," and "we declare the right of the people of Ireland to the owndership of Ireland," and "we hereby proclaim the Irish Republic as a Sovereign Independent State, and we pledge our lives . . . to the cause of its freedom," and finally, finishing this poetry made from real life and written in their own blood certainly, this ultimate dare of a document describes their revolt as an "august destiny."

"1916, they'll always remember this year," I say, continuing to read as drops of tears fall from my eyes to the newspaper.

Tanner and Dinny watch me among the chaos of the city street. I read of America disapproving of the Irish rebels and their acts meaning they stand with the Germans against the allies. This is proven by Sir Roger Casement's arrest for the scuttled German boat carrying arms for the rebels.

"We don't concern ourselves with a war between empires!" I hear a man yelling from a cart addressing a crowd. "Not with King nor Kaiser do we stand!"

I look around more and there are men with their faces in their hands, crying in elation. Old men with silver beards and country hats leaning against the walls and affected so deeply by the surprise attack in Dublin that their legs shiver uncontrollably. They hug one another in tears, a very rare thing for Irishmen to do. I see women throwing paper out their windows above the saloons. Throwing their aprons too. Throwing anything into the bonfire. Everything. Men with tin whistles under their mustaches sing old songs. Very old songs that are so upbeat and happy that it makes the tears turn to cheers, tilts back the drink in them. When the men with tin whistles happen upon a reveling fiddler, they ask in each other's ears what tunes they know, then stand with their backs against the Hudson Street

saloons and play the rebel songs I remember as a child. The
same songs my father hummed as the muscles in his shoulders
swelled from the pulling of peat from the soggy ditches and bogs
outside our home and the songs he whistled as we traveled from
our farm to Queenstown (he always called it Cobh, though) just
six months earlier where I boarded the ship for New York.

"Fookin' Cath'lic moiderin' scum!" I hear a man yelp.

"The surprise of it, eh? Hit 'em when they're busy on the
continent. On our holiday! Easter!" Tanner yells.

"Ya thinkin' about ya father?" Dinny asks.

"Yeah."

"Well, the way things sound, the Brits won't allow this to go
unpunished," one of the men named Costello says. "Doubtful
they'll lay down and let Home Rule take place now. There's
gonna be battles for some time."

I looked at Dinny, who says to me, "We need to think about
gettin' ya family over here, kid. Ya mother and sisters at least."

"I should go home," I say. "Back to my family. To fight.
Ireland needs her sons right now. I've only been here since
October last and . . ."

"Wait, wai', wai', wai'." Dinny steps closer to me, away from
Tanner. "Ya father sent ya here for a reason. He didn' know the
Fenians was gonna strike again? He didn't? Shit, he knew. And
that's exactly why he sent ya here when he did. To get away
from what's comin', a new war."

I looked at him strangely, as he seemed attached to using
that same outdated word again, "Fenian."

"You been readin' the paper about these guys? The Clan na
Gael papers here in the city? These men're ready to die. They
wanna die. Ready to throw themselves against the empire,
ready to be martyred."

"And I am too!" I say.

"Ain't the point, kid. Ya father sent ya here so ya could bring
the rest o' the fam'ly to New York. You don' see that? Ya mother.
Ya two sisters. He wants them in New York. That's why he sent
you here."

I look at Dinny, then think about the Claremen's association down the block and the Hibernians who can help get them here. And then on the letters I'd sent which were never replied. Probably thrown in the trash by my uncle. Over the next hour or so, I remain in shock about everything that has just passed, connecting things in their new forms. All the while, Dinny tells me not to worry, then turns around and keeps talking business with Tanner. I had a hard time paying attention between all the excitement, the beer and my worries. Dinny shows Tanner his scar from being shot by a starker, "One o' the Droppers." Dinny explains.

On the topic of starkers, Tanner explains how the Jews in Greenwich Village have taken over the labor slugging and Tanner's gang is laying low until the right time. Dinny offers assistance and they both agree that when the time comes, they'll break the longshoreman strike that was inevitably going to come, being as though May Day was upon us. Dinny would provide two hundred, maybe three hundred men on top of Tanner's gang and together they would restore the Irish to prominence on the docks of Greenwich Village and work together to keep the docks in Irish American hands.

"You seen Thos Carmody around?" Dinny asks him.

"Sure, what about 'em?"

"Wolcott paid us to kill 'em."

"Kill Thos Carmody? The ILA recruiter? King Joe's guy? Why? He's been down in Brooklyn o' somethin'?"

Dinny nods, "You see'm much."

"Yeah, I see'm."

"I need 'em done."

"Yeah?"

"Don't know where to find 'em around here. You want back in? You wanna job?"

"Looky there, Dinny Meehan offerin' me a job. Tables've turned, haven't they?"

"You take care o' that for me and it's three hundred dollars."

"Three hundred?"

"Done, like done," Dinny says, making sure Tanner understands.

"It's a risk on me, but we'll do it, the Marginals."

Dinny pulls out a wad, hands it over. "Welcome back to the gimmicks."

"Thanks Din, we'll work together good too. Like the ol' days. Except you're the big shot now."

"I don't forget friends," Dinny nodded, then looked at him.

"Done," Tanner confirmed. "I'll give'm a bullet."

"We still got things . . . in a couple days."

"Yeah? A little action? How can we help? Ya wouldn't do it wit'out us, right Dinny? Dinny? Action is action, we're in wit' ya, Dinny. Like ol' days, me'n you runnin' around Hudson Street. You kid," Tanner taps me with his fist. "Dinny tell ya about them ol' days, me'n him? He was my star. He didn' warn nobody, just action. That's Dinny Meehan. No threats, just fists and dornicks in the air," turning to Dinny. "Then ya had to go an' move to Brooklyn."

"Can you send me a few guys?" Dinny asks.

"Sure, just lemme know and we'll be there," Tanner says, shaking Dinny's hand and slapping him on the shoulder with his left hand. "Thos Carmody's done, promise."

"I'll get back to ya about some action."

Dinny trusted Tanner. They embraced. Laughing like old war buddies. Looking down the street at the festivities, I watch the flickering shadows playing off the tall, oranged tenements that line the edges of Hudson Street in the lowering sky. As crazed, drunken men and women flail in front of the fire in celebration, their elongated shadows dancing with them along the face of the old dilapidated buildings like peasant tribal gods of another era, ghosts of themselves from ages ago. Like the ghosts of the war-loving Celts celebrating rebel risings as if it were some farce of reality. It all seems so right these days as I dwell upon the past: fighting against an empire for freedom. Like it was inevitable. Fixed in history. Fated. But back then it was against the grain, against everything that was. The shock

like that of an earthquake tumbling down the ancient edifices
that stand so tall, the symbols for law and order that have
guided the life of generations, only now revealed as fallacious
by the weakness in its fallen state.

I hear the sighing of a mare strapped to a wooden cart
amidst the rumpus, her owner off somewhere with the drink. I
come to her with my palms open to her snout, but she is
untrusting. She bobs her head in the air and turns her eyes sideways to watch me. I talk to her the way my father taught me,
real gentle like, and I open my arms out wide to show her that I
am in control and knowledgable of her kind. Although she is
close on eighteen hands tall to the withers, she has a docile
streak in her. In a moment, she is letting me soothe her, but the
sounds of angry and drunken men make her stamp in place and
I can see the bonfire in her eye like a mirror. Like the ancient
light inside her, and inside me too. She is no pure quarter, but of
mixed blood like the rest of us.

"A beautiful one, you are," I say to her.

Soon she nestles her long face along my shoulder and neck,
pushing me playfully. Then she looks away. Then stamping happily, clicking her shoes on the paving stones. And I have a yearning
to unstrap her from the dray. To let her free from her binds.

"You just want to be free, don't you girl? Don't you? You do.
You just want to be home in the country where you can run and
be yourself, not stuck here in some foreign land. You don't even
know why you're here, do you? You just want to go home, but
your home's not there anymore."

I stand there next to her, and still I am shocked by the awe of
rebelpoets and teachers storming Dublin and the dancing
shadows and the bonfires and Manhattan and the gangs filling
up my new life. Tanner comes upon me among the party to
wrap an arm around me next to the mare, his other hand filled
with a growler of ale. "Kiddo, not to worry. That man will take
great, great care o' ya. Dinny Meehan's a great, great man. No
shittin' ya. He'll love ya so hard he'll squeeze the tears outta ya.
Stick wit' 'em and all'll be good for ya."

Staring into the bonfire, I give a respect to my father who for so long stayed quiet about his plans. And I think on the pookas too, the ghosts that the shananchies told me about as a boy in the fields and hills and boreens of my youth. About how they haunt our successes, bringing us down again in rebellion and in flight too. Haunting us everywhere we go. I could see those ghosts on the walls of the New York tenements dancing above us under the sky. The shadow dancers from the barrel fires. Dancing over me. Dancing around Dinny Meehan's head too. Sometimes giving us hope only to yet again lay us flat on our backs in the slums of foreign lands.

It's family we have to think about first and foremost, I believe. Families. And I still do to this day many years from April 1916. Anything for the closeness felt by the family. All for it. And if Dinny is right that my father is off with the rebels, then that means my mother and sisters are all alone on the farm since my older brother, Timothy, probably went with him to the country-side, readying for the war with the Fifth Battalion of the East Clare Brigade, their brothers in arms for a real republic in Ireland.

And with that, my only goal is for their arrival. All else matters less. The mare looked at me from the side of her head and I could feel that she felt me. That my mind had been made and that I now only have but one purpose, for my mother and sisters' safe coming. And the quicker the better, for everyone knows what'll be done on the isolated farms in Ireland when the Brits come round for their retaliations. One purpose for myself, and nothing less. I hug the mare's head with one arm under her large jaw and smell her mane. It reminds me of home, that smell of a horse. So pure it is too. Nothing purer than the place I'll always call home: the west of Ireland, but that I will never be able to get back to in my long life, sadly. And so it lives so gracefully in my mind and in the odors that sometimes come back to me in the form of burning turf or the wild gorse in the fields or the natural smell in the mane of a cob or a draft horse.

And I remember too one day not long before this April evening of song and drink, when a homeless and hopeless sort I was.

When all that I longed for was a plan. Something to drive me. Because a man without a plan and a fixated need to lead his thoughts is a rudderless wanderer altogether. And now I have it. A plan for my thoughts. A fixation on my mother and sisters' health and well-being for it is I who was always thought of as the one who could open the doors for many, and open the door for my mother I will.

Although Dinny has offered me help, it is my family I need to turn to first. Kin before kith. Blood before all. And so Uncle Joseph, the brother of my father, is my first choice and maybe he has information, letters or news of some sort that will help me get my mother and sisters here as soon as it can be done. Only one goal now, nothing more. One plan for me is all, though a smart man always leaves himself options.

"Dinny," I say, pulling out the knife across my hips. "I know what must be done."

Turning my way among the circle of Tanner and friends, he looks at me with the sense of honor. And so do the others. The first time anyone in New York looked at me with the honor.

CHAPTER 16

A Tug and an Envelope

A SNAP HAD COME IN THE next morning. New York awoke to a mid-April chill uncommon to the city. It wasn't yet cold enough to snow, but the sky threatened a freezing rain in the gray and cobalt covering. The lilacs and the lily of the valleys that had emerged with the weeds recently were laid flat by the gusts and stripped of their scents. Men leaned forward and winced their eyes closed when it kicked up. The scrape of trolleys ached in the back of heads, below the ears.

A few blocks from the White Hand headquarters, inside the pilothouse of a tug backed to the shore alone under the cold clicking of the Manhattan Bridge, Dinny, Lumpy Gilchrist, and The Swede sat and waited, breathing in the flat steel air through wiggling, watery noses.

A little past four in the afternoon Head Patrolman William Brosnan, dressed in civilian clothes with a cap covering the eyes and a collar to the ears, came upon the tug and entered at the bridge. The pilothouse now shrunk as four men of varying sizes stood too close together.

As The Swede stared at the man without his tunic and copper, Dinny gives a few words. "After the shindig, Non Connors takes the fall. We'll have witnesses for yas. When the smoke clears in Red Hook, I want him in front o' Judge Denzinger as the leader o' the gang, photos for the papers'n all, dig?"

There was not a response, only a bobbing of the head and a pursing of the lips. Afterward Brosnan placed the envelope Dinny handed him deep into his trench-coat breast.

"Look at'm." The Swede nodded toward the humbled patrolman. "When his hand's open, his mouth is buttoned."

Dinny did not shut The Swede down.

"Seventeen years at Poplar Street, and ya still just a patrolman."

"Head patrolman," Brosnan said.

"Yeah, ya're a head, all right," The Swede sneered. "When they gonna make ya a detective, Brosnan? That sounds good, don' it, Dinny? Detective Brosnan? Why don' ya make him a detective, Dinny? Why not? He does what he's told."

Dinny just stared at Brosnan, who looked away.

The Swede mumbled, "Maybe den ya won't need us, eh Brosnan? Makin' all that dime."

CHAPTER 17

On the House

PADDY KEENAN ROLLS THE LAST OF six kegs down the double planks at the back of an automobile truck in the alley of the Dock Loaders' Club. In the cutting drafts and in the chill, he and James Hart, the truck's driver, hoist it onto a squeaking wheel cart. Standing upright with hands on hips, their chests heave while the moisture is sucked out of their breathing by the nip in the thin air.

Through the rear room go Keenan and Hart, wheeling the sixth keg passed the stairwell and around the impassive Ragtime Howard, turning left behind the bar where it's to be tapped for another busy night under Dinny's office.

Mick Gilligan has been in the saloon since quarter to noon, drinking off the pay he gained the previous day in the Navy Yard with Red Donnelly. At that time of day there are only eight men scattered along the bar and against the wall, Gilligan is the only standing.

"Whadda fook d'ya think den?" he slurs. "Whadda ya think, Rag? Talk ta me!"

Ragtime Howard sits at the farthest part of the bar away from the front door and window. Not interested in Gilligan's blatting, he keeps his eyes trained on the drink in front him.

"Rag?" Gilligan continues. "D'ya think das right? Do ya? I'm gonna get my honor, Rag. You watsch. Even if I gotter pay a galoot forit. Appare'ly das whatcha gotta do around here to get honor. And I know jusht where da go . . . I do too!"

"Mick," Keenan says. "Have a seat, aye? Here's a drop fer ye. To calm yer nerves, 'tis."

"Ah, one on the house!" Gilligan announces victoriously. "About time I earned one o' dem yokes, ya're a real patriot, Paddy. A patriot! I don' care dat ya from . . ."

"'Tisn't from the house, Mick," Keenan answers. "A man buys that one fer ye."

"Who does?"

Standing relaxed while drying his hands on the apron round his waist, Paddy Keenan looks toward the end of the bar where Vincent Maher sits smiling through his toothpick, the door behind him. Next to Maher is the sandy-haired Richie Lonergan leering Gilligan's way, leaning on the mahogany with not a word to say, a small whiskey glass held limp over his frozen face etched with the cheekbone eyes. He drinks it down slowly, watching Gilligan all the while. Even watches him through the bottom of the empty glass until he rests it on the mahogany. A candle sways between Mick Gilligan at one end, Maher and Lonergan at the other, Paddy Keenan quiet and empty in his staring. The two men between them push away from the bar and disappear from the glares.

"Ahhh," Gilligan says dumbly, unable to give the drink back now that it is in his hand. "Thanks then, Vincent. . . . Thanks."

Gilligan's voice slows off when awareness sets in. The guilt of offering pay to Bill Lovett under Dinny's roof weighs on his eyes now, afraid and self-loathing. Beyond any guilt though, Mick Gilligan knows as well as anyone at the Dock Loaders' Club that Vincent Maher only buys a drink for one kind of man: A dead man. There is no apologizing now. No begging can resolve Maher's summoning.

Adrenaline running through him, coursing in waves and deep shivers like loose nerves on a fresh cadaver, he stands in place in the mesh of his terror. The iron-piped banshees singing at a high pitch when an immigrant walks in the door as a train passes overhead, Maher and Lonergan keep at a stare. Though he cannot move, Mick can feel his bowels turning and bubbling in him. A heat pulls up through his back, beads of sweat form in his hairline. He stands there still. One pace behind Ragtime Howard. On an island as far as he is concerned.

He looks away from the boys at the end of the bar and sees the quiet, uncaring face of Paddy Keenan. Cold. He knows by the look on Paddy's face that the tender is in on the gig too. He then looks toward Maher, who still sits smiling with both elbows on the bar engulfed in a long, terrible stare. Concentrated on him. Mick Gilligan. And nothing else. Behind Maher the gray light through the window offers a saintly appearance. His face almost completely obscured in shadow, the moment has turned religious for Mick Gilligan and the joining of the window joists behind Maher's tilted cap appears like a cross through the dull shine. A putrid epiphany has taken shape in Gilligan's awakening. Silence takes the saloon down to the smallest creaking sounds. That creaking sound! The sound that appears in the ears of travelers stacked inside the belly of a lost clipper. An Atlantic crosser. Like a pooka's whispering. Gilligan shivers. The adrenaline rushing through his body while he keeps still, still standing in the same place. The plot revealed: death in the creaking afternoon.

Someone opens the front door again behind the smiling Maher and the Lonergan kid. The sound of popping metals and rushing trolleys above, the underbelly of the gigantic Manhattan Bridge screaming off the water until the door is shut again. In an instant, Gilligan shoots down the whiskey, throws the glass onto the ground, and runs back through the rear room and out the back door.

Maher jumps up and runs after him while Lonergan swings backward and limps out the front door as if it were all planned beforehand. The alley behind 25 Bridge Street is blocked by James Hart's automobile truck in back.

As Gilligan rips the back door open, Abe Harms laughs and surprises Gilligan by wrapping both his arms around the frantic man. Hart laughs too as he sits in the driver's seat of the truck that forces Gilligan to run one way down the alley, toward the water and the Manhattan Bridge.

"Hello thele, Mr. Mick Gilligan," Harms says with a hun's guttural accent, then pulls out a .38 and points it to Gilligan's throat. "Vat's wrong, man? Not zo much talk flom you now, no?"

Gilligan screams, ducks out of the way of the gun, and runs down the alley toward the water.

As Maher opens the back door and stands next to the young Harms, he pulls out a .45 and takes a potshot from his hip at Gilligan's back. Following Maher's lead, Harms let one go down by his hip as well.

"Right where we want him to run," Maher says, patting the new kid on the back. "Let's go."

Mick Gilligan is running for his life and jumps a fence in a paranoid state as he hears a bang from a .38 in the air, then the bullet smacking a metal garbage can in front of him. Then a second slug goes off behind him. While at the top of a second fence, Gilligan looks behind him and sees Maher and the German kid running after him. Quickly, he crawls up a water-pipe to the roof of a building and jumps across it to the face of the Kirkman Soap Factory and enters through an open shudder at the side of the building on the second floor. Inside, a few factory workers notice Gilligan but keep themselves busy as they are anticipating the end of their workday at the five o'clock whistle.

Richie Lonergan watches from the front of the factory as Gilligan enters at the second floor of the building, which reaches up at least ten flights high. After jumping two fences and waiting for an empty railcar to pass in front of them, Maher and Harms come upon Richie staring high.

"He's inside." Richie motions.

"I saw," Maher said. "Abe, you stay out here and if you see him crawlin' out a window again, start firin'. We'll hear ya. Richie, come wit' me."

Maher and Lonergan walk inside the front door of the old factory and are immediately met by the manager in the middle of a wide, recently swept concrete floor.

"Vincent, 'ow goes it?" The manager asks with a heavy cockney accent. "What can we do for yu? Yu lookin' for that cabbage that just run up 'ere?" he said, pointing up the stairs.

"Listen," Maher said in a low tone. "We gotta runner up here in the upper floors. He's gotta be taken care of. I'm sorry to have to make ya do this, but you know how things gotta be."

"No, no fine," the manager agrees obediently. "What can I do?"

"I gotta have you clear these people outta here. Like now."

"Okay." The manager thought. "We'll knock off early. I'll blow the whistle and everybody'll be 'appy to let outta 'ere early."

"Make sure to lock all exit doors, 'cept this one." Maher points behind him to the front door. "We gotta check 'em all first, make sure this bug doesn't try and sniff the cracks through here."

For the next fifteen minutes, Maher and Lonergan stand on each side of the single-file line of happy workers who got out ten minutes earlier than expected. They come upon the gangsters with a smile, then the smile turns fearful when they see the look on the two guys' faces that stand at the door. Hoping beyond all hopes that they don't get picked out for some unknown reason. After all the employees exit, Maher instructs the manager to lock the front door and for Richie to wait downstairs.

"Nah," Richie says. "I'm goin' upstairs wit' ya."

"I ain't waitin' for ya, Richie," Maher says, walking toward the metal stairwell to the left. "Just so ya know."

"Ya don' have to wait for nobody."

Maher sprinted up the stairs, skipping a step at each leap and was up to the second floor before Richie had made it to the first step. Before starting, Richie looked up. He hated steps, but was forced on them every day of his life, especially the three floors of the Sands Street station.

"Can yu tell Dinny what I done for yus? Can yu?" The manager said. "'E gots me this jobba, Dinny Meehan. Sadie Leighton's me cousin and . . ."

"Who's Sadie Leighton?" Richie asked.

"Oh, sorry," the manager said in a heavy cockney chop. "Sadie Meehan nows'er name, since they married now an' t'all.

So loike I was sayin', 'elpin' yu boys out is just a pleasure since I owe yus. I keeps me 'air on though; don't see nor 'ear nuffink . . ."

"Who are Darby and Pickles Leighton to ya, then?" Richie wonders, putting together the connection.

"Theys me younga brothas," he continued as Richie turned his back and inched up the stairwell. "We came 'ere from St. Giles. Pickles? 'E's barmy; lost the plot a'long toime 'go an' e's banged up now, course. Sing Sing. But Darby narrrr . . . 'e's no plonka, narrrr. Darby's got it right in 'is 'ead. Just nippers off the boat 'ere from Lond'n, they was. Real Brooklynas now, them two. . . ."

Richie had stopped listening after a moment and as quickly as he could, kept himself concentrated on lifting the wooden leg up after planting his normal leg. The manager saw that he was being ignored and turned around, walked to his office by the front door, and waited quietly until the job was done and the two Whitehanders told him it was all right to leave. However long that took, he didn't mind.

Richie looked at the twenty-foot-wide silos that were in the lobby. The silos also connected to the second floor, then the third, and all the way to the eighth. He felt one, they were extremely hot to the touch as the batches were being boiled during the day, left for the next morning where they would be vacuum-sprayed into bars to be shipped up the harbor to the Erie Canal and sold throughout New York and beyond to a thousand different retailers across the state, country.

Richie followed Maher's path and walked gingerly up the stairs, using the handrail with his left hand and his gun held straight out ahead of him with his right hand. He stared upward as he climbed, listening closely to any movements and only hearing the pop of settling hot metal echoing through the halls of the building. Wherever Maher had climbed, Richie couldn't tell. It was quiet in the factory. Quieter by each flight of stairs. All the cackling of the happy workers had dissolved and any sounds Richie heard could be considered the movements of his prey, as far as he was concerned.

While the employees had caused a din of sound and confusion, Mick Gilligan climbed straight to the roof of the building only to find there was no fire escape on the outside. Feeling trapped by height and thinking it too obvious to his predators that he'd be hiding on the roof, Mick had worked his way down to the ninth floor where he was hiding in a closet. There, he hoped Maher and the two boys that had been hired to kill him would quit their search out of frustration, at which time he could make his escape after the soap factory opened again in the morning. Mick knew this was not a good plan. Inside the closet it was hot and his mouth watered for another whiskey, just one more whiskey and he could fall asleep and forget all of this was happening to him.

"Why?" Mick cried to himself under his breath. "Why did ya ever talk like a babblin' idiot? Why? Idiot! And after Dinny sent Christmas tidings and everything? Why did I do that? Why? Idiot."

"*Miiiiiiiccckkeeeyyyy*," Richie yelled as he climbed the stairs to the fifth floor. "Mickey *foooooookin' Gilligaaaaan!*" He sarcastically blew, allowing the echo to work itself into a fervor throughout the empty building.

Mick Gilligan shook uncontrollably as if he'd been stuck in a freezing, icy rain. He could hear Richie walk on the floor, but he couldn't tell if he was on the ninth floor or below. All he could hear was the crack of his right boot on the metal stairwells and the drag of his left leg. It was that crack and drag that drove Mick Gilligan to the point of insanity. Out of nowhere, he felt the need to relieve his bowels. His stomach turned and made struggling sounds in his lower belly. He tightened his cheeks and held them closed with both his hands and shook and shook.

"Mickey fookin' *Gilligaaaaaaaaaaaaaan!*" Richie yelled at the top of his lungs in a seething fury. A voice so haunting and deep, so full of animalistic joy and violent mysticism that Mick Gilligan could no longer hold his bowels. Bursting out, he shat himself in the closet and cried while the relief he felt turned into the symbol of the most absolute terror when he realized that he was now stuck in a closet with the smell of his own fear. His body began to give in. A sweat had pierced his skin and brought over him the greatest heat followed by a wet chill. He could feel the shit sliding down his pant leg toward his boots and again he was stung by the fiercest heat, only to be shimmered with a new freeze. He gagged, burped suddenly, and the whiskey in his belly burst through his fingers. When he smelled the rot of his inner stomach in his hands, his body pushed more vomit through his cough.

He flung the door open and screamed. Running in complete abandonment with the sticky shit slipping down the inside of his thighs until Richie gave him a tackle that partially knocked Mick unconscious and before he could wake, Richie had his head in a lock from behind and a gun at his temple.

"Jesus, did ya shit on yaself?" Richie asked, and let him loose leaving him on his stomach with the gun pointed to the back of his head and his wooden leg stuck firmly in the small of his victim's back.

Gilligan stayed on his stomach completely unaware of his surroundings. Overcome with shock. He lay there shaking and did not respond to any of Richie's questions. A few moments later and Vincent Maher walked up behind Richie, smiling.

"Look at these huge vats o' soap," Maher said looking down. "Eight fookin' stories tall. And bubblin' all over the place. Mick?" he said, standing over him next to Richie. "Why ya so fookin' ignor'nt?"

Mick could not respond.

"Mickey?" Maher yelled, then flicked his toothpick on Mick's back. "Open ya fookin' ears, then ya mouth! Fookin' weak."

No response.

"Whatever," Maher said, and pulled out the .45 from his belt and reached down, pointing it to the back of Mick Gilligan's head, then pulled it away, turned it around, and gave the butt of the gun to Richie.

"You can kill'em?" he asked.

With his pointy cheekbones and unfeeling eyes, Richie took

the gun and with a clamorous bang that echoed throughout, put Mick Gilligan to sleep forever.

Hearing the shot, the manager below stopped his busy work for a moment and looking up, could only imagine what was happening above. Instead, he decided not to think of it. Then licked his pencil and returned to his writing.

Richie at the head, Maher with the feet, the two picked up the body and swayed it left to right on a three count.

"One," they said together.

"Two."

"Three," and with a heave, Richie and Maher hurtled the limp body over the guard rail. With half a head and a seven-inch exit wound in the face, the corpse slowly cartwheeled below and flopped into a boiling silo with a deep plunking sound. The momentum of 146 pounds of dead weight into boiling soap one flight below sent a wave over the side of the vat that exploded on the ground floor of the lobby eight stories below, a few feet from the manager's office.

CHAPTER 18

Ybor Gales

LATER IN THE DAY, A FOG rolled off the Buttermilk Channel and began to engulf the immense structure on Imlay Street in Red Hook. Above Bill Lovett and Non Connors, the cement sign was becoming obscured in the steam's onslaught, but if you looked close enough you could make out the words, NEW YORK DOCK CO.

Lovett and Connors stood next to each other in the dirty gray jackets and black ties of the laborman, but with black scarves wrapped loosely around their necks, trailing behind over shoulders. Cap pulled down over the eyes, Connors leaned on the building and dragged from a paper cigarette while Lovett watched the crowd without moving his head.

"What about Strickland?" Connors mumbled, hand in pocket.

"Squeaks on wops, he'll squeak on anybody. Fuck'em. He's a tout."

Connors dragged, Lovett watched the crowd for the pier house super among the men and women leaving and entering the building at the end of the workday.

"There he is."

The two pulled their hands from their pockets and wrapped the scarves over their faces, leaving only their shaded eyes to be seen like bank robbers from another era. Across the street, three more men covered their faces and moved toward the center of Imlay Street at Lovett's motioning.

A white man with three olive-skinned Italian men were together crossing the street at that moment. One of the Italian men was carrying a box under his arm and wore tight black gloves that made his hands look small. That man looked both ways before crossing, then took off his fedora to wipe the sweat from his forehead and by doing so, revealed a patch of white-streaked hair that reached from a low black hairline back to the top of his head.

Before the white man and three Italians made it across Imlay Street to the New York Dock Company building amid the traffic of automobile trucks and drays, Bill Lovett pulled a .45 from his coat pocket and aimed it generally at the men crossing the street. Connors did the same. Opening fire as they walk quickly, arms out-stretched, the lead Italian threw his cigar box at the two men firing upon him and ran for the Italian enclaves inland toward Union, Sackett, and Degraw Streets up Imlay. The crowd shrieked, the two other Italians went for their guns, but one of them fell to the street as he was shot in the side of the head from Frankie Byrne, who came from behind him. The white man too, among the Italians, fell to a knee a few feet from the downed man. With the streak-haired Italian running away, it left one more Italian who had yet to fire and before doing so, noticed shots coming from behind him to the side, turned to return fire and was shot three times by Lovett and Connors, two more times by Jidge Seaman and Sean Healy, and then fell to his face, flattening the nose on the cement and loosening the weapon from a flaccid hand.

"Him! Him!" Lovett yelled with a muffled voice at the man running up Imlay.

Shots were fired after the man. Sparks jumped at his pawing feet as all five of the scarved men ran after him, crowd parting and ducking and running for cover. Most were unaware of where the sounds come from and didn't recognize them as gunfire anyhow. One woman backed into Non Connors as he was running after the lone remaining Italian. He was sent sprawling to the ground and angrily cursed her, even before he had stopped sliding across the shiny wet pavement, "Fookin' stoopit slattern . . ."

Connors looked up from the ground and saw the last Italian hopping as he had received a bullet in the hamstring. Looking back at the gang of men closing in on him, the last Italian limped toward the building looking for desperate cover, but was soon overcome with bullets and lay crumpled in an awkward corner obscured by one of the building's columns. Satisfied the last Italian was dead, Connors looked back over to the box on the ground, as his scarf had fallen to his chest without his recognizing it. He picked up the box and read aloud, "Ybor Gales."

He then noticed a circle gathering around a moaning man. Connors stood up and walked over for the crowd, pushed his way through. It was Strickland still alive, holding his shoulder in pain and pushing with his leg off the pavement as the concerned tried calming and nursing him. None had recognized Connors as one of the killers among them. He walked up to the injured man on the ground within the circle. "Clouts for touts," he said, pointed his weapon at the back of the man's head, and fired as screams catapulted into the air. The circle of the concerned imploded in all directions, tripping over dead Italians, and before anyone could realize who had executed the injured man, all five killers were running toward the trolley station up Commerce Street on Henry four blocks away.

CHAPTER 19

Fifty Dime, Done

THOS CARMODY WALKED NORTH ON HUDSON Street in Manhattan and turned in to a building at 310 with his collar high, hands in trench coat. Two men sat at a round table by the door inside, looked up unflinchingly.

"Private club, buddy," Lefty said.

"So private it ain't even got a name," Thos smiled, though no one laughed. "Tanner here?"

"Come wit' me," Costello said standing. "Lemme see ya hands."

Thos looked at Costello, slowly took his hands from the trench coat. Lefty stood up and took the gun out of the pocket, "I'll hold this for ya."

Calmly, Thos looked at the door as Costello walked passed him for the stairs. Licking his lips nervously, Thos followed.

"How's T. V. O'Connor doin'?" Costello called back while walking upstairs.

"He's in Buffalo," Thos said, following.

"Yeah? What about that monkey, King Joe Ryan?"

"Waitin' for me outside," Thos lied.

"Yeah? Tell'm to come in then," Costello stopped. "We got drinks for King Joe."

"Just bring me to Tanner."

Costello opens one of the closed doors on the second floor where Tanner Smith sits alone at a round table by an open window, a deck of cards peeled open in front of him.

"This guy says O'Connor's in Buffalo again," Costello laughs, then continues without an answer from Tanner. "Looks like the city is all King Joe's now."

"Thos Carmody," Tanner says, shuffling cards as the door closes them in together. "Popular man these days."

"You back in the gimmick yet, Tanner?"

"Just a dockboss, that's all I am," Tanner answers angrily.

"Good thing, we need honest guys like you, Tanner. Ya can't trust no one no more. Gangs, sluggin' . . . guys'll turn on their friends to save their own asses. Not like the ol' days."

Tanner winced at that, grumbled, "What's wit' the Huns, we strikin'?"

Thos laughed, looked away, "Ain't gonna happen, they got cold feet."

"Good."

"Good?"

Tanner pulled out a rare Russian Nagant revolver from his breast pocket, a seven-shooter, and opened the cylinder slowly, pulled out the bullet that was next in the chamber, and tossed it to Thos. "Done."

Thos laughed nervously.

"Here's fifty dime, Thos. Get outta the city for a few months. Go to Buffalo for the summer. On me," Tanner pushed two twenties and a ten-dollar bill across the table.

The ivy along the walls of the courtyard through the back window was beginning to turn green again even as it was a cold day in April. The sun was disappearing beyond a distant water tower atop a brick building while Thos Carmody nodded his head in acceptance.

"Tell T. V. O'Connor and King Joe I saved ya life. Tell'm to keep me in mind for a job sometime, yeah? I want back in the game, but legit like."

"Who hired ya, The Dropper?" Thos said, holding the bullet between his thumb and middle finger, then snatching it with the palm of the same hand.

"I don' work for sheenies or wops, you know I won't Thos. I tell you what though, I can turn all o' the longshoremen on the

Brooklyn waterfront to ILA," he said, then raised his eyebrows and looked up. "If only I was a ILA man, of course."

"We got a guy for that down there to turn them hayseeds around."

Tanner looked down at Thos coldly. "No ya don't."

Thos looked back quizzically.

"Garrity? Joe Garrity?"

Thos stared back without answering.

"Marked man, Joe Garrity is." Tanner continued, "Any o' my guys see you in New York the next six months, they got orders to kill. Don' tell no one ya leavin'. I wanna missin' persons report for ya. G'on then, ya welcome."

CHAPTER 20

McAlpine's Saloon

It is by now 8 p.m. and Paddy Keenan pushes a poteen across as I pull up to the bar in the candlelit Dock Loaders' Club. The dockbosses are lined along the stretch with serious looks on them: Gibney the Lark, Big Dick Morissey, Connolly, and Donnelly with Dance, Dago Tom, the Chiseler, Philip Large, and others standing behind. Only Harry Reynolds missing, gone after receiving his envelope.

I sip the drop like a man and reach into my pocket. The Saint Christopher Mam gave me. I hold it in my fingers, rub it smoothly. I love my mam and I feel so sorry for her. I only want better things for her and I start believing that to become a man means doing whatever it takes to soothe her. If danger provides the path to her peace, I'll gladly take it. And just like Dinny, I'll never complain about it. That's what a man does, I say to myself. Then I look over to Mr. Lincoln on the wall, so proud and honorable. A beautiful man who soothed many.

"When Lilacs Last in the Dooryard Bloom'd," I say. And just like that, I believe myself a warriorpoet because you can't write beautiful words unless you've seen and done terrible things already. "Have you ever heard of a warriorpoet?" I ask Paddy Keenan who looks at me like he always does when I ask him questions, like he is the one supposed to be listening, not talking.

"Warriorpoet, ye say? Not since the ancient glories have they been round, bhoy."

"Well, at least you don't have to go and get schooling to be a poet."

"'Tis true, from the blood and the bones does it rise, the poetry." Vincent Maher interrupts with concern in his eyes, "Ya seen Lovett? Heard from him in the last couple few hours?"

"I haven't."

"A'right," he says, and with a stony face he takes my hand and shakes it like a big brother. "Good luck, kid. You'll be good." Walking toward the stairwell he shakes his head in Tommy Tuohey's direction. As he swings up for the stairs, Tuohey looks concerned too. I feel something on my hand and put it in front of a candle: blood has been smeared across the palm. When I look up again, Vincent is already upstairs. I take a sip, but can't get his stony face from my mind.

"Well looky 'ere," Paddy says as the door opens behind me. "T'ree members o' Brooklyn's own h'opstandin' citizenry. Come to sing us the werd o' the Lord, like t'ree good 'lil choirbhoys?"

I turn round and see Petey Behan's short little muscular body with the thin hips and wide shoulders. He is wearing my coat, smirking at me. Behind him is the taller, awkward Timothy Quilty, then the nervous but handsome face of Matty Martin. They are all my same age, but have much more experience on the streets than I, working for Lonergan robbing candy stores, jackrolling drunken sailors, and sleeping train riders and such. Not to mention stealing coats from the homeless like myself.

"This oughter be interestin'," Behan says, sitting at the bar as the other two snake around him, taking seats where they'd longed to sit since they were babies.

"Why are you three here?" I ask.

"We're here to make sure you don' fook it up, Dinny says so," Behan smirks.

"Only payin' customers set at the bar, bhoys," says Paddy Keenan. "You bhoys got'ny money?"

"What about him, is he payin'?" Behan whines.

"Certainly is. He's a werkin' man, can't ye tell by the werry on his face?"

"Yeah," Behan said. "He's worried a'right."

"Let's go then," I say, leaving a tip as my stomach turns. "We've a job to do."

As we get up, I see all of the dockbosses looking at me with their wide-shouldered glares and candlelit faces in the dark. I see doubt in them, weary stares. Little Behan then steps in front of me and opens the door for himself, leaving me to catch it. Outside we yell due to the sound of the trolley passing above. "Ya got ya weapon, o' what?" Behan asks.

"I do," says I, and open my coat to reveal the knife Harry Reynolds gave me. "You three got yours?"

"Sure we do. Let's get goin'."

It is good weather to hide weapons and though I have no intention of using mine, I do feel a need for it as a precautionary. I look over at Behan as we walk, then away. Realize that I am in a bad situation, though the police and the law seem farther away than ever. I had planned on going alone to meet my uncle. Convincing him to help me. But Uncle Joseph isn't always the agreeable type and now I have these three enforcers.

"I'll go in first," I tell Behan.

He looks at me hard. "This uncle o' your's, he knows ya workin' wit' Dinny?"

Begrudgingly, I admit he does not. Behan nods his head and I can feel that he sees right through me.

"Let's go in Richie's new bike shop for a minute." Martin asks Behan, seeing it across the street and pointing.

"No," is the answer from Behan. "You only wanna look at Anna. We ain' got time for lookin' at goils now."

Walking up the hill at Bridge Street we move through the neighborhood toward the Manhattan Bridge approach. Cutting through the crowded Sands Street train station, we jump the wooden railings of a long walkway in front of some hurrying travelers and duck underneath the station where only the Lonergan crew would know such a short cut would lead us to the other side by the waterfront. At Court Street, the Fulton El stops above us and I can see people staring down as we three push through the pressing crowd in the dark. I wish I were in that train up there, for I know I am going to a very bad thing. Behind me, up above, the train slowly lurches forward and the clicking is slow at first, but then quickens as it gains speed and is then gone.

"We're gonna see just what kinda man y'are, Garrity," Behan says. "I don' think ya got it in ya to pull it off. Just don' get us in a pickle? 'Cause I'll make sure ya get yours, dig?"

"Just follow my lead," I say daringly.

We stop around the corner from our destination at Sedgwick and Columbia Streets just north of the Italian enclaves of Red Hook where Dinny, Vincent, and The Swede had told me to go. We can no longer see out into the black water behind us, and a cold wind comes from the south and wiggles an aluminum lean-to roof in our ears. It is a barren, industrial-looking dumping ground for rotted wood, useless metal scraps, and fiery barrels with circles of men who have their palms outstretched to its warmth, bottle under arm. This is a place where only the lowest kind hide from some curse or terrible luck. We look down the windy Sedgwick Street where a few men are standing outside a shanty saloon called McAlpine's, a real ornery place.

"That's it," I say.

"We'll be in there in twenny minutes," Behan demands. "Make sure ya ready and don' fook it up?"

"Get off it, you've a loud mouth on you," I snap at him before I realize it.

Behan pushes me against the building. "I'll kill ya if ya fook this up, boy . . ."

"Let go . . ."

"I'll murder ya . . ."

"Yeah," Martin says nervously. "Don't get us in a bad place."

"Yeah," Quilty says, going along with it.

Petey lets me off and I look at the scared faces of Quilty and Martin and try to put a tough face on myself, just like Reynolds taught me.

In practice, I jump for my knife and grab the handle perfectly. Then I do it again. And again. Finally, I make the turn around the corner of the building and start the long walk, one block to McAlpine's. As Behan and the boys watch me from behind, I shiver in the cold breeze. The temperature is dropping, but that's not what makes me shiver. My teeth chatter and chatter against each other as swooshing paper flies by my head, rags tumble ahead of me. My hands shake and they're wet and I suddenly feel hungry. Tucking that hunger away like so many warriors have had to do for so many thousands of years, I keep at my walking with a firm stride. When I come upon the men standing outside McAlpine's, I walk passed them for the door without looking up.

"Who you, kid?" a longshoreman at the door stops me. "No babies allowed in here."

"I'm no baby," says I. "My uncle's in there and I need a word with him. Joe Garrity's his name. Mine is William. Go and tell him to let me in."

He becomes reasonable, "Joe Garrity's ya uncle?"

"He is."

"He knows ya comin'?"

"Look, me da was involved in the h'uprisin' in Dooba-lin," I say convincingly and with a thicker brogue than normal. "I needa spake wid'is brudder: Joe Garrity. Goo and get 'em, yeah?"

"Uhright, kid," says he. "Wait here a minute."

A few moments later and the same man opens the front door for me. "He's over dere."

It is dark inside. Very dark. Candles whip and jerk on the wick as the door closes behind me. I walk by the coatrack, leaving myself fully clothed. Even keep my wool cap on nice and tight and close over the eyes. I feel like everything is bigger than me. Like I am in over my head. A notion comes across my mind, a notion that is not only from Dinny's words to me while walking over the Brooklyn Bridge together, but from his own actions too: men make their own destinies. But this is a fleeting thought and soon it is gone, again I feel like I am small. Waiting for the world to take me somewhere so I don't have to force my will on it, I push on in the dark.

I can hardly see a single man's face among the crowd and along the bar and the smell of smoke is enough to choke a child. I don't recognize my uncle among the longshoremen, but I see wiry Italians, sharp-eyed Germans, tow-headed Nordics, whispering Jews, a couple bulky blacks, meat-fisted Polacks, open-necked Russians, and a few Irish among them. Quickly, I am grabbed and hear a clicking back of a revolver's hammer, "Gimme all yer blunt or I'll tear your togs off ya an' sell 'em rag by rag, ye stupid Mick."

A crowd starts laughing around me like flapping vultures, yet I still have no way of knowing who it is that's grabbed me. My eyes finally focus on the face of the man holding the gun to my nose. It is my uncle Joseph, looking scraggy as usual and drunk on top of it all.

"Well!" he yells, as the men around him continue to laugh. "Hand it over'r else!"

I don't move. I just look in his eyes with the sternness that's so new to me. As a reaction to my stoic response, he pulls the trigger in my face.

"Click," the gun says to me, nothing in the chamber and the dark crowd laughs it up again.

"Have a seat, bhoy," Uncle Joseph announces, pushing a man out of the way and clearing it for me. "Come, come. Set down next to yer ol' uncle. . . . Me nephew from Clare!" he announces to the world with his glass high in the air.

I sit to his left, facing him as he looks toward the barkeep. He can't sit still for a moment and continues cajoling the men around him in a state of drunkenness. I notice that he enjoys some sort of status among them. Honorless as it is to me, the men of McAlpine's see him as a leader, just like Dinny said.

"He wants to join the ILA!" he blares. "Works as hard as any man dat ever broke bread, this one does!" then leads a cheer that was popular in those days. "International Longshoremen Unite!"

"A drink fer me nephew!" another grandiose announcement.

Within a moment, a whiskey is placed in front of me. I have no choice but to throw it down as he eggs me on.

"Anodder!" he yells.

"What's happened with my da?" I interrupt. "Do you know if he was in the Dublin rising?"

"Drink yer drink, kid," ignoring me. "Ye found yerself a new home here."

"What's happened with your brother?" I demand. "Is he still alive? Have you heard anything since the rising about him?"

Frustrated, he slams his drink down on the bar as it spills over his hand, "And what've ye been up to ye'rself since last we jawed, hey? What is it den? Ye beggin' on the street now? Werkin' fer the Whitehanders?"

"I've been working on the docks up in the Navy Yard where they don't bother me, long as you pay tribute," I lie, just as Dinny coached. "Red Donnelly's a good guy, he pays his dues and goes about his own up there."

"Pays dues to the wrong kind. The ILA'll help a man, Whitehanders' days are numbered."

I don't say anything back and when he looks over to me again his face is awash in shame.

"That's nice then, real nice. I guess ye t'ink I'm a wort'less ol' drunk, do ye? Ye do . . . ! I don't care, bhoy. Fine. I'm sorry I gave ye the boot like I did, I'm sorry fer that. I've been t'inkin' about it and, yeah. I was wrong. Did all go well after that then?"

"Fine," I said, then lie some more. "I don't hold it against you. I was stupid then, you know? I didn't know anything. I still don't. But I'm trying. I'm trying to learn something."

"That's a good lad. Yer fadder raised a good bhoy in ye. A good lad!"

I look around the bar. Most men are paying no attention to us any longer. The drunkenness has taken over and there doesn't seem much guard to anyone. We are sitting toward the middle of the bar, only about fifteen steps to the front door through a dense crowd of torn-seamed union men. Smoke

settles toward the roof from the many pipes and paper cigarettes and every man holds at least one drink in his hand.

"So, have you any letters from my ma?"

"Yeah, plenty. I didn't open 'em . . . Well, I opened one of
them. On accident 'cause I t'ought t'was fer me since the letter
had gotten wet so yer name was wiped off it clean . . . So I
opened it and after, I realized. . . . Anyhow, she says she misses
ye and wants to know if ye can send 'er money, maybe."

I thought for a moment, almost bubbling up in cry.

"I was goin' to send'er some money, ye know," he slurred.
"But I didn't have much extra on me, so I figured I'd wait 'til ye
send some and I'll add to it, yeah?"

"Uncle Joseph," I say with as much persuasion I have. "You
have to help me. I have to get my mam and sisters here. Do you
remember Abby and Brigid? Do ye? They were just tykes back
before you left for New York."

He winces while looking away, bobs his head.

"Uncle Joe, I'll join the ILA and be your best man here.
Please help me, though. There's a war coming. You know what
the Brits do when you stand up to them. I'm afraid for the girls'
fate, Uncle Joe. My da sent me here for a reason. When they
had that funeral for O'Donovan Rossa in Glasnevin last year, it
was then my da decided to send me here. And send me here
only to bring my mam and sisters he did, after the uprising . . ."

His face went sour, "Why ye so werried about that? Ye didn't
come all this way to werry, did ye? This is a new life, kid. No
more farmin'. No more wet shoes all day and all night. No more
barren country and small town minds. This is New Yark, kid.
We're home now and there's a lotta money to be made here in
arganizin'. I'm clearin' t'irty dullers per week just in recruitin'
alone. I met King Joe too, the vice president o' the ILA and he
says T. V. O'Connor wants to meet me too! Congratulate me for
takin' over for Thos Carmody here in Brooklyn. Why don't ye
work wid me, kid. Let's do somethin'. Ye know there's a rumor o'
a million dullers bein' sent our way by the Germans fer a general strike. We might do it, ye know! Can ye imagine Brooklyn,

Manhattan, and New Jersey longshoremen strikin'? We got a great opportunity here. The shippers and the stevedorin' companies would have no choice but to raise our wages to whatever we demand. They can't stop the war effort because they don't pay the longshoremen a right wage! They'll have no choice. Its big money, kiddo! Our day is comin'! Forget about the past and the old and the women. They're a burden on ye, and they'd burden me too. I'll not help ye bring them here. . . . Just send'm money here and there and leave'm far from us, bhoy."

Then I see Petey Behan and the others outside the bar talking with the same bouncer that greeted me. I turn to my uncle desperately. "What happened with my da? Uncle Joseph, I need to know what happened to my da. Did he join the uprising? Is he in hiding? What happened! Won't you please help me get Mam here."

Disgusted that I am unaffected by his recruiting speech, he turns his back to me and looks away. I can hear men laughing with a sinister accent behind and to the side of me. A second later, he turns back round, "Yer da's dead! A dead man! Killt en Dooblin like all de other Fenians o' the auld world. Dead! Yer ma an' sisters too! Ye heared me? Dead! All of 'em!"

He turned again to the tender and sits coolly.

There was only one other moment in my life when everything stood still: the moment my first child was born and, of course, at this very moment here. I can picture it as I sit here at the typewriter punching words out in front of me, pausing now. Closing my eyes: the darkness of the bar pervaded much of that night. There was almost no light in there at all, no electricity at all along the old waterfront of the time. None. Just darkness. Like a forgotten time so long ago. Happily forgotten in the darkness and the fading of ancient memories. I can hear the clanking of bottle to glass though, the old man behind the bar with his big, bushy mustache from another century, the smell of pipe-smoked tobacco, and the cheap clothing of immigrant labormen huddling in the tiny bar shoulder to shoulder. I can see my uncle's bald spot too, his back turned to me in true dishonor. And I remember too, that urgent feeling to prove my own honor. "Mystifying," I say aloud, shaking my head. These men with broken beaks and broken backs lining up for a drink long after the shape-up whistle had rung out in the morning. It's always mystified me. The humble beauty of it. They were all wounded in some fashion, physically and more. I can hear them singing in that silent moment. Their well-journeyed souls unkempt and uncared for. I knew then that I was alone in the universe. Like a man knows and finds out along his own travels. And I knew that no one was allowed to live alone in such a place as New York where every other saloon you walked by had a piano man plucking the same old nostalgic tune, "The Sidewalks of New York." Standing still in my memories, I cry at the loneliness of the place. At the contest of it where oftentimes loyalties were more powerful than family. My friends were now my family, and family is survival. It really was that simple. The clan mentality, clans existing to fight together for survival in an unforgiving circumstance.

I look up.

The bouncer starts walking toward me through the din of sounds and right behind him sneak Petey and the others. Some other drunken longshoremen start yelling that the kids are storming the place. The bouncer turns around and I know that in any second all hell is about to break out.

In one motion, I stand up and yank my left elbow down, pushing my uncle Joseph's head to the bar, then I rip out my knife as I'd practiced many times over, and reach back. I reach back farther. Reaching back so far and so high that I probably looked like a baseball pitcher for the Brooklyn Robins. When I come down, I hear a gunshot in the air. But that doesn't stop my momentum. I come down so hard with that knife, just like Harry the Shiv had told me, going straight for the neck. The knife comes in so deep that I can feel the hilt of the blade press squarely against his skin. It had gone through the back of his neck, out the front and stuck into the mahogany bar with a banging sound. Maybe more like a deep thud on the bar that makes the drinks around us jump in a scare.

Then I remember seeing Timothy Quilty decking men twice his age, left and right. He was a real puncher, that kid. Every man he hits goes to the ground. Another gunshot rings out and next thing I know, Matty Martin grabs me by the collar as I stand over my dying uncle, stuck to the bar by the knife in his neck. Just for good measure, Petey Behan comes up from under the darkness or someone's armpit and sticks his own blade into my uncle's side, reaching out from below. Another gunshot rings out from Matty's snub .38 and down goes another man. A riot breaks out, but no one can see who the enemy is, and with everyone drunk to the gills, it takes many of the men several moments to realize what is happening. Some smart ones start stealing drinks from underneath the tables where they hide, like it isn't such a big surprise to be suddenly overcome with a shooting brawl in the place. Others just start punching anyone around them to protect themselves as they've been ready for a rollick after their third drink anyhow. Now they jump at the commotion and give a licking to anyone around them.

A bottleneck is created since there is only one exit. Men start to realize that those who came in shooting and stabbing are trying to make it out the same exit as them. This fact puts a spook in them. Finally, someone throws a chair through the front window with a big splash. I look back one more time at my uncle who is alone in the room save three men that lay on the ground either knocked cold, or dead. The old scrag knows he is dying and doesn't have a say in it. Stuck to the bar, I see him reaching back with the tips of his fingers for his chair so he can sit and wait it out in peace, I supposed.

When we finally make it outside, Matty yanking on my collar, I see the remarkable faces of Cinders Connolly, Petey's big brother Joey Behan, Dance Gillen, and Dinny Meehan. When they see me and Matty exit the saloon among the chaos and the mayhem, they motion to each other. "They're all out, the boys are out!"

Flame throwings being his expertise, Cinders has lit the rag that sticks out of a glass bottle of gasoline, then runs toward the bar and whips it inside the open front window. Behind him come Joey Behan and his, then Dance sprints up with the biggest smile I've ever seen on his dark face with the last as Dinny is directing traffic. After Dance throws his flaming bottle, which explodes with a big huff inside McAlpine's Saloon, he screams at the top of his lungs and tackles two or three frantic men running from the flames. The force that he uses in hitting men is so vicious and comical that he can bring four men to the ground with the punishing blow. Stomping on one after another, I run by him a little dazed.

Connolly comes running up to Matty and myself and asks where my uncle is and what has passed. Matty speaks up and tells about how I'd speared him like a fish.

"Is 'e dead? Dead?" Connolly frantically asks.

"Dead, oh he's dead a'right!" Matty laughs. "Real dead!"

When the fireworks begin, the Whitehanders all start yelling in congratulatory tones, then heel-toe it out of there in a big hurry. I'm not sure if it was the rollick in the air and the rumpus among us, or just an anger that comes bursting out of me, but at that moment I search for Petey Behan among the running crowd and the blazes. When I find him, I sprint full speed at him, just like Dance Gillen does, and I tackle Petey with a thump.

"That's what'll happen with you too, you son of a bitch, you!" I scream and batter him for a good few punches until his big brother grabs me. "Don't ever . . . !" I scream, but can't get all the words out. "Ever . . . ! I'll give you one of these real hard if you ever think of putting yourself over me again!"

"Jesus Dinny, why the hell's this kid gone crazy abusin' Petey?" Joey asks while holding me as tight as he can so I don't kill his little brother right then and there.

But I have grabbed ahold of the coat by the collar and refused to let it loose. I see Petey's eyes light up in anger. He yanks at my hand while his brother tries pulling me away.

"Let it go, kid!" the older brother yells in my ear.

Cinders Connolly, suddenly on my side yells also, "You let it go, Petey."

"Fuck no," Petey grits, then yanks at my hand again.

I have that coat so firm in my hand that it's the death grip. I'll not let it loose no matter if Dinny himself demands it of me. I yank back hard while in Joey Behan's hold, and soon I can hear the alpaca's seams come loose at the shoulder.

"Let it go!" Petey yells and takes a swing at me, which lands on my arm.

I kick up at him as his brother tries pulling me backward and soon enough the coat gives way, tearing into pieces.

"Ya're a fookin' asshole!" Petey yelps, throwing down half of the useless coat.

Dinny Meehan smiles and in a moment we are all running back up north for the Bridge District as Cinders Connolly looks back in awe at the flaming night sky.

CHAPTER 21

Donnybrook in Red Hook

"WAKE UP!" DINNY BELLOWS, ENTERING THE room. "Wake up boyos, time to get up! Let's go, we gotta big day in front of us. You're official kiddos now! Wake it up!"

He jumps on the bed where huddled close are myself against the wall, Timothy Quilty and Matty Martin in the middle, and Petey Behan straddling the edge. We are sleeping as quietly as growing young teenage boys do, but with our boots still at the ready. All four of us. The previous night our apparent initiation and with congratulatory drinks at the Dock Loaders' Club afterward, we drunkenly agree that killers sleep with their boots on, so we keep them laced.

It's true. We are Whitehanders now. Like real men. I not nearly as thrilled as the others of course, and as the pitter-pattering of the rain at the sill argues against Dinny's exuberance, I try to turn to the wall.

"Let's go, let's go!" Dinny yells, pushing on our chests and slapping our faces in the dark morning.

I open my sandy eyes and look up to Dinny holding a candle to his face in the darkness, standing above me on the bed. His smile has never been wider. He bounces on the bed and Petey falls off, still asleep.

"We got places to be, boys, now get yourselves up," Dinny encourages.

As Matty and Tim get out of bed, I see Vincent Maher appear with a wooden box in his hands. He whispers to The Swede and an approaching Dinny that it was outside on the stoops, empty and wet.

"Ybor Gales," Dinny reads the smeared but colorful papering around it.

Before The Swede cusses Lovett, Dinny hushes him so as not to let the young ones hear of dissension in the gang. But I know it means Lovett got the job done. And in his way, sends the message that he, Bill Lovett and his own crew, take the credit for it. Without tribute to Dinny's hand. It means that Lovett's act is seen as bravery and daring among his own men, traveling to Dinny's home to make a point about his gang's accomplishment. It means treachery to The Swede though. To Dinny, a demand for honor by the old ways. The ways that Dinny too honors.

"He's got disrespect," The Swede mumbles, pointing at the box in Dinny's hand.

Unfazed, Dinny looks away. "He knows what sway is."

I hear them whispering, The Swede angrily, but act as though I can't.

"It's all about the Leighton brothers," The Swede growls. "As long as Pickles sits in Sing Sing and Darby's eighty-sixt, he'll never get wit' us. Even after givin' it to McGowan like they did."

"He'll never be wit' us," Dinny whispers while looking over at me. "Just have to keep him weak."

I'm the last out of bed, but when I finally raise myself I head to the bathroom and open the door where standing three wide over the toilet and pointing their peeing puds at it are the sleepy-eyed young gangsters little Behan, Martin, and Quilty. In a rush, Sadie shoves a piece of toast on my chest with egg stuffed in it, scruffs my hair a bit, then doubles back and looks at my face. "Y'even look bigger, William."

It is the first time she ever called me William. And it wasn't until that very moment that I realized I was taller than her, as I must have grown three inches in the four months that I'd been sitting at her table.

Next thing I know and we're all sprinting down the stairwell with a cluttering, then striding with a furious pace up Henry

Street in the cold, rainy morning air with the gray sky above none too happy neither. Since most of us have holes in our boots, we jump the rain-dotted puddles from the cobblestoned street to the broken-paved sidewalk. Little Petey screws on his tough face again while Quilty, the tallest of the kid clan, dangles behind wiping the sleep from his eyes.

Dinny is surrounded ahead of us by Vincent Maher and The Swede who have apparently been up since even earlier apprising Dinny of the situation ahead of us. When we get to Tillary Street and take a right toward 25 Bridge Street instead of a left toward the water, I start hearing a strange sound. A big, rumbling sound. The sound of many men speaking at the same time in the distance. A clamoring of voices and as we come upon the Sands Street station and cross Adams, then Jay Street, it becomes apparent that there is something very large on the agenda for the morning.

Between the yells of the many, I hear Chisel MaGuire with his shrill voice barking at the heels of the crowd until it again booms in the distance. As we near the corner to Bridge Street, I see Dinny look back to me among the shoulders of The Swede and Vincent Maher. There is sadness in the look of Dinny as he glances back at me. I know that. But that was Dinny. A man smarter than all the rest, yet haunted by all the responsibility behind it. But now that I'm old and knowing, I recognize that in his look was a hope for help from me. Sure I was young. Too young to help much, but there was a powerful need in him, Dinny Meehan. It was too much for one man to hold down an entire gang and long stretches of territory with multiple enemies. Too much. But I had young thoughts then. But not too young to see the sadness in his glance. Then he is gone around a brick-faced corner while Petey and Matty follow up ahead. As Tim and I round the corner behind the rest, I can't believe what I am seeing. The voices cheer so loud it sounds like a stadium of fanatics. Chisel MaGuire has pointed at us as we come around the corner and announces, "There's Dinny Meehan! There he is!"

The rain comes down in a mist on the Dock Loaders' Club which is flooded with men waving fists and sticks and hooks and shovels in the morning air for the leader of the White Hand Gang's arrival. It must be below thirty degrees, but that doesn't stop three hundred, maybe three hundred fifty men from jumping up and down wildly, ready to go to war. Their breathing smokes in the cool air as they scream. With the misty rain, they receive the best cleaning they've had in months. Red Donnelly, Gibney the Lark, Big Dick Morissey, Harry Reynolds, Philip Large, Dance Gillen, and a few others wait at the edge of the mass of men to help Dinny wend through the revelers to get to the makeshift podium where Chisel has been antagonizing the crowd into a blood-thirsting fervor. But the podium is nothing more than a couple crates stacked in front of the saloon.

Cinders Connolly emerges from the excited men and stops us before we follow Dinny and his protectors into the crowd and tells us to wait at the periphery and before long Richie Lonergan and Abe Harms appear to stand among us. Cinders gives me the firm shake that men give each other and pats me on the shoulder with a smile.

"All is well witcha den? It ain't nothin', doin' what ya did, ya know? Things like what ya did ain't easy gettin' over."

I nod to him and yell in his ear, "This is my family now!"

As he smiles at me, I see behind him Bill Lovett and Non Connors smoking big fat cigars. Frankie Byrne and his old gang too, Jidge Seaman and Sean Healy. There are so many faces of men I have worked with in the past month, yet I never realized they are part of the overall gang. Some of their commitments to it so loose that I hadn't thought them loyal to Dinny. Many of them are nothing more than laborers and longshoremen, or truck drivers, warehousemen or pier house superintendents, factory managers, and the like, but they all report eventually to Dinny Meehan. All jump at the chance to repay him for his helping them get jobs in the neighborhood. It takes me a long while to understand the web Dinny spins in Brooklyn quietly